DEALING WITH THE OTHERS

No matter what I did, who I chose to work for, or what choices I made, I'd be pissing somebody off. I had my pick between The Circle, Royce, or the White Hats. The White Hats were obviously an unstable element, considering they thought I'd be more amenable to joining their fun and games at knifepoint. The Circle had me in a contractual pinch I wouldn't be able to break out of with any ease. Royce would probably hit the roof as soon as he figured out what I was really after. Each and every one of them had the resources and clout to make my life miserable or even make me disappear. One, or more, of them would have a reason to want me to, once I made a move.

I wandered back to my bed and sat down on the edge, staring blankly at the wall. My hands had started shaking again. Right now, Royce seemed like my safest bet, seeing as he was the only one of the three who hadn't threatened me.

Yet.

I was so dead . . .

HUNTED BY THE OTHERS

JESS HAINES

ZEBRA BOOKS
KENSINGTON PUBLISHING CORP.
http://www.kensingtonbooks.com

ZEBRA BOOKS are published by

Kensington Publishing Corp.
119 West 40th Street
New York, NY 10018

All Kensington titles, imprints, and distributed lines are available at special quantity discounts for bulk purchases for sales promotion, premiums, fund-raising, educational, or institutional use.

Special book excerpts or customized printings can also be created to fit specific needs. For details, write or phone the office of the Kensington Special Sales Manager: Attn.: Special Sales Department. Kensington Publishing Corp., 119 West 40th Street, New York, NY 10018. Phone: 1-800-221-2647.

ISBN-13: 978-1-4201-1187-3
ISBN-10: 1-4201-1187-6

First Printing: May 2010

10 9 8 7 6 5 4 3 2 1

Printed in the United States of America

ACKNOWLEDGMENTS

To my unofficial number one fan, Binah, and all the friends who supported me through the publishing process. You know who you are. To my tireless cheerleader, Mom. To my compadre, caffeine, followed closely by his sidekick, chocolate. I love you guys!

A special word of thanks to my agent, Ellen Pepus, and to my editor, John Scognamiglio (along with the rest of the team at Kensington). Words cannot express my appreciation for all your time, advice, patience and hard work. Thank you so much for helping me bring the world of the Others to life.

Chapter 1

Long, delicate fingers caressed the stem of a wineglass, trailing upward to catch a few small beads of condensation on the glass. Sultry eyes the color of the sky during a summer storm bored into me from across the cloth-covered table, with all of the woman's not-inconsiderable power of compulsion behind them. I knew what she was trying to do, which didn't make it any easier to resist.

Taking a deep breath, I forced my gaze away as nonchalantly as I could to look through the bay window beside our table. Staring at the rippling black waters of a little man-made pond, dotted with reflected lights and a single white swan, beat falling into a black enchant by looking into Veronica's eyes. The bird floated, serene and oblivious, as a laughing young couple threw bits of bread at it to try to lure it closer.

Swans were pretty but vicious if you got too close. Much like my dinner companion.

She was still waiting oh-so-breathlessly for my

reply. With a sigh, I dragged my attention off the sights outside and back to the mage, careful not to meet her gaze directly.

"Look, it's not that I don't need the money, but I don't kill vampires for magi. First and foremost, I'm human. I can't compete with you guys. Second, I'm a private detective, not an assassin. Not to mention that it's still illegal to kill vamps without a signed warrant."

It took every ounce of willpower I had not to look into those overbright eyes and change my mind. Hey, I hated vampires as much as the next human, but I wasn't about to go *hunt one down* like a crazy person and get myself killed. My job was scary enough as it was without adding angry vampires to the list of stalkers trying to get a piece of my hide to make up for the grief I caused them.

"Shiarra, I'm not asking you to kill him. Just," Veronica paused, her persuasive tones trailing off into a throaty "hmm" before she continued, "just find out what he's up to. Detain him if necessary. Find the location of a little trinket for us. My coven will take care of the rest."

Her cherry lips curved in a smile more predatory than any vamp's, her pinkish tongue darting out to run suggestively along her upper lip once she noticed that was where my attention was focused. God, I hate magi.

In the back of my mind, I wondered darkly why Jenny, our receptionist-slash-bookkeeper, had set this appointment without checking with me first. Belatedly recalling that she went over the bills with my business partner on a regular basis, I realized she must have decided the need to pay our bills outweighed my likely moral outrage. Under any other circumstances, the moment I found out a potential client was an Other, I walked. Jenny knew this. She also knew that since money was so tight, I'd probably at least agree to hear the mage out.

After finding out what she wanted, though, I was starting to regret agreeing to stay through dinner.

"I know I made the news with that whole Were incident at the Embassy last month, but honestly, that was my first run-in with supernaturals. I don't have the experience or the equipment to deal with vampires."

I tried to sound reasonable, though I was afraid I was coming across more testy and frightened. This woman really put me on edge, though I tried to tell myself it was what she was asking me to do, not the aura and crackle of magic surrounding her, that did it. Maybe it had something to do with her coming on to me? Either way, I didn't like it.

"Frankly, I don't think you could pay me enough to put my life on the line against a vampire. Shouldn't you be getting a half-blood? Or another mage to deal with him?"

Little furrows appeared between those perfectly shaped brows of hers. Her hair was a lovely mahogany shade that didn't quite match the dark brown of those eyebrows, framing her delicate, oval face. I hated that she could pull the look off so effortlessly. My hopelessly curly red hair would never look as sleek and sophisticated as her artfully careless 'do. It was probably spelled to look that way.

"The Ageless would know us for our magic. That wouldn't work at all. A half-blood would kill first, ask questions later. Same with a Were." She paused, thinking. "Unless, of course, he killed them first."

I leaned back in the chair, crossing my arms over my chest. "Not really helping your cause here."

The woman started tapping her perfectly manicured nails on the table, leaning back as she eyed me anew. Something in that look told me wheels were turning and her plans were changing. Uh-oh.

"A human is our only chance. You have no taint of magic, no scent of change on you. You also now have some familiarity with, and have proven yourself capable against, supernaturals."

For a moment, Veronica's lip curled faintly in a sneer, venomous but gone almost as soon as it appeared. I would have missed it if I hadn't been staring at her lips and nose, avoiding looking directly into her eyes. Her features resumed that intent predatory look that told me she was only barely hiding her contempt for the lowly pure-blood human, doing what she could to put me on edge. Sadly, it was working.

"As I said, we do not want him dead, just watched. You can get close without fear of injury, since he has plenty of willing donors and is known for his restraint. The worst that could happen is you being banned from his places of business."

It was my turn to tap my nails. "Aside from an abrupt, painful death, that *is* the worst thing that could happen to me. Alec Royce owns half the nightclubs and restaurants in the city. Those are the places I go to track my marks."

I glanced at my watch in an effort to give her the hint that I wasn't going to stick around much longer for this crazy talk, even if she was picking up the tab.

She gave an overly dramatic sigh, no longer hiding her annoyance. She dropped the sickly sweet tones she'd been affecting and finally put a cap on the damn aura she'd been exuding since this dinner started. No wonder the waiter hadn't come to refill our glasses in almost an hour.

"Shiarra Waynest, you forget yourself. The other half of the city belongs to The Circle, and we are more than prepared to compensate you. Fifty thousand, plus expenses, and an extra ten thousand if you find what we're looking for. Five thousand up front, and your pick of equipment from The Circle's own security vaults. We'll give you protection, and more work if you do well at this job."

I sat back, speechless. Five grand to start? My usual take only came out to two thousand, sometimes up to four if it the job was tricky or somewhat dangerous. Plus equipment? Expenses? Maybe this really *was* a godsend in disguise. I wondered if she might know that I had debt up to my ears and a car payment that was killing me. Plus I think my PI license was about due for renewal, and let's not forget taxes coming just around the bend. Mental note: get Jenny a very, very nice thank-you card and a bonus.

Taking my stunned silence as a bad sign, Veronica

narrowed her eyes and threw another bone on the table. "Is that too little? Fine, make it ten if you get the information, and another twenty if you find the location of the artifact."

Lifting my napkin up to my mouth to hide the fact that I couldn't snap my jaw shut, I took just a moment to close my eyes, take a breath, and remind myself that I'd be walking right into a death trap if I took this job. I thought bleakly about the stack of bills that seemed to grow larger every day. Most unsettling was the one from my landlord that had appeared in my mailbox a few days back. I hadn't quite been able to bring myself to open it yet. My cut of the deposit for this job would be enough to cover the demands of my landlord, and maybe a few of the other creditors demanding a good chunk of my income.

"Well?"

Though I couldn't help but feel I was betraying something inside myself, something important, I gave her the words she wanted to hear, however grudgingly. "I'll do it. What is it I'm looking for?"

Veronica leaned back in her chair and smiled grimly, a sly light in her eyes. I really hoped I would live long enough to regret this.

Chapter 2

The next morning, my partner stared at me in shock over the scarred and pitted kitchen table in the tiny break room of our office, coffee mug paused inches from her lips. Sara Halloway blinked as if trying to clear her vision—to make sure she was really seeing what was in front of her.

"Run that by me one more time. Slowly."

I rubbed a hand down my face, groaning as I tried to figure out how to explain my reasoning to her without sounding like I'd finally gone off the deep end.

"I know. I can't believe I took the job either."

I reached into the back pocket of my jeans and carefully smoothed out the crumpled check on the table, staring down at the five grand under my fingertips so I wouldn't have to face Sara's disbelief. I had enough of my own.

"What is it you're supposed to be looking for exactly? You know it's got to be dangerous if they're paying so much."

"Paying so much? This is a drop in the bucket to The Circle."

Shaking my head, I brushed a few loose tendrils out of my eyes before reaching for my own coffee on the table. "Anytime a vampire or spark is involved, it's dangerous. You mean more dangerous than that? Sure, I'm positive whatever it is will get me killed if I don't watch my back. It may be worth the risk. I can always back out if things get too hairy."

She made a rude noise, but at least she wasn't giving me grief for my little racial epithet, calling the mage a spark.

"It's part of the arrangement. I can keep the nonrefundable deposit on my services." I flicked a few fingers, while carefully cradling the coffee mug, to point to the check. "I can end the contract at any time at my discretion if it looks like my life is on the line. Veronica e-mailed me the paperwork right after dinner. I looked it over last night; it's clear and concise, and damned if it isn't actually a fair deal."

Sara's clear blue eyes narrowed, thoughtful rather than annoyed. "What equipment are they going to give you? Did she say?"

I shrugged. I had plenty of my own equipment, so it was doubtful I'd be using any of The Circle's stuff anyway.

"No, not really. Just 'my pick of the security vaults'—whatever that means."

Her soft harrumph was reassuring. That meant she was mulling it over and wouldn't bug me about it too much more until she had a chance to work it out in her own head. Maybe she was starting to see the same twisted sense in the plan that I had.

Pressing on, I added, "Honestly, it doesn't seem that dangerous a job. All she asked me to do was find out what I could about some artifact."

The speculative look returned. "Did she tell you anything about it?"

I nodded. "A little. She showed me a picture. It's a black stone about the size of a man's fist, carved into a lizard-bat thing. Little rubies for eyes. Older than dirt, powerful, priceless, blah blah blah."

Sara narrowed her eyes again, only this time in that dangerous don't-even-try-me look. "Elaborate on that blah, blah, blah thing."

"She didn't tell me what it's for or what it can do. She did say I'll have to get my way into Royce's good graces to find out more about it. Including where it might be hidden."

A look of horror crossed her face. It would've been comical if my own face hadn't mirrored her expression last night when I'd come to the same conclusion she just did. "You mean you'll have to talk to the leech directly? Face to face? You're crazy!"

"Not that crazy." I tried to keep from showing outward signs of the sudden fear-induced surge of adrenaline her words gave me. "Reporters interview him all the time with no problems. He frequently makes appearances at his nightclubs and restaurants. There's never been any kind of incident except last year when that White Hat tried to stake him at the opening of his new restaurant, *La Petite Boisson.* Remember that?"

Wow, go me. My voice didn't crack or quiver even once getting all that out.

She chuckled, her crystalline blue eyes glinting with mirth. "Oh yes, I think I do. The one who knocked the mayor's wife into the punchbowl, right?"

I smiled back, losing some tension. "That's the one. Everything went backward for the White Hats after that. Poor, misjudged, minority vampires . . ."

"Yeah, I think she even kissed him on the cheek after for helping her up and making light of the whole thing. The tabloids loved it." Sara's expression hardened, and I braced myself for what I knew was coming next. "You know he's still dangerous. I mean, Christ. Come on. A vampire?" An ominous, suspicious pause. "How exactly were you planning on meeting him anyway?"

I couldn't help but redden a bit under her scrutiny. It doesn't help that I blush easily with my pale skin, but the topic was making me more uncomfortable by the moment. "I was going to go in as a restaurant and nightclub guide reviewer or journalist. There's a whole calendar of events on his website on when he makes appearances at his clubs. I figured it would be the best way to go in and get a chance to talk with him."

She shook her head, frowning. I was about to protest, but she cut me off. "That will never work. He's got press agents and marketing people to deal with the journalists. Not to mention his security. They'd spot you coming a mile away since you work that beat, and you're more high profile after that thing at the Embassy. You may not have noticed since they usually leave us alone when we're in his clubs, but that's only because we generally don't hassle the clientele."

It was my turn to frown, more in consternation than anything. I'd thought the journalism thing was a stroke of genius on my part. "What do you suggest?"

She grinned at me in a way that suggested I really wasn't going to like her idea. "Go exactly as you are. No pretenses."

An incredulous laugh burst from my lips. "Are you kidding me? First, he'd laugh in my face before banning me. Second, what in the nine hells makes you think he'll actually talk to me if I go now versus the other few hundred times I've visited his clubs?"

"Shia, don't doubt me." That know-it-all look somehow managed to get even more smug. "I know exactly how to do it."

Chapter 3

The rest of the day seemed to take an age to creep by. I was inundated with paperwork to fill out from the last couple of runs I had done, so that kept me busy until a little past lunch. Afterward, Jenny wanted to crunch some numbers with me.

I usually let Sara do all of that, but she left after lunch to go do some recon on her latest mark, a charmingly lecherous teenager who'd run off from his parents about three weeks before. It wasn't the first time he'd run away, but it *was* the first time he'd done it with a vamp. That the parents knew of. Seeing as how the parents were rabid White Hats (card carrying, with little antivampire legislation pamphlets they carried in their pockets—I kid you not) and the teen was a Goth, judging from his picture, this was neither surprising nor entirely unexpected. At least for Sara and me.

Since the boy was nineteen (and the parents were psychotic), the police didn't give much of a hoot that he'd gone missing. They'd gone through the motions of searching after the missing persons report was filed, but that basically just meant an APB went out, some flyers were posted, and that's about it. So now the kindly Mr. and Mrs. Borowsky waited until the trail was almost cold to set us on his tail.

Hence Sara's bright idea for how I could meet Royce. I go in, ask around after the kid, ask for the management and whatnot. After all, he was the most influential vampire in the city. Almost every bloodsucker for three states had to clear their movements, purchases, political aspirations, and most important, who they "turned," through Royce. If nothing else, he might at least be able to point the way to the sire of the vamp who ran off with the teen.

So now I had a perfectly legitimate reason to talk to him. The idea didn't make me feel any better about it.

"Shia? Did you hear what I just said?"

Whoops. "Sorry, Jen, what's that?" It took a real effort to actually concentrate on the figures in front of my eyes. I hate bookkeeping. Hate, hate, hate it.

"I was saying that two of our permits are due for renewal next week, and even with what you brought in on that deposit, we're going to run shy unless we skip part of the rent or insurance payment. We're really in the red here."

I blinked. "Excuse me?"

Jenny sighed, turned, and pointed to the computer screen across the desk, jabbing a finger at a couple of figures on a spreadsheet column.

"See this? Between what you pay me, gas, electricity, and a few other things, we're running at a loss. Hasn't Sara been over this with you?"

I shook my head, ire rising. "How long have you known this? When did you first let Sara know?"

"After we almost failed to pay the rent about seven months ago. I don't know how, but Ms. Halloway . . ." Oh God. If she was calling Sara "Ms. Halloway," we were really screwed. ". . . dug up the money from somewhere and saved the day. She's managed to scrape us out of a tough spot a couple of times. I'm sorry, I would've mentioned something sooner, but I thought you knew."

Which meant Sara was dipping into her coffers to keep us afloat. Great.

One of the benefits to working with Miss Sara Jane Halloway was that her parents had been very successful in their investments in stocks and real estate before they were killed in a horrific accident—a drunk driver on the interstate who careened into theirs and three or four other cars—three years earlier. Sara and her younger sister, Janine, split the estate; it left both of them very, very wealthy.

It cheesed off Janine and the surviving relatives that, instead of carrying on the family tradition in real estate, Sara had partnered with me in this private investigations venture. Janine hadn't taken up real estate either, but for some reason she expected Sara to pick up the slack and run everything.

Though she'll never admit to it, I'm almost positive that pissing off her family was why Sara did it.

We first met five years ago in college; I was working on a degree in criminal justice, she was halfheartedly pursuing a joint business and corporate law degree. I was frantic to keep my grades up so I wouldn't lose my scholarship. She was considering dropping out and taking an extended vacation in the Hamptons.

Since we had a few classes together, I helped her out and urged her to at least finish up the term. By the end of the following year, we both had our degrees and had cemented a friendship. I met her parents a handful of times when she invited me along to parties or other outings at one or another of her family's properties. The parents were nice enough but the rest of her relatives kind of left me cold, especially the neurotic, whining Janine.

More often, I invited her over to my parents' place—a little ramshackle house on a hill overlooking the Sound. It was tiny compared to what she was used to, but the warmth and affection my Irish-Catholic family showed her made her far more interested in going to my clan's gatherings than her own.

While I loved it that Sara helped finance the start-up of this crazy idea of mine, I told her all along that if it didn't look like we were going to make it financially, we'd have to just sell the biz and start something fresh. I didn't want to be a burden or a freeloader. I hate being indebted to people.

She protested and bitched about it a bit, but in the end we came to terms. I even paid back most of my half of the start-up money she'd fronted me. A couple more takes like my latest and I'd have the balance paid off in no time.

I really didn't relish the idea of selling the business, but I also didn't want it to be said that I was a hanger-on to Sara for her money. I got enough of that back in school. Plus, with two successful brothers, I wasn't thrilled with the idea of letting on to my parents that my biz was a failure. They already gave me enough crap for being a PI instead of a lawyer like Mike. My mom was fond of dishing that one out, along with the whole don't-you-think-it's-about-time-you-settle-down-and-pop-out-a-few-grandkids-for-me speech. Sara gave me hell for that, laughing about it and bringing it up every few days for weeks afterward.

Rather than keep Jenny waiting, I took a breath to get some semblance of control over my temper and told her not to worry. "I'll go over the numbers with Sara when she gets back. Look, it's Friday. Why don't you go ahead and take off. I've got to go get ready for tonight anyway; I'll just wrap up here and lock up."

Behind her glasses, her brown eyes held a hint of sympathy, though I had the feeling she'd head straight home and start posting her résumé all over the Internet. She was probably convinced we were going under. But between Sara's generosity and my latest contract, I was sure we'd be able to pull out of this mess just fine.

So why did the whole situation still rankle so much with me?

"I heard you took a job doing something with that vampire who owns all those nightclubs. The one who's in the news all the time. Is that right?"

I grimaced and nodded, avoiding her questioning gaze.

"Be careful, Shia. Those things are dangerous."

"I know. Don't worry. I don't plan on doing any

more than asking a few questions and leaving. They give me the creeps."

She put a hand on my arm, surprising me with her serious expression and the touch of worry in her voice. "I'm not kidding, Shia. My cousin died about two years ago while she was dating one of those—those things. Those monsters."

My eyes widened and after a moment I remembered to close my open mouth. "I'm sorry. I didn't know. When? Why didn't you say anything?"

She shook her head, not quite looking at me now. Her voice grew into a quiet, broken whisper, and terror gleamed in her soft brown eyes. "It was a couple of months before I started working here. Shia, you need to know this. You need to be careful. The coroner—he said it took her hours to die, bleeding out like that. The way it left her . . . after. I can't bear the thought of it happening to someone else I know. Not again. Not you, please don't let it get you, too."

Almost involuntarily, my hand came up to gently wipe away the single tear that trickled down Jenny's pale cheek. The feel of her trembling even under that light touch was frightening all on its own. For her sake, I smiled and took up her cold hands in both of my own to try to put her at ease, steeling myself against letting any of my private doubts come to the surface. Despite that, I knew the sincerity in my voice never touched my eyes. There was too much fear in them for that.

"I won't. I promise."

Chapter 4

Royce's clubs are a shade more risqué than his restaurants, though all of them are usually packed. Vamp-run establishments are "the thing" right now. I guess to some people, the idea of rubbing elbows with a leech is titillating.

His newest restaurant, *La Petite Boisson* (I suppose "The Little Drink" sounds more tacky in English), is the kind of outfit where you'd spot people like the mayor, celebrities, visiting dignitaries from other countries, that sort of thing. I would stick out like a sore thumb there. Not to mention that even a glass of water from that place was way outside my budget.

Luckily, his website said he was going to make an appearance tonight at The Underground, one of his less expensive nightclubs. I'd been there plenty of times. The bouncers know me on sight, and usually let me through at the front of the line as long as I wave some money at them. It's not my favorite hangout, mostly because of the BDSM theme. The music is heavy industrial or dark techno stuff, and they have scantily leather-clad male and female dancers in cages hanging up near the ceiling, high over everyone's heads.

Maybe that's some people's idea of a good time, but it usually just gave me a headache.

Unfortunately, it seemed the majority of my "find-that-cheating-rat-bastard" clients (as opposed to "find-that-rat-bastard-that-owes-me-money" and "watch-that-shifty-eyed-rat-bastard-for-me" clients) thought their significant others were hanging out in establishments like this. What was even more unfortunate was that they were usually right. Every once in a while they'd prove me wrong by actually working late in the office. Once the boyfriend I was checking up on was working a second job in secret so he could pay for the engagement ring he wanted to spring on his paranoid soon-to-be fiancée. Yes, really. There may be some hope for humanity yet.

After tidying up at the office, I locked up and headed home to change. Pressed slacks and a business jacket wouldn't fly at The Underground. Now, standing in the cold about a half a block away from the club in the reassuring pool of light of a streetlamp, I was glad I'd taken the time to change. Staring up at the garish neon sign flickering over the entrance, in one of the two pairs of black leather pants I owned, with a white button-down shirt that flared at the wrists and waist, topped with a black wool peacoat to keep warm, I shoved my hands into my pockets and shivered against more than the biting winds coming in off the river.

The line was long. I guess I wasn't the only one hoping for a peek at the owner of the club tonight. My feet were already hurting, too. The heels on my boots were a little higher than I normally cared for, but I wasn't planning on dancing. Much. This was work, after all.

Muttering under my breath, I withdrew a slightly trembling hand from my pocket to clutch my jacket collar closed around my throat before resignedly clomping across the street and past the leather and PVC-clad crowd chattering behind a length of black velvet rope. How cute, someone had chained little handcuffs to the support poles for the rope since the last time I was here. I also picked up the scent of some smoke on the air that smelled suspiciously unlike cigarettes.

Yup, it was the same old club scene I knew and loved. There wasn't much difference between the vamp-run establishments and the human-run ones, honestly. These days, the pedigree of the owner was all it took to make the difference between what was cool and what was not. Were-run bars and restaurants weren't as common, but they also seemed to get more business than those run by us poor humans.

Oh well. Bruno, the blond bouncer on the left, who was built like a truck and probably hit with those ham-sized fists like a ton of bricks, gave me a once-over when I brashly stepped around the front of the line to greet him. He cracked a Hollywood smile, all gleaming rows of pearly whites, when I held out a hand to shake. I was holding the requisite bills in my palm to bribe my way past the two-block-long line of complaining would-be patrons, who'd probably been standing in the cold waiting for entrance for at least a couple of hours already.

"Hey, Red, lookin' good tonight." Waving off the other three guys working security and unclasping the velvet rope for me to step through, he engulfed my hand in one of his. It looked like a shake, but he was really just palming the cash. I couldn't stop from shuddering when he ran his thick, calloused thumb over my wrist. I wondered briefly if he could feel the staccato beat of my pulse before quickly drawing my hand back and shoving it back into my pocket.

"You gonna take me up on my offer yet?"

I laughed, though it was a little forced. Ugh, I'd tried so hard to forget that "offer" he'd made me last time I was here.

"Not yet, Blondie. Maybe next time."

One of the other bouncers, new from the look of him, was holding the door for me. I didn't keep him waiting and hightailed it inside to the sounds of catcalls and pissed-off complaints. Maybe I shouldn't have worn the leather.

Walking into the entrance was always a little intimidating. It was a short, pitch-black hallway, occasionally lit by the hint of a strobe light creeping under the thick metal door at the end. I could already feel my bones vibrating from the bass of the music inside. Taking a breath, I slid my hand into one of the pockets of my leather pants and drew out a silver chain with a matching silver cross. Not much in the way of protection, but at least it should prevent Royce from getting any ideas.

Once I'd settled the necklace around my throat, the cross prominent against my breastbone, I pushed my way past the door and dropped off my coat with the checker, a heavily tattooed boy with a blue Mohawk and more piercings than I could count.

The first bar was far too crowded, so I brushed past the first hurdle of bodies crushed against each other and worked my way toward the dance floor in the next room. The place had four floors. There were three dance floors, one with a stage, and a number of quieter rooms with plush couches and sideshows and whatnot for those who wanted a break from dancing or just wanted to get their rocks off watching the exhibitionists that came out of the woodwork for the sideshows. The rumored "private" show rooms and employee's offices were all upstairs as far as I knew. Never been in them, never planned on being in or even near them, thank you.

I'd made nice with one of the bartenders a while back. James often helped me find my marks and made for good conversation when said marks were no-shows. Unfortunately, he was completely inundated when I made my way to the second floor, barely having enough time to return my wave of greeting. There went my bright idea of asking him where to find Royce.

Looking around with distaste, I figured I might as well work off some of my jittery energy on the dance floor for a few minutes until some space cleared up at the bar. If I didn't calm my nerves, I'd probably end up looking and sounding like an idiot once I finally found the vamp anyway.

I headed to the one that was playing the least obnoxious remix, relieved to see that the third, smallest, dance floor was also the least crowded, as was the bar. Glory hallelujah!

After two songs without a partner to dance with, I was bored out of my skull. There were only a handful of other people dancing here, and there was plenty of room for us all to leave a good deal of personal space between one another.

Weaving past the gyrating bodies on the dance floor to get to the tiny bar, I waited just a couple of minutes to get the attention of the bartender and shout an order for a bottle of water. Much as I would've liked something with a little more kick to it to steady my nerves and give me a shot of much-needed liquid courage, I didn't think it would be a good idea for me to interview a vamp while toasted.

One of the men who had been leaning indolently against the wall watching the dancers walked over to me, and I had to fight back a sigh and an eye roll. He was taller than me, though still average in height. He was dressed much like the other Goth posers on the floor, albeit without the heavy white makeup, dark eyeliner, or multiple piercings. At a guess, judging by his smooth, slightly dark-toned skin, he was in his late twenties, early thirties, tops.

I braced myself for what I was sure would be a

cheesy pickup line, but the guy surprised me with a much more subtle opening.

"Alone, are we? You don't seem like one of the usual crowd. What brings you here tonight?"

The directness of his question was what caught me. I took a quick sip of my water to hide my indecision. Well, I didn't think it would hurt too much to tell him the truth. It'd probably work to make him move on to greener pastures.

"I was hoping to catch the club owner for a few minutes. I would've asked one of my friends who works here, but he was busy. Just killing some time until some of the bodies clear out."

On closer inspection, I saw he had thick dark hair that hung down to his shoulders and partially obscured equally dark eyes, though in the dim lighting I couldn't tell if it they were pure black or simply a dark brown. His features were strong, as were those well-defined shoulders and taut, flat stomach I could see through the netted black shirt he wore. Those leather pants seemed painted on, showing equally muscular and painfully well-defined legs. He was, dare I say, devilishly handsome?

He arched a brow at my answer, his gaze shifting from mine to the cross. It was a brief glance, not lecherous, simply speculative. I flushed a little anyway. Come on, the guy looked at my (albeit small) chest. Also, knowing I was coming to speak to a vamp with the cross on was pretty much blatantly stating that I was either a White Hat or the closest thing to it. Very cliché, and, depending on who you asked, very rude.

I didn't mind committing the social faux pas as long as it meant Royce would keep his fangs to himself.

He surprised me further at his next words. "I can help you with that. Follow me."

Chapter 5

Follow a stranger in a vamp-run bar? I hesitated, but only for a moment. Figuring it beat waiting around to try to spot Royce myself or for James to have a spare moment to help me, I did as he asked. As I followed him toward the back of the club, I managed to take note that he looked almost as good from the back as he did from the front. My, my. If these were the sorts of people in Royce's entourage, maybe I needed to come by more often, if for nothing more than the eye candy. I wondered if the guy was security or vamp chow.

We weaved through the crowds, working our way to an elevator hidden around a bend I'd never cared enough to explore before. Once inside, he pulled out a key and used it to unlock the button for what I noted was a heretofore-unknown fifth floor. Even in the elevator, I could hear music pounding through, making it seem somehow uncomfortable to start talking just yet. As the elevator "pinged" almost imperceptibly, he reached forward to hold the doors and gestured for me to precede him.

I stepped into a silent, well-lit hallway with a number of thick mahogany doors leading to what were presumably management offices. It felt like stepping into a different world. The austere design would have looked more at home in a well-to-do law firm than a nightclub. There was no music once the elevator doors slid shut, only the soft burble of water flowing over rocks from a little fountain sitting on a low table.

The man slid past me and led the way to the last of the doors at the end of the hall. There was no sign to indicate whose office it was. He opened the door, flipped the light switch, and stepped inside.

It was a pristine white-carpeted, white-walled space, with two chrome-and-leather chairs facing a sleek black desk, and two black leather couches surrounding a gleaming marble table. He gestured for me to sit on one of the couches, which I did, a bit stiffly, holding on to the bottle of water since I didn't see any coasters and wasn't about to chance pissing off the vamp by getting spots on his nice, shiny table.

As I sat, I noticed a little wet bar in one of the corners, with two gleaming chrome barstools set before it. There were no papers on the desk, nothing but a pen, a desk calendar, and a silver paperweight shaped into a little pyramid. No computer? No phone? Odd.

The walls were hung with tasteful paintings of English riders and hunting scenes. A few potted plants, mostly ivies and ferns, added some color to the room. The view behind the desk was fantastic, overlooking the moonlit river spilling out into the ocean. Somehow the mix between sleek modern sophistication and rustic English lord came together into an unexpectedly comfortable workplace. I don't know what I expected of an office for Royce, but I don't think this was really it.

After I'd taken it all in, I said, "Thank you for showing me up here. I hope this isn't much trouble for you. Will Royce be long?"

He chuckled, pulling the door shut and walking over to take a seat on the couch next to the one I'd chosen. He surprised me yet again when he leaned back and propped his combat-booted feet on the table.

"He's here. What did you want to ask me, Ms. Waynest?"

Oh God. Oh God, oh God, oh God.

Alone in his office. Alone with a vampire. *Oh God,* I'd checked out his butt!

Seeing my mouth drop open and my sudden speechlessness, he grinned, giving me an unnecessarily good view of sharp, pearly canines. They weren't much longer than a normal human's, since they weren't extended to feed just now, but the razor tips were obvious, if only to me.

"Surprised, I see. Not to worry, I know you're here for business rather than pleasure. I take it you weren't expecting to see me under quite these circumstances, hmm?"

"Uh, no, not exactly."

Not in leather pants and a netted, see-through shirt. Not looking quite that good, or so . . . alive, I suppose. Which for some reason made me sort of suspicious. He had approached me first and now called me by name. I knew I'd never met him before. Why would he come to me?

"How did you know who I was?"

He shrugged, sitting back comfortably and lacing his hands behind his head. His eyes never left mine, though, and it was getting more unnerving by the second.

"I make it a point to familiarize myself with others using my places of business to further their own ends. Forgive me for saying so, but you are much more lovely in person. Your picture in the paper last month did not do you justice."

Argh. I could feel the heat and color rising in my cheeks. I would *not* let his flattery sidetrack me. Turning my head so my red curls hid the obvious blush on my pale skin, I started fumbling in my pockets to find the photo I'd brought with me. How could a vamp's skin tone be darker than mine?

"I—listen, I actually wanted to just ask for your help. H&W Investigations has taken on a client whose son is missing. He was last seen fleeing his home in the company of a vampire."

"I see."

The flat words weren't encouraging. He didn't move, or say anything else. It was almost eerie. That was when I noticed out of the corner of my eye that his chest did not rise and fall to take a breath. He wasn't bothering to "play human" for me now. Great.

Finally finding the picture, I dragged it out of my back pocket, only slightly creased from the abuse I'd put it through by carrying it back there. "This is the boy, David Borowsky, and his girlfriend Tara. Do either of them look familiar to you?"

I couldn't help but shudder when his fingers brushed against mine as he leaned forward to take the picture. His gaze flicked from the picture to me, then returned to focus fully on the photograph. A low "hmph" escaped him, his coal black brows slowly furrowing and a frown forming on his forehead. "She's not one of my number. Nor one of any of my current guests' flock. She's poaching."

Poaching. Just hearing him use that word so casually to mean taking the life of another human being made me feel ill.

At my silence, he glanced back to me again, still frowning. "I will assist you in finding her. You should get a warrant for her extermination. Do you have the connections?"

I shook my head, almost unable to believe my luck. This would tie him to me for a few days at least, possibly leading to the opening I needed to find that little figurine. I wondered why he recognized me but didn't already know that I don't do exterminations. H&W specializes in lost persons, tracking, surveillance, and photographing and videoing our marks. Sara and I left the rest up to our clients or the police if we discovered wrongdoing in the line of duty. My contacts at the local police stations were all pretty casual, not enough to get a warrant on short notice.

"Then I shall handle that for you." He pointed at the photograph. "May I keep this?"

"Sure," I croaked, feeling way in over my head. What the hell was I doing, partnering up with a vampire on a run?

"Very well. I'm sure we have the information on file somewhere, but would you mind giving me your card in case I need to contact you on the matter? I'll give you my direct number as well."

He rose with glacial slowness to head over to his desk, pick up the pen, and open a drawer to pull out a business card. Probably moving that way on purpose to keep from scaring me further. He scrawled something on the back of it and came back over to the couch. We exchanged cards, and this time I managed to keep from having a physical reaction when our fingers brushed again. Outwardly, anyway. I was pretty sure my stomach was still somewhere in the region of my knees.

Once that was done, he held out his hand. It took a long moment for me to realize he meant to help me up. I hesitated at the idea of putting my hand in his, and worse yet, it was noticeable. He actually smiled, amused rather than annoyed.

"I don't bite without permission, Ms. Waynest. Or did you want to stay and chat?"

Oh no. No, no, no. I shook my head vehemently, probably too much so, taking his hand and rising quickly to my feet with little help on his part. He probably felt me shaking despite how brief the contact was. I certainly felt how cool his flesh was; it made my skin crawl.

"Do you need me to see you out?"

After swallowing my heart, I managed a few words. "No, I can find my way." I hesitated again. What I said next felt like the equivalent of forcing ground glass out from behind my teeth. "Thank you, Mr. Royce. I'll be in touch."

I got a glimpse of fang as he grinned again before he turned away and moved toward the windows overlooking the river. He clasped his hands behind his back, his words seeming distant through my haze of fear. "The pleasure was all mine, Ms. Waynest. I'm sure we'll speak again soon. Good night."

Chapter 6

When I got home, all I wanted to do was collapse in bed. I had the shakes in the car all the way across the river. I still had them when I shoved the key in the lock after the third try. Even after I turned on every light and snapped every lock and deadbolt in the apartment, my hands wouldn't stop shaking.

What the hell was it about vamps that scared me so much? They'd come out of the closet, so to speak, along with the rest of the supernatural community shortly after 9/11. It was pretty creepy for most people to find out they'd been doing lunch with an elf in the next cube for the last few years and that a Were had been giving them their manicures. That the janitor was a vamp flunky. The plumber was a warlock. That the state representative they voted for was a mage and the one they didn't was a Were. The initial panic that hit most people settled down when a handful of prominent celebrities, businesspeople, and even some government officials all came forward to let the world know they had supernatural origins.

Actually, that kind of explains a lot.

Anyway, it was common knowledge now that vamps, along with the rest of the underworld, have been around for ages plodding alongside the rest of humankind as we worked together and shaped what now passes for civilization. Even though they hid their identities and usually no more than scraped by in the past, making a living as best they could without giving away their origins, the layers of secrecy surrounding their existence are slowly coming undone. They've been here through our good times and bad, fighting and bleeding and dying alongside us in our wars, not to mention in their own secret turf wars in the shadows.

In the aftermath of the World Trade Center attacks, a Were known as Rohrik Donovan came forth, offering the aid of his pack members in searching the rubble of the Twin Towers for survivors. They worked hard and long into the night side-by-side with the police and firefighters, digging desperately through the remains of the collapsed buildings and using their superior sense of smell, blinded as it was by the toxic mix of chemicals and ash thick in the air, to find any signs of life. Actually, some of the firefighters first on the scene *were* Weres, and only revealed themselves after Rohrik announced the Moonwalker tribe's offer of assistance that day.

At the same time, magi and vampires found it became necessary, because of their ties to the financial sector, to reveal themselves once the World Trade Center collapsed. While the stock market was already in flux over the act of terrorism, The Circle stepped forward a few days later with offers to dip into their coffers to give the halting economy a much-needed boost in the days following the country's near collapse, as well as to use their supernatural skills to fortify strongholds in some major cities in the event of future attacks.

Royce, soon followed by a few other vampires, also stepped into the limelight to add his support to The Circle and speak on behalf of other vampires their wish to see the United States fortified against future acts of terrorism and rebuilt stronger than ever.

Their acts of charity in the name of patriotism and the deep shock people the world over had already suffered from the terrorist attacks was probably the only thing that saved the Others from the hysterical panic of the masses. Those who had stepped forth in other countries were not so fortunate.

Owing to their efforts, these days racism was simply *not done* when it came to creatures not fully human. It had become more than just a social no-no. If you were going to discriminate, you needed to be prepared to deal with it in court. Royce was the one who brought that about, actually. *A. D. Royce Industries v. Amaretto Confections* was notable not only because the plaintiff was a vamp, but because the vamp was suing a distributor for discriminating against his restaurants by jacking up their prices and treating his staff like crap whenever they placed an order. He'd gathered the evidence and proven that they, along with a number of other businesses, charged more to Other-run establishments. Word on the street said The Circle was still bitter that he got to keep the majority of the winnings from the case since they hedged too long about joining the potential class action suit.

The result was more rights and privileges for our undead or otherwise nonfullblood citizens. There were other supernaturals who had made it a point to push for equal rights, and after the first few riots and massacres that broke out, things were settling down and they were actually getting their wishes. In the United States, at least, the Others are now considered to have the same rights as fullblood humans, perhaps more because of their minority status.

These days, it was illegal not only to inquire as to potential employees' national origins or religion, but also to ask whether they were "daylight impaired" or for other clues to their not-quite-fullblood status, since Weres and vamps now fell under the Americans with Disabilities Act (don't ask me how, I'm no lawyer). You couldn't kick someone out of a theater or off a bus for being Other-blood. You also couldn't expect to hunt or assault an Other without consequences, or vice versa. When a vamp sucked someone dry or turned the person without signed papers, they got staked after a quick, low-hassle trial. When someone staked a vamp without a signed warrant, in thirty-four states they got twenty to life for murder. The way the other sixteen states handle killers of Others varied between lethal injection and a bounty from the local authorities for "getting rid of varmints."

I wanted to be enlightened and tolerant about vamps, but all I could do was be scared shitless when met face-to-face with one. Me and a good percentage of the human population were extremely thankful for the legislation that had been rushed through Congress to both protect them from us fullbloods, and vice versa. At least it meant Royce couldn't legally touch me without my written consent. Though whether that written consent came before or after the fact could be fudged, I'd sooner cut off my own hand than sign *those* papers.

Don't get me wrong. I'm not completely anti-Other. I only had a minor spastic fit when I found out that my last boyfriend was a Were. We still talked now and then. I haven't quite gotten around to forgiving him for *showing* me instead of *telling* me what he was. He did a great job hiding it from me and lying about all the little tell-tales right up until he wanted me to sign a contract. Instead of leading up to it in conversation, his way of explaining was to suddenly turn into a timber wolf in my living room.

It was good that he at least knew better than to take his freaky half-man, half-wolf form in front of me. If the cops had shown up with him like that, they would've shot first and asked questions later. I mean, they would have seen this big, hairy *something* straight out of an eighties B-movie lumbering around my living room. Okay, maybe not an eighties movie. The special effects in those films don't do justice to the oddly sleek and graceful in-between form Weres can assume.

Either way, he scared the bejeezus out of me, and—worse—shamed me by effectively hiding any sign of his true nature for months. The Others had grown adept at hiding themselves from mankind out of necessity, and I certainly wasn't the first girl in the last decade to find out her boyfriend wasn't a fullblood human. That had ceased to be a novelty on daytime soaps and talk shows five or six years ago. It didn't make it right, but it stung when I realized I was just another statistic, and hadn't been observant enough to spot any warning signs.

His motives for hiding his nature from me were even somewhat understandable. Besides being worried about my personal feelings on the matter, there were an awful lot of people out there that would happily hunt him down or ruin his business reputation if they found out what he was. I wasn't one of them, but I knew they were out there.

The group who thinks every last supernatural should be exterminated call themselves the White Hats. There are others, but they're the most vocal and active of the lot. Last I heard, they were lobbying to reinstate segregation laws for separate dining and public transportation facilities for Others. That was since their attempts to lobby for mass extermination (read: genocide) was shot down in flames before it even reached the floor in Congress. Their new idea has about a snowball's chance in Hell of passing, too.

Not that they always use the legal route to get

their way. Every few weeks there was something else in the papers about a building being burned down, some poor wretch being beaten or even killed just for being Other-blooded. The cops in this part of the state didn't take kindly to that sort of thing, and if a White Hat was caught in the act of vandalism, slander, or assault, his butt was toast.

So. Why was I terrified of Royce, what with all of our progressive achievements where his kind were concerned? I like my bodily fluids just the way they are. Inside me. The fact that vampires are stronger, faster, and very often smarter and craftier than your average human gives me the willies. It wasn't unheard of for them to use guile or even black enchants to get those contractual papers signed so that your blood, your life, and quite possibly your eternity rested in their hands. Yes, they are people, and not all of them are bastards, but their bodies are mostly dead. They have to feed on other people in order to survive. Cannibalism and black magic, no matter how you couch it, is still wrong and downright scary in my book. Sure, the man looks pretty, but knowing what he has to do in order to stay that way, and knowing also that he has his own brand of dark magic, is more than deterrent enough.

Frankly, I was lucky to get out of there without being spelled. Veronica the mage wasn't the only one who could cast a black enchant with eye contact alone. It was well and truly unwise of me to stare into his eyes like I did, but of course the thought of what could have happened only occurred to me after the fact.

It didn't help that I had read in the papers about that one vamp who went off the deep end about three months ago and went on a rampage. She started—literally—tearing the limbs off the White Hats who were (granted, illegally) accosting her and her flock of followers (read: food) at a downtown restaurant. The papers really spiced it up with unnecessary details, but most didn't mention the fact that one of the White Hats had been holding a knife to the throat of her latest boy toy.

I heard the whole story when I dropped off some evidence down at the police station the night it happened. When I walked in, the blood-spattered White Hats who hadn't been torn up by the vamp and shipped to the hospital or morgue were all in cuffs waiting to be processed. So were the vamp's followers. The vamp herself had been staked in the line of duty by some of New York's finest.

The vamp's followers were either weeping their eyes out or screaming and shaking their cuffed wrists, basically pitching a fit over the loss of their leader. The running mascara and caked white makeup, black clothes, and multicolored dyed hair contrasted sharply with the clean-cut White Hats, all pressed shirts and crisp jeans or slacks. So did the heartwrenching cries for their lost "master."

That was the thing. It wasn't the sensationalism of the newspapers, or even the fact that the vamp had been throwing body parts around like a child's discarded toys. Hearing more than one of my fellow humans cry for "master" was probably what got under my skin the most. Slavery, like cannibalism and black enchants, is not only illegal but wrong on every moral and ethical level, no matter which way you look at it. Whatever she did to them, even after taking their blood and seeing her tear apart other living people, instead of being overjoyed when she died for having their freedom back, they were utterly despondent. Whatever hold she had on them was still hooked deep, urging them to protect and love a leech even after her death. The memory still gives me nightmares.

I'd never let that happen to me. Never.

With all these cheerful thoughts in mind, I undressed, pulled on an oversized T-shirt, and got into bed. I left the lights burning in all the rooms, the cross still around my neck for comfort, and lay staring up at the ceiling as I drew the blankets up to my chin and shivered with more than cold. I'd effectively tied myself to Royce now, and willingly, too. Even if it was only for a short while, I would really have to watch my step. The minute I started feeling any kind of draw to him, that's when I'd know it's time to hit the brakes and back out. Now if only I could manage to fulfill the contract before that happens, and get the money in the process.

That gave me a moment's pause.

What if backing out pissed off The Circle? If Royce *and* The Circle both got ticked at me, I would be royally screwed. I had no trouble admitting that I was small fry and so was my business. I wasn't so egotistical as to think one short clip and my picture in the news was enough to make H&W Investigations a Fortune 500 firm. Hell, we'd be lucky to make the Fortune 50,000 at the rate we were going.

A. D. Royce Industries and The Circle were both incredibly affluent and politically powerful factions, not groups I wanted to come between. The only wealthy contact I had to speak of was my business partner, and she didn't come with the contacts or political muscle to flex that Royce or Veronica had at their fingertips. This meant I'd also be bringing down the house on Sara if I did decide to cancel the contract. Being my partner, even though it wasn't her run, meant that she was tied into this mess almost as much as I was. Crap.

I had no choice. I couldn't back out of the contract now. For the time being, I had the dubious safety of The Circle to run to if Royce got pissed. Right now, he thought I was an ally or at least a business associate of some kind. If what I was doing for Veronica was a betrayal of some sort (and I had no doubt in my mind the vamp would view it that way if he found me out), then I had no choice but to carry things through or I'd lose that protection, however minimal it might be. If I broke the contract I'd have not one, but two, incredibly pissed-off powers-that-be after my hide.

Which brought up another great point. Royce knew me, and acted almost like he was expecting me when I showed up at the club. It would be foolish to believe that he'd simply recognized me from the papers and that his "helpful nice guy" show was little more than coincidence. Sure, the Were thing was on the front page, but that was over a month ago. I'm not *that* memorable, and neither was the take.

Was he taking that old saying "Keep your friends close, but your enemies closer" to heart? Did he know I was actually working for The Circle? Was he going to try to play me somehow?

What the hell had I gotten myself into?

Chapter 7

Something woke me in the middle of the night. I cracked my eyes open, not sure whether a feeling or a sound had disturbed me. Squinting out from under my cocoon of blankets, I saw that my digital alarm clock read 3:17 in very large red numbers. I grimaced. Oh well, at least I wasn't expected to go into the office later.

Throwing off the covers, I glanced over at the window and noted absently that light from the streetlamps was filtering in between the blinds. Pausing, I looked up at the ceiling.

The light was off.

"The hell?" I muttered, getting out of bed. Hadn't I left all the lights on in my moment of insecure paranoia after meeting with the vampire? I had just changed the bulb not that long ago. Did it burn out from being left on all night?

I moved to the door. As my hand rested on the knob, about to turn and open it, a very large, very male hand clamped over my mouth as another snaked around my waist and yanked me back, pinning my arms in the process. I didn't have time even to gasp in shock, my eyes widening as I was pressed back against the guy's chest. His sour breath slid over my cheek as he whispered in my ear, "Don't move, or we'll gut you like a fish. Are you one of his whores?"

Another man became visible, stepping around the guy who'd grabbed me so I could see the hunting knife glittering in his gloved hand. It was too dark for me to see his face. "She's not. Not yet. Look what she's wearing."

My eyes were open so wide they stung. I didn't want to hyperventilate and pass out, but I was scared shitless and couldn't move. The guy's gloved hand stayed clamped over my mouth while his other hand slid between my breasts and fingered the cross at my neck. He gave a little dissatisfied grunt. "Doesn't mean anything."

"Sure it does. It means she saw him, but she didn't let him touch her. Isn't that right, princess?"

I made an incoherent sound of confusion against the glove held to my mouth, rolling my eyes to the side to try to make out the features of the other man. What the hell was going on?

"If we let you go, do you promise not to scream or run? My companion wasn't joking. I don't want to hurt you, but I will if I have to. Blink once if you agree."

I did. He nodded, and his beefy companion reluctantly let up his grip on me. The second the man let go, I rounded and slapped him. "Don't *ever* touch me!"

The big guy staggered back, a hand lifting to his

cheek in shock. Seemed like that was the last thing he was expecting. Turning back to the smooth talker, who appeared to be the leader, I balled my fists at my sides and seethed, "What the fuck are you doing in my apartment, threatening me? Get the hell out!"

"That's quite a mouth you've got on you. Don't worry, we'll be gone soon enough. We just want to know if you're one of us or one of them."

That gave me pause. Us or them? "What are you talking about?"

He laughed softly, the sound for some reason making me shiver. This guy was nuts, completely unhinged. It was his companion who answered me, his low voice rumbling in a growl deep enough to do any Were proud. "Are you a donor? Do you work for or with the corpses?"

Oh no. White Hats. Not like the uptight Mr. and Mrs. Borowsky. These were the right-wing, gun-toting, business-torching kind. The ones who made vamps and their people disappear.

"God, no. Of course not, I'm not psychotic." Not like you, buddy.

He nodded, gesturing with the knife for me to back up and sit down on the bed. I did, yanking the sheets over my bare legs and wondering what was coming next.

"You saw him tonight. The leech. What was your purpose?"

Well, this was just a peachy keen development. Was I being followed, or did they just happen to be scoping the place out when I got there?

"I was there on business. I'm a PI, and I'm trying to track a missing person for a client." I took a breath, noting the unspoken condemnation in their postures, and plunged ahead, hoping I wasn't digging myself a deeper grave. "He was last seen with a vamp. The leech's contacts may be the only way for me to find the kid in time."

Maybe using the offensive slang for vampires would help my cause. Maybe making him think the kid was in danger would make him back off. Yeah, and maybe they'd put on top hats and coattails and start singing showtunes for me while they're at it.

The bigger guy glanced to his partner, who didn't relax. "That's only a half-truth, Ms. Waynest. We've been watching you. I know you have some ties to The Circle."

Shit.

"That's true," I muttered warily, trying to swallow back the sudden surge of fear those words caused in me. Some White Hats were more liberal when it came to magi than they were with Weres and vamps. What type were these two?

"We want you to join us."

More than a little nonplussed, I stared in the general direction of his shadowed face. Would he take a stab at me if I let out the hysterical laughter that threatened at his words? It took more than a little effort to swallow my first reaction back.

He slid the knife into a sheath at his belt before spreading his hands and taking on an apologetic tone.

"I can only imagine what you must think of us,

but we had to make sure you had not gone over to the vampire. As I said, we've been watching you. You are capable of dealing with and against the Others, and you have an excellent front of a legitimate business to carry out our line of work. You simply forced our hand by going to the leech so soon."

Good God. This was getting more and more like a bad gangster movie by the minute.

"Look, no offense or anything, but no thanks. I'm just trying to do my job." Man, I could be remarkably polite when under threat of having my throat slit. "I didn't ask to get involved with these things, and I have no plans on ever working for either leech or mage ever again once I finish out my contract."

Since my eyes were adjusting to the dark, I was finally able to make out the small white cowboy hat pins at their collars, and some of the smooth talker's features. Tall and skinny White Hat was about as white bread as they come, probably blond and blue-eyed though it was still too dark to be sure. Mr. Deep Voice had mahogany skin, blending well with the shadows. They were both wearing dark clothing, leaving most of their bodies indistinct, though I could now see well enough to note that Mr. Smooth Talker was frowning.

Thankfully, it didn't seem like they were going to press the issue. After the two shared a look I couldn't read, Mr. Deep Voice spoke up.

"We'll give you some time to think about it. Remember what you're dealing with, little girl. Leeches and sparks are dangerous. They both play for keeps. Be a real pity to stumble over your body in an alley somewhere."

"Thanks for the advice. Get out."

Under the circumstances, that was about as polite as I could be. I wanted to add a few colorful expletives, threats, and suggestions of my own to the mix, but I figured I could do without the gaping stab wounds I'd likely get for my efforts.

The two of them quickly exited the bedroom, fading into the deeper shadows of my living room. I got up and rushed over in time to watch them slip out a window and onto the fire escape. Damn, they'd cut a neat little hole in the glass and simply flipped the lock over to let themselves in. I considered calling the cops, but chances were I could call in an order for pizza, too, and the food would get here first. The trail would be stone cold by the time they arrived.

Just great. Slamming the window shut and locking it behind them, not that it would do much good with the four-inch hole in it, I thought about what the two men had said and how exactly I would explain the damage to the window to my landlord.

No matter what I did, who I chose to work for, or what choices I made, I'd be pissing somebody off. I had my pick between The Circle, Royce, or the White Hats. The White Hats were obviously an unstable element, considering they thought I'd be more amenable to joining their fun and games at knifepoint. The Circle had me in a contractual pinch I wouldn't be able to break out of with any ease. Royce would probably hit the roof as soon as he figured out what I was really after. Each and every one of them had the resources and clout to make my life miserable or even make me disappear. One, or more, of them would have a reason to want me to, once I made a move.

I wandered back to my bed and sat down on the edge, staring blankly at the wall. My hands had started shaking again. Right now, Royce seemed like my safest bet, seeing as he was the only one of the three who hadn't threatened me. Yet.

I was so dead.

Chapter 8

After a very long, very sleepless night, I finally broke down and called Sara around 7:30. That was pushing it on a Saturday morning, but I desperately needed some reassurances. She picked up on the fifth ring.

"Ugh. Yeah, what?" Her grouchy, morning-gravelly voice was comforting in its familiarity.

"Sara, someone broke in during the night. I'm in deep. I met with Royce last night, and now I've got White Hats on my tail."

Yeesh, and I'd thought the White Hats were being melodramatic last night. Must be rubbing off.

"What?!"

The edge to her voice made me cringe. I hadn't quite meant to get it all out in a rush like that, but there was no help for it now.

"Shia, what the hell? I mean, great, you got ahold of Royce, but what's with the White Hats? Are you okay? Anything stolen?"

Sighing, I rubbed a hand over my face. "No, nothing

stolen. I'm okay. These two guys broke in through the fire escape and politely asked me at knifepoint to join their cause."

Her silence was making me nervous.

Then she said quietly, "And what did you tell them?"

"I invited them for tea and crumpets. Give me a break, Sara, I told them to get the hell out and leave me alone."

She sounded more relieved than anything. "I was just checking, chill out. So what're you going to do?"

"I don't know. Probably go down to see Veronica today and take her up on that offer for equipment. Might as well take advantage of it. Maybe they have something useful against vamps and rogue zealots."

After a short bark of laughter, she asked, a little more normally, "Do you want me to come with you?"

"No, I'm okay. I just needed to tell someone."

My turn to hesitate. I didn't like having to say the next part, but the White Hats didn't leave me a lot of choice after last night. Not that I'd had a choice since agreeing to work for The Circle.

"Listen, watch your back. I know this is my run, but I've got a bad feeling this one's going to go wonky and I don't want you getting hurt because of me."

"Hey, what are partners for? If you need a place to crash until this blows over, just bring some clothes and come by. Oh, and check in with me before sunset or I'll come looking."

"Thanks, I may just take you up on that. I'll call you after I see what The Circle's got to offer."

"Be careful, Shia."

"I will. Thanks, Sara."

Only after I hung up did I remember that I was supposed to chew her out for not telling me about the financial straits our business was in. Oh well. I'd bug her about it when I had a few less important things on my mind. Things like my impending demise and need to decide what side of the supernatural fence I was on.

I still had the jitters and didn't feel like lying around, so I got up to shower and get dressed. After pulling on a comfortable pair of jeans and a sweatshirt, I made myself a bagel with lox and cream cheese, a cup of coffee, and headed over to my computer. A few clicks and passwords later, I was staring at my e-mail.

Two were from Mom, one a joke and the other a reminder for Sara and me that my brother Damien's birthday barbecue was on Sunday. Spam. Spam. More spam. A note from my brother Mikey asking if I knew what Damien wanted and if I wanted in on a joint gift. A few offers to enlarge my PEN15 and get a better mortgage rate. Lo and behold, my in-box also had an e-mail from Veronica Wright sent early last night, and another from Alec Royce from less than two hours ago.

The sun had risen about three hours ago. Did that mean vamps could move about in daylight? Great, that was more than I needed to know.

I clicked open Veronica's e-mail first.

TO: S. Waynest
FROM: Veronica Wright
SUBJECT: Update

I haven't heard since you signed the contract Thursday. I am concerned. Update?

Irritated at her impatience, I clattered out a quick response.

Met with our subject last night. Progress being made. I would like to get together with you this afternoon RE: equipment. Are you available?

Next came Royce's message. I remembered belatedly that he'd written something on the back of his business card before he gave it to me, and wondered if that had anything to do with it.

TO: S. Waynest
FROM: Alec D. Royce
SUBJECT: Security

I have received word that our friends the W.H.s have paid you a visit.

That was scary. How the heck did he know about that already? Chilled, I pressed on, scanning the rest of the note.

I would be displeased to see our business relationship terminated prior to completion of your assignment. I will extend you some measure of protection against the W.H. element and give you an update on the missing boy.

The requisite forms are filled out and the warrant should be signed by noon. Call the number on the back of my card if something comes up during the day.

Please come to my office on 52nd as soon as convenient after sunset. Present my card at the security desk for entrance.

Cordially,
Alec D. Royce
A. D. Royce Industries

Well, that was a development. Why was he offering me protection now? What exactly did he plan to do to keep the White Hats off my back? Something about the letter struck me as off, aside from the fact that I was reading an e-mail from a friggin' vampire. Royce was supposedly older than dirt, but he didn't appear to be the technophobe I would've thought considering the height of technology at the time he was made a vamp was probably a sundial.

Reading it over a second time, I decided that there were two things about it that bothered me. First, he was being far more formal in writing than he'd been in person. Second, "prior to completion of your assignment" didn't quite make sense. It was just a little too carefully worded. It was the sort of thing that made me think he might really know about the agreement I had with The Circle and that he was planning on using me to get to them somehow.

Maybe I was reading too much into everything.

I jotted down a quick "I'll be there" reply and sent it. Just as I was about to turn off the monitor, another e-mail popped into my in-box. Veronica was an early riser, apparently. I opened the e-mail.

> Come by at 2PM. Ask for Arnold at the front desk. He'll get you whatever you need.

Nice. Things were starting to look up. Maybe when I met with Royce this evening, I'd actually be prepared for it.

Chapter 9

Even though I'd forced myself to lie down and take a nap so I wouldn't be a complete zombie later that night, I was still feeling groggy when I entered the lobby of The Circle's downtown office tower. I'd almost slept through my alarm and ended up hurriedly throwing on presentable clothes, fluffing my hair and slapping on some makeup before running out the door. Traffic had been hell, and even though I knew it was better to park somewhere and take the train, I just didn't want to deal with it. So between traffic and finding parking, I was twenty minutes late.

The design in the lobby was impressive: lofty ceilings; high windows that allowed sunlight to stream in; low-slung red couches; and intricate arcane symbols inlaid on the floor. Feeling hassled, rumpled, and cranky, I approached a sleek, polished desk where a bored-looking receptionist tapped away at her keyboard. She didn't bother to look up.

"Excuse me? I'm here to see Arnold."

The girl slowly raised her eyes from her flatscreen monitor to look at me over the rim of her glasses with cool, studied contempt. I couldn't help but notice that her clothes were all trendier and nicer than mine and that her expensively dyed blond hair framed a thin, elfin face with heavy, but expertly applied, makeup. She was stick-thin and pretty enough to be modeling those clothes on a runway somewhere.

She looked me up and down and cocked a dismissive eyebrow before sliding her eyes back to the screen. Obviously, I failed her inspection.

"You're late."

More tapping on the keyboard. A pause.

"He'll come get you in a moment. Please have a seat, ma'am."

The bored voice couldn't hide the underlying irritation. I'd probably interrupted a game of solitaire.

Making a heroic effort not to flip her off, I hefted my purse higher on my shoulder and had a seat on one of the uncomfortable but stylish red couches. The magazines spread on the table were up to date, but stuff I'd never read. *Arcana Quarterly* and *Familiar Fashion: How to Accessorize Your Fae Focus* just isn't my cup of tea. I pulled out my cell and started fumbling with the text messages, trying to find something to focus on other than the rapid clicking of nails over keys coming in rattling spurts every few seconds from the reception desk.

Arnold kept me waiting exactly thirty minutes. His way of telling me off for coming late, I supposed. I looked up at the sound of him clearing his throat from the glass double doors next to the receptionist's desk.

He was tall, skinny, with thick glasses perched on a narrow nose and an untidy mop of sandy brown hair, and wearing jeans and a faded T-shirt that read JESUS SAVES. THE REST OF YOU TAKE DAMAGE. Oh great, a geek.

"Ms. Waynest?" He appeared distracted, glancing at me from a thick sheaf of papers he clutched in one ink-stained hand, offering the other to me to shake. His shy, somewhat weak smile was genuine, however, and I realized he hadn't been keeping me waiting on purpose. He was probably just tied up in his work. He actually looked a trifle apologetic under all the distraction.

"Thank you for seeing me, Mr., uh . . . *Arnold.*" I realized I didn't know his last name. "Veronica told me you'd be able to help me."

He nodded, reddening a bit at the mention of Veronica. A crush, perhaps? Poor guy. That love was destined to remain unrequited, and for more than one reason if her hitting on me in the restaurant the other night was any indication.

"Yes, ah, Ms. Wright told me you were coming. She said you needed something from our security vaults, is that right?"

"Yes, that's right."

I found myself liking the guy despite his geekiness. He was nice enough. Too bad he worked for scum like Veronica.

"This way, please. Follow me." The receptionist

didn't look up once, still tapping away as I followed the guy into the room behind the glass doors.

Inside it looked pretty much indistinguishable from any other cube farm in corporate America. Gray and drab, with a few amusing cartoons tacked to cube walls or mildly entertaining screensavers on the computers we passed, but otherwise unremarkable. I couldn't hear the sounds of anyone working, and it looked pretty deserted. Guess even magi took the weekends off.

He led me to an elevator oddly stuck in the middle of the floor between two rows of cubicles. I wasn't going to question it. Magi could do whatever the hell they wanted with their architecture.

As we stepped inside, he pressed the button for the lowest basement level instead of one of the double-digit high-rise levels I was expecting. All the corporate bigwigs must get the view.

He didn't speak during the short ride, just zoned back into the papers he was holding. When the doors opened, he looked up with confusion, as if surprised we had arrived so soon. Weird.

Stepping out, he led the way down a damp, obviously underground hallway. Thick insulation pipes ran overhead and the paint was dull, institutional gray-blue. We passed a number of doors, one or two with strange inscriptions where one would expect a name tag or some such. Then I noticed we passed one that had a nameplate for the boiler room. Lovely. Poor Arnold must be among the lowest of the low on the corporate ladder to be stuck working down here.

We rounded a bend or two, then he abruptly stopped at an unmarked door with peeling paint. I probably would've walked right past it. There was nothing special about it that I could see, but he opened it anyway and stepped inside.

Following him into the room, I was a little disappointed to see it looked like an entirely unremarkable, if high-tech, security office. A collection of monitors gleamed against one wall showing various scenes inside and around the building. A guard in a slate gray uniform glanced over at us briefly at the sound of my heels clicking against the floor but soon returned his attention to the monitors. A couple of fans were running, keeping the computers under the table cool. I noted with some amusement that the guy was hiding a paperback under one thick palm against his leg, probably hoping we wouldn't notice.

Arnold continued walking, nose in his papers, and I have to admit to being surprised when he walked without stopping into the blank far wall and disappeared. I paused, mouth agape, not sure whether to attempt to follow or just stand there staring like an idiot. Guess which option I took.

"You can follow him. Just keep walking straight ahead, you'll be fine."

The guard's voice was bemused but kindly, and I felt just a little foolish for being so shocked. Magi do magic. Duh. I should expect that here. It still gave me the willies.

Swallowing my discomfort and putting on a brave face, I took the guy's direction and kept walking. I shut my eyes when I got close, expecting-but-not to have my face smashed when I walked into the wall. Nothing happened. Well, nothing except a slight tingling sensation against my skin and my footsteps suddenly being muted by carpet.

Opening my eyes, I saw Arnold watching me expectantly from across the room. I took it all in, feeling a mix of elation at having survived walking through the wall with my dignity intact and disappointment for the plain homeliness of the room he'd brought me to. There was a big, beat-up desk in the middle of the room, one leg propped up with a bit of cardboard to keep it level. There were tons of papers scattered around the room and on the desk, piled on a table off to the side and on top of the two tall filing cabinets shoved into a corner. A pizza box was perched on top of one pile, an open box of Chinese food, and a couple of coffee mugs on the desk. One held pens and pencils, the other what looked to be very old tea. The smell was a mix of old pizza and gym socks, with a very faint undertone of incense.

I knew it was Arnold's office almost immediately, not because of the clutter but because of the scatter of dice on the desk and the dinosaur and alien action figures on top of his monitor.

"I just need you to sign a form for me, then we can go into the vault."

I shrugged and took the form he deftly pulled from somewhere in the middle of the stack in his arm. Looked like a standard requisition form, nothing terribly exciting. I signed and dated it and left it on the desk. He dropped the rest of his stack of papers next to it with a muted "thump" and moved behind the desk, twisting a ring on one of his fingers before placing a hand against the wall. I blinked as he revealed another wall behind it as the first simply blinked out of existence at his touch.

This one looked like the back of a cave, all sandstone and multicolored layers of reddish rock. It curved inward a few feet behind the desk. There were a pair of arched double doors made out of some kind of gray stone, closed tight and covered with intricate patterns—runes or something like them, I supposed.

The hair on the back of my neck rose when I realized the runes were moving and changing even as I stared at them. Solid stone is *not* supposed to move.

An idle wave of Arnold's hand and a short "*Aperto*" and the thick, rune-inscribed doors slowly opened inward.

Chapter 10

"Don't touch anything while we're inside without asking first," Arnold said before we walked through the doors. "Some of the stuff in here is dying to get out and might try to attach itself to you."

Oh great. Sentient artifacts, just the sort of thing to make my day.

He led the way inside. The walls here were of red sandstone marked with runes similar to the ones on the doors. Every few feet there were arches with burning torches for light. The flickering lights drew my attention to the runes that moved and swirled in a way that was making me feel dizzy. I had the sick feeling we left New York behind the minute we walked through those arches.

"What did you need exactly anyway? Vero didn't tell me what to give you."

I sighed, hoping I wouldn't sound too ridiculous and unprofessional. "I was hoping you might be able to tell me. I was hired to find a statuette in the possession of a vampire."

He snorted laughter, drawing my attention sharply to him and off the weird walls. "Oh, that. I've got just the thing."

We continued on for what seemed like forever. I should've worn flats instead of heels. Abruptly, the tunnel opened up into a large circular chamber with other tunnels branching off in four other directions. I noted the five-sided star etched into the sandstone, each point set before a tunnel opening, including the one we now stood in. There were fat candles set on each point of the star, none lit.

"Luminare," he whispered, and I took an involuntary step back as the candles simultaneously lit themselves up. *"Guidare."*

One by one, the candles flickered out, leaving only one with a steady flame. He gestured cheerfully, his voice resuming normal tones. "That way. Follow me."

I did. My curiosity was really getting the best of me. "What's down the other tunnels?"

"Traps. Death for the really stupid." He was pretty nonchalant, considering the topic. "Most of the ones who make it this far don't know enough or are too arrogant to ask for guidance. We put that little safeguard in a couple years ago. Works like a charm."

I swallowed hard. "Who comes down here? Aside from you, I mean."

"Oh, I don't know. Disgruntled former employees, rival corporations and covens, people like you who get a glimpse once and think they can make it past our safeguards." He laughed softly, the sound making me shiver despite the nasal quality. "Greed getting the better of them, I suppose."

"People like me?"

I knew my voice had an edge, though I didn't mean it to come out as harsh as it did. The way he said "people" led me to believe he didn't think very highly of us plain ol' magic-less humans. It's one thing when you voice your little bigoted thoughts in private, quite another to do it to the person's face.

He laughed again, a little more heartily this time. "Don't take offense. I meant outside contractors."

"Oh." My turn to be embarrassed.

"Here we are."

He waved me into another large cavern, this one positively overflowing with junk. It looked worse than his office. There was old dusty crap scattered everywhere, all over the floor, piled on tables, everything from books and scrolls to rusty suits of armor and old-fashioned weaponry. There was jewelry and vials and gems and statues and coins strewn as far as the eye could see.

Despite the mess, I had to admit I was impressed. The Circle had literally tons of junk. And because it belonged to The Circle, all of it, every piece, had an element of magic to it. My respect for them went up a notch, despite their obvious lack of housecleaning skills.

Arnold waded into the mess, carefully stepping over and around the stuff on the floor. He picked up a little stick-looking thing from underfoot, made a surprised "huh," and continued on. I stayed behind, not sure I'd be able to follow in my heels.

He disappeared around a mountain of books. I'm not kidding. There were so many, I couldn't even begin to count them.

"Wait there, I'll be back in a sec." His voice sounded far more distant than I would've credited, considering he was only a few yards away.

So I waited. And waited. After a little while, I pulled out my cell phone and checked the time, noting with dismay that it was nearly five o'clock. Had we really been down here that long?

"Arnold?" I called, hoping he hadn't gotten distracted and forgotten me down here. I'd never find my way back to his office, not without help.

"Just a sec, almost got it!" came a faint reply from somewhere in the midst of the mess.

Despite his words, I was sorely tempted to go look for him and see if I could maybe help move this along a little faster. I still had to meet with Royce tonight, and didn't want to keep the vamp waiting too long after sunset. Who knew how he'd take it if I showed up late to our scheduled meeting.

From somewhere out of my sight, I heard a prolonged crashing and clattering. It sounded like the whole place was about to fall down around our ears. A minute later, dust-covered and triumphant, Arnold appeared from behind the books and carefully picked his way back to where I stood.

He had a few things in his scrawny arms and cupped in his hands. I reached out as soon as he was close enough to take a few from him, and he looked grateful for the help.

"Thanks. Sorry for the wait."

"No sweat. What is all this?" I looked down at what we were holding, a little confused. None of it looked very useful.

I'd taken a couple of delicate crystal vials filled with an amber-colored liquid and a plain-looking silver chain with a tiny black stone pendant hanging from it. He was still holding the stick he'd picked up earlier, along with a leather belt folded over one arm and a dusty book and loose papers cradled in the other.

"Got some good stuff for you. That perfume is faint to someone like you or me, smells a little like cinnamon." He nodded at the crystal vials. "It depresses a vamp's appetite and makes you smell less like food to them. Alchemists came up with it a few hundred years ago."

I raised my eyebrows at that, examining the sloshing liquid with interest. In that case, I'd bathe in the stuff before I went to see Royce.

Reading my expression, he grinned. "You just need a dab at the throat and wrists, against the skin. Works best over a pulse point and it'll last until you wash it off. Next," he continued, starting to walk back the way we came, "I got you that necklace as a deterrent against any mind games the vamp or even one of us might try to pull on you. You'll see through illusion and can't be forced with magic to do something against your will."

Jackpot! "Wow, thanks," I couldn't believe my luck. This was great! "That's amazing, I never knew there were such things."

He grinned, apparently pleased with himself.

"Yeah, The Circle's pretty good at keeping secrets. You won't find any of this stuff on the market; it's all made in-house."

I hid a pang of worry. Did this mean I'd have to keep quiet about the items, or could I tell Sara? I decided to leave that problem until later.

"Anyway, that's not all. This belt was a lucky find, I thought we'd given the last one away a decade ago. The stakes will always return to the belt after use. Oh, and remember, don't wear it until you're ready to use it."

My elation suddenly dried up into something nearing terror. "What? No, no stakes. I don't do exterminations. I told Veronica that when we met on Thursday."

"Trust me, you'll want these." Arnold wasn't ruffled by the panic in my voice. We'd reached the double doors leading into his office, and I couldn't help but be further alarmed noticing that the walk took a lot less time, and we hadn't passed the star and candles this time around. "Maybe not right away, but they'll come in handy."

He thrust the bundled-up belt at me, ignoring my protests. Reluctantly, I picked it up, surprised at how heavy the silly thing was. I hadn't seen the three solid metal stakes attached to it since he'd had them pressed up against his chest. Peachy keen.

Sourly, I gestured at the book, papers, and stick he was still holding. "What about those?"

He shook his head and dumped them unceremoniously on top of the papers on his desk. "These are for me. You've got Veronica's e-mail, right? If you need anything else, just have her give me a little forewarning and I'll have it all ready for you. It'll save you the walk next time."

I sighed. "Okay. Thanks Arnold, you've been a big help. This was way more than I was expecting."

"Don't sweat it." He grinned again, his gaze shifting down to the dice on his desk. He picked up a few and rolled them absently against the desktop. I noted the bright little bits of plastic came to rest with the 20-side, the 10-side, and the 1-side up. His voice was faint, and probably would have gone unheard if I hadn't been so on edge, taking note of every detail. "And they say divination is a dead art."

The look he turned to me was speculative, intrigued, and something else I just couldn't read. Clearing his throat, he walked me over to the blank wall we'd entered through earlier.

"Let me know if this job gives you trouble. You can just call our main number and ask for me."

I walked through, looking back at him over my shoulder. "Thank you very mu—"

My last words were cut off abruptly as I stepped through the wall and into the main lobby, right next to the receptionist's desk. She was still typing, and didn't look up at the sound of my voice. I reached up a hand to lightly run a finger over the huge Impressionist mural on the wall that I'd stepped through. Solid.

With a slight shudder, I rearranged the stuff in my arms, stuck the necklace and vials in my purse, and wrapped the belt up into a loop made awkward by the stakes. As I headed toward the exit, the girl looked up.

"Have a nice day!"

I was so edgy that the sound of her voice cutting through the silence made me jump. She smirked, then focused back on her screen, content to pretend I didn't exist.

What a day this was turning out to be. I cringed when I realized it had barely started; now I had to face Royce.

Chapter 11

When I left the building, I saw Veronica standing off to one side near a planter, talking to another woman I didn't recognize. Both of them were wearing chic business suits, and it looked like the other lady's charcoal gray pantsuit was even more expensive and well tailored than Veronica's navy blue skirt and jacket. The two of them had cigarettes in hand and were in a heated discussion. Veronica did not look pleased.

I started to approach but she saw me out of the corner of her eye and shook her head at me, mouthing "later" and turning back to the other woman. The woman turned to me, her startlingly bright green eyes staring at me from a lined, frowning face. Her graying hair was pulled tightly back on her skull into a severe bun, making it impossible to miss the disapproval in her gaze, like the teacher that just caught you playing hooky.

If I'd done something wrong, I might have felt uncomfortable. As it was, I just shrugged and kept walking. Maybe she didn't like my clothes. Yeah, that was it. I'd just call or e-mail Veronica later.

Thinking better of showing up to meet with Royce with stakes on my person, I returned to my car, parked a couple of blocks away, and hid the belt under the front passenger seat. I wanted it out of my hands as quickly as possible. Next I poured a few drops of the perfume onto a finger and dabbed at my throat and wrists, finding the cinnamon-and-cloves scent curiously pleasant. I could get to like this alchemy stuff.

Rather than carry those delicate-looking crystal vials in my purse, I put them in the glove compartment, figuring they were less likely to get jostled around that way. Digging the necklace out from the depths of my purse, I put it on and locked the car up again, hefting the bag over my shoulder. Royce's downtown office wasn't too far from The Circle's high-rise. I'd hop on the subway and be there in no time.

The ride was quick, but I had time to send a text message to Sara to let her know what was up and give her a brief description of the loot Arnold had given me. When I stepped back out onto the street, the sun was still just barely hanging in the sky. I figured I might as well grab a bite to eat before dealing with the vamp. I wanted to be as clearheaded as possible.

I found a café half a block from my destination. By the time I finished my overpriced sandwich and coffee, it was fully dark and I was feeling that familiar gut-wrenching fear settling into my bones.

The food hung heavy in my stomach as I pushed through the revolving doors and stepped into Royce's office building.

There was no snide receptionist in this place, only a guard in a sharp-looking suit who got up to greet me from behind the security desk. "Can I help you, miss?"

I dug into my purse and pulled out Royce's card. "I have an appointment with Mr. Royce."

He gave the card a cursory examination before handing it back with a nod and a smile, pointing to a bank of elevators. "Eighth floor and to your right. You can't miss it."

"Thanks," I said, and meant it. Praise all for good service.

The eighth floor wasn't terribly exciting. When I stepped out of the elevator, there was a pair of double doors to my left, and a similar pair to my right. A little plaque on the ones on the right read A. D. ROYCE INDUSTRIES. Guess I found the place.

There was a sticky note stuck to one of the doors. I peeled it off, figuring it was probably for me.

Ms. Waynest:
Please come in. My office is in the back.
—Alec

Well, that was nice, going from "Mr. Royce" to "Alec" in the space of one meeting and an e-mail exchange. I guess he wanted a more casual business relationship than his last e-mail implied.

The front office looked deserted but I could hear

voices coming from the back. Following the voices, I recognized Royce's in short order. I soon found myself standing in the doorway to his office, peering in.

". . . will work just fine, and I'll bring the paperwork with me. Thanks, Jim, I'll see you Wednesday."

"You got it, Alec. Take care."

He had his feet propped up on his desk, and he gestured for me to come in as he tossed the pen he'd been toying with on top of the papers scattered there and reached to turn off the speakerphone. This office looked a little more like somebody worked in it, phone and computer included this time. The furnishings and view were still nice, but not as impressive as the one over The Underground. I noted the low bookshelf in the corner had a curious mix of cookbooks and classic literature. Guess he was a fan of cheesecake and Shakespeare. Who knew?

There was no conference table here, no couches or wet bar. The walls were hung with corkboards covered in papers and Post-it notes instead of paintings. From the look of it, he didn't get visitors here very often. This was obviously where the real work got done.

I noted with a touch of amusement that he was just as casual today as he'd been in the club. This time he wore blue jeans and a plain white T-shirt instead of leather pants and a netted shirt, but he still looked good to me. Damnably so. Undead, bloodsucking fiend, Shiarra. Remember that.

He rose and moved around to pull out a chair for me, a warm smile curving his lips. I felt pretty overdone in my makeup, pantsuit, and heels, but a second later my fashion worries were overtaken by a surge of unreasoning fear at his approach.

"Ms. Waynest, thank you for coming."

I took a seat, relaxing slightly when he slid back around to sit at his desk. I kept my purse clutched in my lap, however.

He leaned back comfortably in the chair and regarded me with heavily lidded eyes. I wasn't fooled. He looked more like a waiting python than a relaxed businessman to my eyes.

"Have you eaten? Can I get you anything?"

"No, thank you, Mr. Royce."

What was with the formality and looking after my happiness and well-being? Was he trying to put me off balance with his solicitousness on purpose?

"Did you get any news about the missing boy or the girl he was with?" I asked.

"Yes, actually. The girl's name isn't Tara, it's Anastasia Alderov."

I nodded, impressed despite myself. His people must move fast to get that kind of information on such short notice.

"She's the progeny of one of my competitors in Chicago. I imagine she was here to scout the area when she met the Borowsky boy."

Yeesh, he was doing me out of a job. "That still means that she's . . ." The words died in my mouth. I just couldn't say it.

He seemed to sense my discomfort and his tone

turned serious. "Yes. It's still grounds for disposal. She has no guest permit to hunt in this state."

Good God. He made it seem like he was talking about deer season. I swallowed hard, trying to calm the sudden racing of my heart.

"Unfortunately, we have not pinpointed her resting place yet. She'll turn up, and so will the boy."

I nodded, not quite trusting my voice just yet. He sighed, spreading his hands in a helpless, frustrated gesture. He looked so human and convincing, for a moment I forgot my fear.

"What is it about me that frightens you so? I am not about to leap over the desk and go for your jugular, Shiarra."

Now that was embarrassing. I must have been exuding nervousness more than I thought for him to be remarking on it. Turning my eyes away, I forced myself to relax a little, leaning forward to put my purse down between my feet to show that I wasn't about to make a run for it.

"It's not you exactly, Mr. Royce." How could I explain my fear without sounding like an unenlightened racist idiot?

"There is no need for the formality; call me Alec. Has someone at The Circle been filling your head with stories about me?"

I started. He smirked. Damn it, he knew, he already knew what I'd gotten myself into and was just toying with me now. I started to rise, but he held out a staying hand.

"Please, sit. I know you're doing something for them, and I know it has something to do with me.

I'm prepared for that. What I don't understand is why it is you. You're obviously terrified to be here, yet here you are. What hold do they have on you? Perhaps we can come to an arrangement."

An arrangement. Would he be able to keep The Circle *and* the White Hats off my back? Doubts immediately assailed me. I didn't have much to offer a vampire like Royce. He had more money than God, owned a good chunk of prime real estate in several states, and had more flunkies and fawning donors than one would think he'd know what to do with. I didn't have anything to give him that he didn't already have, except maybe a line into The Circle.

Not to mention he'd probably be pissed once he knew what I was really after. Plus, I was contracted. There were all kinds of confidentiality clauses tied into that contract, and I could lose my license if The Circle didn't just splatter me out of existence for turning on them. Oh, and let us not forget that this was a vampire I was dealing with. Judging by our previous encounter, he'd probably try to charm me into revealing what I was really after. The devil was a sweet talker, too.

Thoughts racing almost as fast as my pounding heart, I chose my words very, very carefully. "With all due respect, Mr. Royce, I can't divulge my other clients' information without their blessing. I wouldn't last long in this line of work if I did that."

He leaned forward on the desk, folding his hands and propping his chin on his knuckles.

Those black eyes narrowed as he took in my words, weighing what I did and didn't say.

"I would hate to see you come to some harm on my account."

Oh great. That was comforting.

"My resources are considerable, Ms. Waynest. I'm not withdrawing the offer of protection, even if you choose to continue this farce and work against me. I take care of my own."

What the hell was that supposed to mean? I wasn't one of his donors, or even an employee.

"I appreciate that. I'm sorry I can't give you what you're looking for in return."

About as sorry as a kid caught with her hand in the cookie jar. I still wanted my cookie, er, money, damn it. I had bills to pay.

He inhaled through his nose deeply, eyes closing. I wondered why. Vamps didn't need to breathe like a living person did.

"The Circle wants something badly if they're giving you Amber Kiss perfume. I thought the alchemists stopped making it centuries ago. It does an admirable job of hiding your scent, but your heartbeat gives away your fear."

Hairs on the back of my neck rising in renewed terror, I tried to quell the shakes that started up at his words. What the hell was he playing at?

"I'm not sure I understand where you're going with this." That sounded safe enough. Except that I really, really wasn't sure I wanted to know where this conversation was going.

His eyes stayed shut. He didn't look at me at all,

or speak right away, instead kept taking the occasional deep breath to, I guess, see what he could smell on me under the perfume. Talk about creepy.

"You're attracting the attention of vampires, The Circle, and the White Hats. You've managed to upset the power structure of a local Were pack. You are human, and yet you find yourself caught up with those like myself. You do it despite being afraid for yourself. It is interesting to me."

"And we all know how much you value that which cures your boredom, however momentarily." The bitingly low feminine voice came from behind me, startling me so badly I had to stifle a cry.

Royce's eyes finally opened as he looked to the door, his expression going carefully blank. I turned in the leather chair to look and see who had come to join us.

It was The Circle's receptionist!

Chapter 12

The girl sauntered over to Royce, dropping her purse on his desk and giving him a friendly kiss on the cheek. I don't think I could have been more stunned and horrified if she'd grown horns and a tail and started singing "New York, New York."

Through the shock, part of me distantly noted that the girl didn't look quite so skinny or perfect as she had behind the desk at The Circle's headquarters. Her hair and makeup weren't quite so flawless. She was still pretty, but not the runway model she'd appeared to be earlier.

My fingers itched to touch the charm around my neck, which I remembered was supposed to let me see through illusion. I suppressed the urge with difficulty and kept my hands primly folded in my lap. Seeing the girl this way made me wonder what Veronica must look like under the veneer of magic.

"Ms. Waynest, this is Allison Darling. I believe you've met." Royce's voice couldn't have been more carefully noncommittal and disinterested. Was that for my sake or hers?

Though I would rather have stuck my fingers in an electric socket after how she treated me earlier, I leaned forward across the desk to offer her my hand. As long as Royce was here to referee (imagine that), I'd play nice. She waited longer than was strictly polite before offering me her limp-wristed shake.

"I can't stay long," Allison said to Royce, leaning against his chair with an arm casually flung around his shoulder. As she spoke, her bright blue eyes were locked on mine, glinting with malice behind those trendy glasses. "I thought you'd want to know that she was given the hunter's belt today."

Royce arched a brow in surprise, turning to look up at Allison questioningly. She shrugged and nodded, and I noted with growing alarm the almost imperceptible shift in the air as anger stirred below the frighteningly blank mask of his features.

"Allison, love, go on back to the restaurant. Let me finish my business here and I'll speak with you later." His voice had taken on a dangerously silky undertone, a promise of something unspoken. What worried me most was that I couldn't tell if it was me or her that he was mad at, and what exactly he was planning to do if it was me.

She shrugged, uncaring, as if this happened all the time. Acting like she had all the time in the world, she lightly patted his shoulder, picked up her purse, and made a hip-swaying exit. I watched her go, still in a state of shock trying to figure out the convolutions and consequences behind whatever this relationship of theirs was. The look she threw him over her shoulder at the door was unbelievable, a mix of warning and what looked like lust. I sincerely hoped it wasn't really some of the latter. Gross.

"Don't keep me waiting too long," she purred.

Didn't she realize she was provoking an already pissed-off vamp? Probably doing it on purpose, knowing she was leaving me to deal with it.

Tense and unblinking, I shifted around in the chair to face Royce. He stayed silent and unmoving until the muted sound of Allison's heels on the carpet faded and the front door of the office suite opened and closed. When I say he was unmoving, I mean no twitches, no fidgeting, no breathing, still as a stone. It was creepy as hell. His pitch black gaze soon slid back to focus on me, and I felt myself contract, as if I could disappear into the leather chair if I pressed against it hard enough.

"My, my. The facets of your personality become more and more complex with each passing moment." His tones stayed dangerously soft, thoughtful, and contained a hint of that promising lilt. I was so dead. "You have not yet made any overt moves against me. You are smart enough to be afraid of me, but beyond stupid to think you could take on an assignment as my assassin and survive the attempt. What is driving you? Your family line has no history of mage blood, so it can't be the carrot of an apprenticeship with The Circle. You don't have any known ties to the White Hats. Is it a threat on someone you love? Greed, perhaps?"

I went cold at that. He'd researched my bloodline? Oh no, if this went bad, that meant he knew where to find my family. It took quite a long moment for me to find enough of my voice to speak.

"It isn't like that. I didn't want the belt. He made me take it. I didn't take a contract on your life."

He said nothing, simply stared in silent accusation. I could feel the anger building under the veneer, and it made me feel even more panicked than if he'd dived across the desk for my throat.

I plunged ahead, heedless of what the cost might be. Screw my license, and screw the contract. I wanted to live. I'd figure out some other way to pay my rent and keep all my creditors from camping on the landing—my life wasn't worth this kind of trouble for a few thousand dollars.

"I swear, I never agreed to hunt you. All I agreed to do was help find some little statue thing." If anything, his anger seemed to grow at the mention of the artifact. I knew I was babbling, but I was scared out of my mind. "I need the money or my business is going to go under. Please, don't be angry with me, I swear I never meant to do anything more than this job and then leave you alone."

He rose slowly, unfolding from the chair like some great predatory bird preparing to dive down on its prey. I shrank back even further as he came around the desk, slowly and deliberately setting his hands on the arms of my chair and leaning forward right into my face. Both of my hands involuntarily came up to shield my neck as I slid back in the chair. My knees drew up to my chest as he glared down at me, my mouth dropping open and eyes wide in shock and fear. His breath, when he finally spoke, smelled like a mix of mint and copper, cloying and chokingly thick.

"I am buying out that contract. Whatever they offered, I'll triple it. With a few added conditions, in case you're thinking of running back to The Circle."

I didn't know what I could say without making him even angrier. From the sound of it, I wouldn't have a choice in the matter. A hint of fully extended fang behind his lips was even more reason to keep my mouth shut until he said what he had to say and, hopefully, calmed down.

"One—you're to turn over the hunter's belt to me. You may keep the Amber Kiss, and whatever else they gave you. Two, you are to end all contact with The Circle except to tell them that your contract with them is null. Direct any questions on why to me. Three, you may not speak of the focus to *anyone* other than myself. That includes your business partner."

This didn't sound so bad. He stared down at me expectantly, like he was waiting for something. I belatedly figured out that he was waiting for an acknowledgment, so I stammered one out. "Oh—okay. I can do all that."

He pulled back from the chair. Instead of aggressively standing right over me, he aggressively folded his arms and stared down at me from a few feet away, leaning back against the desk. It looked like his anger was abating but not entirely gone. Not gone enough for me to feel comfortable about removing my hands from my throat or putting my feet back on the floor. His eyes were narrowed, black pits boring into me, keeping me pinned in place with their intensity.

"One last thing. To ensure your loyalty, you're to sign papers by the end of the next business day. I want a notarized copy in my hands by no later than Monday night."

A sudden sick feeling swept over me. I could literally feel all the blood drain from my face.

"P-p-papers?"

He nodded tersely, his gaze staying sharp and pitiless. "I won't have you turning back to The Circle or the White Hats for help. You're mine now. The Circle can't touch you if I lay a claim, and the White Hats won't come near you if you bear my mark. Your partner may want to consider doing the same."

Bear his mark. His bite, he meant. Oh shit.

"By Monday, Shiarra. If you don't deliver them, I'll come looking. Trust me, you don't want it to come to that."

"No, please!" I had to fight this. I couldn't let it come to that. Death would be better. "Please, you don't need to do that, I won't go back to them! I swear!"

He actually laughed at that, the sound soft and bitter. "Begging is in poor taste, lovely. You should've thought of that before you stepped outside the bounds of your confidentiality agreement. You broke under pressure. Right now, your promises are just words. The claim will ensure it doesn't happen again."

He wasn't just talking a little love bite. He meant a full-fledged bond, tying me to him until my death. Bloody hell. There had to be a way out of this. There just had to be. Panic was making me feel ill, and I was afraid I might end up losing my lunch on his nice, clean tennis shoes if I didn't find a way out of this, fast.

"It doesn't need to come to that, please. You don't need to do this. Give me a chance, I'll prove it to you somehow."

"I'll be in this office Monday night. Meet me here."

Strain made my voice crack. "Please!"

He shook his head, unmoved by my pleas. Pushing off the desk, he moved around it and pulled out one of the drawers. He thumbed through some folders, finally withdrawing papers from one and returning to press them into my trembling hands.

"This is for your protection as well as mine. Come on now, I'll have someone take you home."

I jerked back from his touch when he reached for me, and he withdrew, waiting patiently for me to rise on my own. The thing that bugged me most was that he now seemed so bored with the situation. It was like the anger never existed. Like he'd planned this from the start, knowing I'd break.

When I looked at the papers he'd put in my hand, my stomach gave a sickening lurch as I saw they were already filled out with both our names in all the right places. I flipped to the last couple of pages and saw that the part for the vamp to sign had already been filled out and notarized earlier today. All that was left was for me to sign on the dotted line and get my portion of the agreement notarized.

Damn him to hell, he'd known I wouldn't be able to keep my cool if he got in my face or flashed his fangs, and he used that fear to put me in this position. This wasn't a burden to him; he'd wanted to put me under his thumb from the start. No wonder he wouldn't even consider giving me the chance to prove I could be trusted. The worst part of it was that I still wasn't any closer to knowing *why,* or what he expected to get from me or use me for. Blood aside, there had to be a reason for his actions. He had too many willing donors, so he wasn't doing this just for a chance to sink his fangs into me. There was something else he wanted out of me that he hadn't put on the table yet. Judging by the lengths he went to and the methods he used to put me in this position, he probably wouldn't lay it out in the open until I was bonded and didn't have the will left to oppose him.

I slid from the seat with as much grace as I could muster under the circumstances, grabbing my purse from the floor and turning away from him to wipe at the hot sting of tears in my eyes before they could fall. He would *not* see me cry. I'd disgraced myself enough already tonight.

"Wait downstairs in the lobby. I'll have my driver get you."

I kept walking, almost running to get out the

door. He didn't follow, thankfully. I'd be damned if I waited around for Royce's driver. Forget it, I'd take a cab back to my car and then go straight to Sara's. She'd know what to do.

There had to be a way out of this. There just had to be.

Chapter 13

The security guard wasn't at his desk when I stepped out of the elevator. I practically ran to the revolving doors, glad there was no one to witness my ineffectual palm swipes at the tears streaming down my cheeks. The cold spring wind made me shiver, and I looked around dismally for a cab. I knew I looked like crap but fortunately there were few pedestrians meandering around this time of night.

It didn't take long for several yellow cabs to prowl around the corner. I flagged one down and it came to a screeching halt at the curb, narrowly cutting off another driver who had seen me first and was trying unsuccessfully to cut across three lanes of traffic.

The cabbie was a Were. I knew immediately from his faint scent of musk and the thick mat of dark hair poking out from under the sleeves of his jacket and running along the backs of his hands. The hair and the dark stubble on his chin was probably more prominent than usual, not because he hadn't shaved, but because the full moon was less than a week away. There was also a sticker plastered to the Plexiglas between the front and back seats that I recognized as a local Were pack's symbol, a moon with a wolf paw print in the center for the Moonwalker tribe. The back of the cab was clean, but there was an undertone of cigarette smoke and fast food that clung to the interior, mingling with his musky scent in a way that wasn't doing my already queasy stomach any favors.

"Where to?" he growled, twisting in the driver's seat to look back at me.

I gave him the cross-streets where I'd parked and turned my gaze to the window, rolling it down a crack to see if the fresh air might help settle my nerves a little. The cabbie pulled out with a glance at me through the rearview mirror. I pointedly ignored his questioning looks. I'm sure I looked terrible, makeup smeared, eyes red, and mascara running from my crying.

"She's not worth it," the guy said, startling me.

"What?"

"I said, she's not worth it. Whoever made you cry. Move on."

Oh great. He thought I'd just had a bad breakup. Better yet, a bad breakup with a girl. For whatever reason, that started up the tears again.

Taking a few deep breaths to avoid having my voice crack, I managed to say, "It's a bad business deal, not a relationship."

"Yeah?"

Great, a cab driver who thought he was a therapist. Just what the doctor ordered. For some reason, I did want to talk about it, if only to get some of the immediate weight and terror off my chest.

"If I agree to this deal, my life is over. If I don't, it's still over but I'll be dragging all of my friends and family down with me. No matter what I do, I'm screwed."

He nodded, his gaze sliding back and forth between the road and the mirror. After dodging an idling truck, he put a little more attention on me again.

"Sounds rough. Pack business is like that sometimes. You either go with the flow, or you stand up to the alpha, at least take a shot at getting your way. May take a few lumps in the process, but when you look back, at least you know you tried, eh?"

I couldn't help but laugh, choking on my tears. That was good. Comparing my screwed-up business relationships to a Were pack's internal politics sounded just about right, the way things were going for me the last few days.

"I'm not alpha enough to stand up to the people putting me in the middle of this mess. I don't have that option."

The Were laughed and returned his gaze to the road, not looking back now that he was probably sure I wasn't going to have a mental breakdown in his car.

"Even the smallest runt in the pack can take a shot at standing up to the alpha. He may know he's going to lose if it comes to a fight, but oftentimes it's seeing that he's stood up for himself and has his own teeth that makes the alpha give way."

That wasn't the way I thought wolves did things in the wild, but since Weres had the intelligence of a human blended with, and usually overcoming, their wolf instincts, maybe he was right. If I showed Royce and The Circle I had teeth of my own, it was entirely possible they'd back off. I just wondered what would be threatening enough to pass for said teeth, and how I could do it convincingly without getting myself or my family killed in the process.

"There, see, got you thinking of a solution to those worries of yours."

I smiled thinly, though the Were was right. He gave good advice. "Thank you. I only hope it's as easy as you say."

He gave voice to a barking laugh, making my hair stand on end. "Sure it is. Even a leech will listen if you make them think the potential profit is outweighed by the trouble you give 'em."

I sat bolt upright, eyes widening in alarm. He still didn't look back at me, eyes on the road like a good driver should be. I was almost sure he was grinning, judging by the tone of his voice.

"Don't get yer panties in a twist. I smell it on you. That and the fear-smell, and a touch of someone else's perfume. You're also wearing something that makes the scent of your blood and skin faint. Mage-work, seems like."

Annoyed, I sat back, folding my arms and glaring at the back of his head. "Is every Other I run into going to know I've been dealing with vamps and magi?"

"Until you shower, probably." He looked at me through the rearview, and I could see the twinkle of mirth reflecting in his eyes. "Shows you're smart, that you're afraid of 'em. Not afraid of me, though. Why's that?"

A little nonplussed, I didn't answer right away. Now that he'd put my attention on it, I realized he was right. I wasn't afraid of him.

"I don't know. I guess I've just known enough Weres to be used to you guys by now. My ex-boyfriend runs with the Sunstrikers."

I was careful not to mention that I'd broken up with Chaz after he changed to wolf-form in my living room; his way of explaining why he was never around on certain days of the month. Prior to that, he'd told me he'd been busy delivering private sessions with clients, not running around with his buddies as a wolf-man. Considering I was normally so busy I barely knew what day of the month it was, let alone whether the moon was full, it wasn't that unusual that I'd missed the signs. He got up the nerve to tell me the truth after we'd been together a few months. Though he admittedly scared the hell out of me when he shapeshifted, he had never quite clued in that I was more pissed at him for lying and hiding things from me than anything else. Ass.

He scoffed at that. "The Sunstrikers are a bunch of good-for-nothing showoffs. Good thing you two broke up."

I made a noncommittal sound, wondering what

the friction was between the clans. Local Were politics were none of my business, and I had enough problems of my own.

"So what're you going to do about this business deal you can't refuse? Tell him to shove those papers where the moon don't shine?"

I looked down at the now-crinkled and slightly sweat-stained papers I still had clenched in one hand. Funny thing was, the Were's words had given me some hope. And an idea.

"Yeah, looks like I'll be doing that."

He pulled to the curb and I saw we were already at the block where I'd parked my car. After stopping, he put his hand on the passenger headrest and twisted around to beam at me, looking all too pleased.

"You'd make a good bitch in our pack. Good luck dealing with that leech."

"Hey, thanks." I think.

I put the papers down and dug some cash out of my purse. I gave him a good tip; he deserved it.

"One more thing," he said, taking the money. "Even if it scares you, don't show it that. Wear that stuff you've got on now and it should help confuse your scents enough that it won't be able to bully you as easy. Not unless you let it."

"Oh, thanks!"

I hadn't realized that. Maybe that was part of why Royce was so direct this time. He couldn't tell by my scent what I was feeling so he went for more obvious tells, like my trembling and attempt to curl into a fetal ball to hide.

The guy started to take off before I'd even fully shut the passenger side door. The door slammed shut as he flipped an illegal U-turn and slid a hairy-backed hand out the window to give me a cheerful wave, disappearing as he turned a corner.

The advice he'd given me was actually comforting. I'd figure out a way to best Royce at his own game yet.

Chapter 14

By the time I reached Sara's, I was feeling much more calm and collected than I had when I left Royce's building. The drive and some good music helped put things in perspective. The lack of traffic also helped.

Sara lived closer to the office than I did. She had a nice little two-story house out in suburbia that was humble enough to keep her family from visiting too often. She also had a scary-looking but completely harmless and affectionate pair of pit bulls that she let the neighbors' kids come over and play with. They made good guard dogs since they barked at anything from the ice cream truck that passed by every afternoon in the summer to the mailman that snuck them treats every other day or so. They also had a habit of jumping on and slobbering all over anyone who walked through the front gate.

I was pretty sure the dogs were a better deterrent

to prying family members than the ordinary suburban house.

Grabbing all my stuff from the car, including an emergency bag of clothes I kept in the back seat and, after a moment's hesitation, a vial of that Amber Kiss perfume and the belt, I opened the wooden gate and headed up the walk. As predicted, the dogs started barking the instant the gate squeaked open, charging out from their doghouse around the side of the house and practically bowling me over in their enthusiasm. For some reason they seemed more interested in how I smelled than usual.

Laughing, I rubbed their big ugly faces and struggled past to the door, trying to keep their drool off my clothes. "Go on, get down, you two. Buster, sit! Damn it, Roxie, that belt isn't a chew toy, let go!"

The porch light flicked on, and I squinted at it as Sara pulled the door open. She had on jeans and a scarf tying her hair back.

"Hey," I said.

She gave me a sympathetic smile as she let me in. I had to hustle so the dogs wouldn't squirm past me and go tearing through the house.

"I take it there's trouble?"

She turned off the porch light and locked the door behind me to a chorus of disappointed howls and scratching at the door. I heard music blaring from the kitchen, and the scent of some pine cleaner. Yeah, when Sara got bored, she cleaned. She'd probably make a great housewife someday, after she got over the wild and crazy "take-the-wackiest-jobs-I-can-find" private investigator phase.

Nodding, I led the way to her living room and plopped down on the couch, letting my stuff fall. Her eyes widened at the sight of the trio of stakes on the belt, and she held up a hand.

"We need coffee for this. Two sugars?"

"Make it three."

She disappeared into the kitchen, cutting the music and tinkering around. I closed my eyes and listened, wondering what exactly I should do with the papers currently getting even more wrinkled and probably ripped from being shoved into my duffel. I thought about what the Were had said back in the cab, what Arnold told me when I left The Circle's tower, and how Royce had manipulated me so neatly. The Were was right. I needed teeth. Which meant Arnold was right. I did want the stakes.

"So what's the deal?" Sara asked a few minutes later, coming back from the kitchen with a steaming mug in each hand. She settled down in the recliner across from the couch and handed me one. It was my favorite, a black mug with white letters that read DO I LOOK LIKE A #*%!ING MORNING PERSON?

I reached over to the duffel, dragged out the papers, and tossed them on the coffee table for her to see. Her eyes widened immediately in recognition, and even more so when she picked them up and saw my name and Royce's neatly typed in all the appropriate places. I waited for her to riffle through and see that he'd already taken care of his signature and now it just needed mine. Then I quickly filled her in on everything that happened at The Circle and my meeting with Royce.

". . . so I broke when he flashed fang at me. He's got me pinned in a bad place. I can either go to him willingly, sign the papers, and make everyone but me happy, or I can piss off everyone at the same time by cutting loose from both him and The Circle. However, Royce made a very effective threat. I don't want to see you or my parents or brothers get caught in the crossfire." I sighed deeply, feeling about three times my age and very tired all of a sudden. "I need help."

Sara had been listening intently, nodding or giving an encouraging word here and there, but hadn't interrupted. Now that I was done, she gave a little *hmm* before turning back to the *Notice of Mutual Consent to Human/Other Citizen Relationship and Contractual Binding Agreement* in her hands. Her brows were furrowed, and her shoulders tense under the flannel T-shirt, her coffee in its ASK ME ABOUT MY EVIL PLAN mug untouched by her side.

"Well," she said cautiously, "I don't know exactly what to do either. Did you have any ideas, or are you still in panic mode?"

"More like apathy than panic now. I might be able to arrange my own funeral to keep everyone else out of the picture, but I don't see any happy endings with any of the plans I've come up with in the last couple of hours."

Sara grimaced, but kept her gaze on the papers. "What do you think?"

"I don't expect I'll have much in the way of a

chance physically fighting against either The Circle or Royce. However, if I take on one, I think the other might back off. The Circle gave me the means"—and here I pointed to the belt—"to fight Royce, if I've got guts enough to use it. However, they both have the means to fight dirty, which I don't. Both organizations have more clout than you or I do. The thing is, I can't legally use weapons against them either, and even with the threat against my family, I haven't got enough evidence to go to the cops for help."

She looked pale and drawn, about as good as I felt. "Royce did a pretty good job of backing you into a corner."

I cleared my throat and looked away, knowing she wouldn't like this part of my idea. Steeling myself against the shivers wracking me at the thought of what I was about to do, I bowed my head over the coffee cup and took a deep breath before I answered.

"I think I can win my way out of this, but I'd really need your help to do it."

Her gaze shot over to me, the abject fear and desire to help I saw etched on her features not making me feel any better about what I was going to ask of her.

She said, "If it'll get you out of this mess, I'll do anything. How can I help?"

"You're much more versed in contract law than I am. That's what I need your help with. I can sign the papers, but I need you to doctor them first." I could see her incredulousness and went on the defensive. "Look, it's just an idea. You don't have to go along with it. Just hear me out."

She was forcing herself to relax, taking a few deep breaths before nodding for me to continue. She tried hiding her expression behind her coffee mug as she took a sip, but I caught the look of displeasure that crossed her face. I knew it went against her morals, but this was the only chance I could see to get out of the hole I'd dug for myself.

Gesturing at the contract in her hand, I stared right into her baby blue eyes, holding her gaze so I wouldn't lose my resolve.

"Word it so that it swings both ways so I can injure or kill Royce with impunity."

She choked on her coffee. "What?!"

"You can do it. I know you know how. I'll help you reword it and we can print a new document that looks just like this one, except tweaked enough so that instead of it reading like a living will and me being completely under his thumb, it'll go both ways. It won't take much to do it, and I doubt Royce will read it once I deliver the signed copy. All he'll look for is my signature on the last page."

Papers usually read like you were signing over your body, mind and soul, mostly because some of the Others couldn't feed without taking one or more of those things from a human in the process. It was so tightly regulated because, like any other citizens, Others needed to be held responsible for their actions up to and including emotional distress, stalking, and assaulting or killing a human in a frenzy of passion, anger, hunger, or whatever it was that drove them. The mystery I've yet to figure out is why people sign the papers letting them do those things in the first place. I mean, I know the Others don't want to be hunted down and exterminated, but why would a rational human being willingly agree to something sucking their blood or initiating them into the world of the terminally furry?

Anyway, generally the contracts read that the Other could destroy your will, drink every last drop of blood in your body, and rip you to itty bits in the process, and they are considered free and clear from all wrongful death suits. These days, when they could get away with it, they also added in a clause giving immunity from any lawsuits that might result from turning the person with irreparable damage. After that suit last year, when some kid who had been left for dead turned Were without a hand, facial scarring, and a horrific chunk of flesh taken out of his arm, and sued the pants off the pack of the Were who infected him, any human who would sign a full immunity pre-/post-death clause was considered a highly prized commodity among the more feral Others.

In addition to all of that, if you (permanently) died while under contract, all material possessions were turned over to the "partner" if you failed to turn into an Other. Most of the time, the agreements were not worded to work both ways. Meaning, if I signed the document as is and I survived an attempt to kill or hurt Royce, I'd get thrown in jail, and my shares in H&W and my apartment and belongings would get turned over to him. But if this worked out the way I was thinking and I was successful, killing him instead, everything he owned would fall into my possession. It would also leave me free of any assault charges or wrongful death suit that might be brought against me for trying to kill an Other without a valid warrant.

It also gave me leverage to get him to just leave me the hell alone. While he was powerful, much more powerful than me, physically and otherwise, vampires don't live as long as Royce had without having a strong sense of self-preservation. If he thought of me as a threat, he'd back off. With the contract worded to my benefit and the addition of the stakes to urge him to reconsider, this just might work. Not to mention if I got Royce to back down, it would more than likely cause The Circle to back off as well. They'd hopefully see me as more trouble than I'm worth.

I could see that Sara wasn't happy with the idea, though she knew the dangers of signing the contract as it was, ignoring it entirely, or doing things my way. Probably better than I did. Still, I understood what I was asking her to do. If it ever got out that she did such a thing, she could be disbarred, fined, probably jailed, and lose her reputation as a fair and law-abiding citizen. She wouldn't look at me when she finally spoke.

"Shia, I know I'm not a practicing lawyer, but I could lose my license over this. It could destroy the reputation of H&W. We may lose the business over this."

I took a deep breath before answering, keeping my voice quiet and level so I wouldn't betray my own feelings about the whole mess.

"I know. Believe me, I know. I wouldn't ask if it wasn't important. Isn't my life worth more than the business?"

I didn't have to say it, and I felt horrible for even letting the words cross my lips, but without Sara's help, I'd never survive this nightmare.

Eventually, she managed to drag her gaze from the ground to meet my eyes again, looking more drawn and pale than I'd ever seen her before.

"I'll do it. This once, I'll do it. But don't ever, ever ask anything like this of me again."

I nodded agreement, breathing a deep sigh of relief. With that out of the way, now I just needed to figure out how I could make an ancient vampire view me, a normal human, a woman, food, as a threat.

Chapter 15

I slept fitfully on the couch in Sara's living room. She had guest bedrooms, but I wanted to be woken up if the dogs started barking at any intruders. After a little more talk and planning, she'd gone upstairs to work on the contract on her computer. I didn't envy her having to retype the whole thing, not only that but then having to use her skills to edit the document just enough that Royce and I could legally go for each other's throats without worry of legal interference.

I stared at the ceiling for a while, finally drifting off a little past midnight. Then I scared the crap out of myself when I rolled off the couch onto the floor in the middle of the night in the throes of a nightmare. The bruise on my hip from landing on my keys did not improve my mood one bit. The dogs barked for almost fifteen solid minutes, too. Thankfully, Sara must have figured there was no problem since she didn't come down to check on me and grind my embarrassment home any further.

Two nights in a row of too little sleep didn't make it any easier to answer Sara's cheerful "G'mornin'" when she came downstairs around eight o'clock. Muttering darkly under my breath, I dragged myself off the couch and followed her into the kitchen, blearily watching her make coffee, scramble eggs, and toast bagels for breakfast.

"Hey, it's Sunday," she said.

I didn't say anything, just stared back for a minute before riveting my gaze on the Mr. Coffee. I really, really wanted my caffeine fix.

"Sunday," she said, grinning at my lack of response, "as in, it's Damien's birthday and we're both expected at your mom's house in a few hours."

I started, practically jumping out of the seat I'd slumped into at the kitchen table. "Holy crap! It's that Sunday?"

Dismayed, I looked at the clock on the microwave. I wouldn't have enough time to get the gift from my apartment, shower, change clothes, call The Circle, and explain to Veronica why I was reneging on the contract while still making it to the party on time.

"Yup." She shook the spatula at me threateningly. "Don't even think about it. Deal with work tomorrow. Today's supposed to be your day off anyway."

I slid back into the chair, running my hands through my hair in agitation. Well, as much as I could with the unbrushed, tangled curls.

"It's not just that. I need to get Damien's gift. It's in my closet at home."

She shook her head. "I wouldn't. Not since the

White Hats broke in the other day. If they've been watching you, they may have tried something drastic since you met with Royce again."

Damn it all to hell and back, I'd forgotten about them. "Don't suppose you've got any bright ideas for that, too?"

"Well, sure. We can swing by the mall on the way over to your mom's."

I meant the White Hats, but her idea to handle my brother's gift made me feel a bit better. Though I soon remembered the contract, my not-quite-good mood shattering. "Did you finish with the papers last night?"

"No, not yet. I have to tweak the fonts and cut out a little of the wording to make it all fit right and say what we want it to say but still look enough like the old contract to pass a casual inspection."

I nodded, wondering miserably how I was going to stand up to Royce. I quivered just at the sight of him, let alone his fangs. What would I do if he actually jumped at my throat?

"Do you really think he'll just lodge them with the court without looking at them?"

She laughed at the worry in my voice. "Of course. Nobody but lawyers ever wants to read this kind of stuff. The form he used was really cookie-cutter, too."

That made me wonder how she was familiar enough with this type of contract to know that it was cookie-cutter. "You've worked on these before?"

"Yeah," she said, looking more sheepish than I've ever seen her. Was that a touch of red in her cheeks?

"I took a job for a Were about six months ago. She thought her contract partner was cheating on her with another Were and wanted to know what he was up to. Turns out he was cheating, just not with another Were. She wanted to know what her rights were, so she showed me the fill-in-the-blanks standard form they had signed. I helped her a little since the guy she was dating was scum and I felt bad about having to break the news."

Gross. I made a face and shook my head. "You pick the weirdest jobs."

"Heh, yeah, I guess I do." She grinned, plucking the hot bagels from the toaster. "Trust me, he'll just look for your signature. You're going to have to act *really* reluctant to hand them over if he's going to believe you've given in, though."

"That should be the easy part. I *am* reluctant to hand them over."

The coffeemaker beeped. Finally. I rinsed out our mugs from last night and poured fresh coffee into both, picking through the cabinets, drawers, and fridge to get spoons, sugar, and cream. After fixing up our drinks, I handed one over to Sara before settling back into my seat at the table with a mug cradled in my cold hands.

Relaxing back into the chair, I shut my eyes, only to be startled by the earsplitting sound of one of the dogs going mental right under the window next to me. Some of the coffee sloshed over onto my hands, dragging a pained curse out of me as I sucked my burning fingers into my mouth.

"Shut up, Buster!" Sara shouted, handing me the

spatula on her way to the front door. "It's probably just the paper."

I got up to tend to the stove, alternately sucking the fingers of one hand while poking and prodding at the eggs with the other. Sara walked back in a minute later, ashen and pale.

"Shia, what was the name of that woman from The Circle you met on Thursday?"

I glanced back at her over my shoulder, wondering at the slight waver to her voice. "Veronica. Veronica Wright. Why?"

She tossed the paper down next to the stove. I dropped the spatula and grabbed the paper, reeling in shock.

MAGE FOUND MURDERED!!! ARE THE OTHERS AT WAR? screamed the headline splashed across the front page. Right above Veronica's smiling picture.

Chapter 16

I didn't have much of an appetite, but I picked at the eggs Sara set down in front of me. I don't even remember staggering to a seat, but somehow I managed it.

Whatever the cops found must have been pretty bad for the papers to jump on it that quickly. Apparently a neighbor complained about some strange sounds coming from Veronica's apartment late last night. When the police showed up to investigate and no one answered the door, they busted in and found her body, mutilated and drained of blood. No witnesses and no leads except that it "looked like an Other attack."

Of all the Others, magi were the closest relations to fullblood humans, according to the hematologists who had done studies. Despite that, any high school kid could tell you that we were still so fundamentally, biologically different that it was almost impossible for us to interbreed. Not impossible, but almost. We weren't the same species, though we were closer in physical similarities than to once-human Weres or vampires.

Vampires used to be human, but like Weres, what turned them was a magically enhanced virus. It made them both completely different, biologically and metaphysically, even while, for the most part, retaining the physical structure that let them appear nearly human.

The vamp virus animated dead tissue, giving it the semblance of life only without the ability to retain or process certain proteins and enough oxygen to keep it "alive" without periodic infusions of fresh blood.

With Weres, the virus fundamentally altered the structure of their DNA so that they turned furry a few days out of the month. They were still *basically* human, and the males could and often did have kids with normal human females, with a seventy-five percent chance of said kids also turning furry on the full moon come puberty. Female Weres couldn't have kids due to the fact that shapeshifting was so violent it generally ended up killing the fetuses well before they came to term.

Due to their "normal" appearance and fewer inhuman characteristics, magi weren't normally treated like the rest of the Others, instead being considered to have the rights of humans. You didn't need to sign any contracts to work with or have a relationship with a mage, unlike vampires and Were-folk. The White Hats, Mothers Against Others, Concerned Human Citizens, and other similar groups were mostly pissed off about vampires and Weres, and rarely lumped magi into their overzealous rants and witch hunts. However, when something freaky happened, you could rest assured the newshounds and extremists would slot mages into the "Other" category as quickly as a vamp or Were.

Hence Veronica being thrown into the "Other" mix in the headline. The news really didn't give me much to work with. "Drained of blood" sounded like a vamp attack, but "torn to bits" sounded more like something a Were would do. Vamps didn't have claws to shred with, and were generally too "refined" to bother using their strength to tear the limbs off their victims. However, Weres generally weren't aggressive enough to do that kind of damage unless they were being threatened on their own turf while under the influence of the full moon. Plus, if they were shapeshifted, most types of Weres didn't have the right mouth shape to suck blood out of a body.

"What do you make of it?" Sara asked around a mouthful of food.

Harrumphing, I laid the paper down and sipped gingerly at my coffee, reaching for my fork to poke at my eggs again. "I'm not sure. The police don't have any leads. The way the paper makes it sound, it's like a vamp worked together with a Were to tear her apart."

Which isn't technically possible, since vamps and Weres are pretty much natural enemies and get into pissing contests with each other at the drop of a hat.

Sara reached across to drag the paper over,

skimming the article while she munched on her bagel. "We'd probably have more luck if we get the police file."

I snickered, shaking my head. "Good luck. Unless you're still dating Officer Lerian, I don't see how you expect to get ahold of that."

Her stiff silence told me enough.

"Oh my God, you are? I thought you two split for the last time like a month ago! 'I'd rather chew my own arm off than go out with him again,' you said."

Muttering, she shoved her plate and the newspaper away, not meeting my eyes. "Yeah, well, so what? I changed my mind, big deal. He's a nice enough guy."

Yeah. The "nice enough guy" that tended to leave her in tears within a week or two of their falling back in bed together. I didn't understand it. Mark Lerian was the proverbial tall, dark, and handsome man, though despite his profession and looks, he was one of the nicest guys I'd ever met. There was no conceit in him at all. He didn't drink, smoke, or so much as cast an eye at other women whenever he was dating Sara. I know she thought she loved him. That's what she said anyway. If not for the spats they inevitably had, they'd make the perfect couple.

Why these two couldn't get along was beyond me, but I hated to see Sara cry. What drove me nuts was that she kept going back to him. They'd split up for a few weeks or a couple of months over something or other, usually because he disapproved too vocally of her lifestyle. Sara wasn't the only one who disagreed with his views that being a detective was "too dangerous for a woman." Instead of coming to terms, they inevitably fought, broke up, and within a few weeks were acting as if it never happened. Sara would come in to the office one day gushing about how everything was all better between them—then, BAM! It'd be over. Spectacularly over. Again. The record so far was twenty-two days between the rekindled romance and breakup fight. Wonder how long it would last this time.

I shook my head, figuring I'd give her a rough time about her love life when my own priorities were straightened out and I actually had some moral high ground to stand on. "Will he be able to give you anything on it?"

She shrugged, obviously relieved I wasn't going to pursue the subject. "I don't know without talking to him first. Since it's all over the front page, he may not be able to get any useful info if he's not assigned to the case. He also may not be willing to talk about it."

Sighing, I finished off my bagel and got up to take my dish to the sink. I busied myself with the dishes as I tried to figure what Veronica's murder might have to do with me. Who should I contact at The Circle since she was dead? Maybe Arnold would know what I should do. He might even be able to give me some help with Royce, since he'd offered.

That in mind, I turned back to Sara, who was trying to pull out the funnies without being too obvious about it. "Do you mind if I go upstairs and check my e-mail?"

"Nah, go for it."

She settled back in the chair and I headed up to the office. She'd left the contract open on the monitor, and I skimmed the first couple of paragraphs, feeling my stomach churning with unease. Rather than freaking myself out any further, I minimized the window and opened up the Internet browser, logging into our work e-mail remotely.

I felt my stomach give another lurch—there, amid the massive amount of spam, was an e-mail from Veronica. It was from last night, around the time I was meeting with Royce, and from a personal e-mail address instead of The Circle's corporate account. She was still alive while I was spilling out The Circle's secrets to the vamp.

It took a minute for me to focus beyond her name and see what else was there. There was one from this morning from "ArnieGoblinSlayer20," which I figured had to be from Arnold.

Feeling ill at reading a message from someone I knew was dead, I opened Veronica's e-mail.

TO: S. Waynest
FROM: Veronica Wright
SUBJECT: RE: Update

Arnold told me you met with him. I know you're probably with our subject as I write this, and I can only hope you remembered what I told you in our first meeting. I've also got some news you need to hear ASAP RE: this assignment. When/where can we meet?

It's probably too late, but remember, *watch* and

> *listen.* You *must* find the mark. Time is of the essence, and it may mean the life of you and everything you love if it isn't secured in time. I'm not threatening you, just letting you in a little late on the importance of this mission. I'm sure you're smart enough to have realized by now that there's more to this project that I haven't told you. Unfortunately, I haven't been left with a choice and need to give you some additional details and instructions before you continue looking for this thing.
>
> Also, don't antagonize the subject. You shouldn't be in any danger, but I've gotten word that your cover may be compromised. Wear the perfume and charm at all times after nightfall. The belt may be overkill, so don't wear it unless your life is truly in danger. Consider them gifts from The Circle.
>
> One last thing—if you're feeling in over your head, you are. There are more players in the game than I initially thought. I'm trying to buy you time. Don't screw this up, or losing your PI license will be the least of your worries. That *is* a threat.

I reread the message. And again. Damn, that woman was good at making me uncomfortable, even when she was dead.

Shaking off the willies from reading a dead person's e-mail, I clicked open the one from Arnold. I was mentally counting down the minutes until the police might start looking for me in connection with Veronica's death, since I was probably one of the last people she called or e-mailed before she was killed.

TO: S.Waynest
FROM: ArnieGoblinSlayer20
SUBJECT: V.W. and the belt

Hi, Shiarra, hope this makes it past your spam filters. I am e-mailing you from home, I just saw the news. If you haven't already, pick up the paper or check the local news on the Net, you'll see.

I figure by now you're probably in a tough spot. I might be able to help.

Start wearing the belt at night, no matter what. Don't leave home without the necklace or perfume on. You might be in danger during the day, too, so call my cell as soon as you get this (212-555-9035).

Arnold

I sighed deeply, running my hand over my face. This whole tangled mess just kept getting better and better.

Chapter 17

I printed out both e-mails and brought them downstairs, going straight to my purse and digging out my cell phone. Sara came into the doorway, leaning against the frame to watch what I was doing.

"Anything interesting in the mail?"

Punching in Arnold's number, I listened to the other end ring while holding out the printouts for her to read. She sat down next to me on the couch, propping her feet up on the coffee table while she read them.

Arnold picked up on the fifth ring.

"Arnold? It's Shiarra."

"Oh, thank God." He sounded both rushed and relieved. "I was afraid you might be dead, too. Listen, if you're at home, get out. Go somewhere safe, somewhere no one knows you. A hotel maybe, out of the county or even out of state would be best."

"What?" I knew it sounded stupid, since I'd heard him clearly. I was just so incredulous.

He sighed into the phone, making me cringe at

the crackling sound right in my ear. "Look, there's some crazy stuff happening. Word must have gotten out that Royce has the focus. We were trying to keep it quiet, but somehow a couple of packs of Weres, another coven of magi, and a whole shitload of other vampires found out about it. Even some of the White Hats might know something about it by now. They're all gunning for it, and him. I wasn't expecting this or I would've given you more firepower when you came by."

I propped my elbow on my knee and held my head up with that hand, closing my eyes as I tried to think of something useful to say. "What the hell did you guys drag me into?"

"Not 'you guys,'" he said, annoyed. "Veronica hired you, not me. I never would've gone this route if I'd been in her shoes, but she thought she knew best. I tried to tell her the probability of success was less than thirteen percent doing it this way, but no, I'm just the Head of Security for the Arcane Division and she's the Assistant VP of Purchasing and Acquisitions. Apparently I don't know squat about these things."

"Yeah, right, be quiet a sec. It's a little late to hold a grudge. Not to sound like an unfeeling bitch, but she's dead and I'm not. I'd like to stay alive. Can you help me?"

He took a deep breath and once again let it out right into my ear. I held the phone a few inches away until he started talking again.

"Yeah, sorry. Yeah."

"Great. So what can you tell me about this thing?"

I asked, trying to rein in my temper. A headache started pulsing right between my eyes, not improving my mood one bit.

"I can't," he said, sounding nervous now. "Not over the phone. Where are you now? I'll come meet you."

I thought about what I had to get done this morning and gauged the urgency of his tone and what I knew of the situation against the probable amount of hell I'd receive if I missed Damien's birthday bash.

Sara took my moment of silence to interject a few words. "Hey, what's he say? Is he going to talk?"

Arnold must have overheard her voice, because he spoke up immediately, his nervousness even more pronounced. "Who was that? Who's with you?"

I waved at Sara to be quiet while trying to make my tone of voice reasonably soothing. I don't think it worked. "Don't worry about it, she's on our side." My side anyway. "I'm supposed to go see my family in just a couple of hours. How long do you think this will take?"

"Oh, geez, don't let the possible end of the world as we know it get in the way of your family plans." I could almost see him on the other end of the line waving his hands in the air dramatically to punctuate his words. "Your life is about to be taken and probably everyone you know is in danger, but hey, by all means go to the movies or whatever."

"Are you finished?" I asked, more than a little annoyed. I didn't ask to get dragged into this, and I was getting pissed off that everyone I dealt with the last couple of days assumed I'd do things their way. That or they bullied me into it.

He growled something harsh under his breath, but a second later he said calmly, "I'm done. But I'm thinking it would behoove me to stick with you for the next day or two, at least until this blows over. Especially after what happened to Veronica. I don't want to see the same thing happen to you, and I feel partly responsible for putting you in this danger in the first place."

"Uh, yeah, about that," I started, suddenly remembering with crystal clarity and a sinking heart how Royce had laid down his terms. "I'm kind of in a tough spot at the moment. Royce found out what I was after, and he said he's buying out The Circle's contract. He wanted me to tell someone if there were questions, refer them back to him, but afterward cut all ties with The Circle."

Arnold went quiet. I could have just about died of embarrassment, sure he must have figured out that I broke under pressure. When it came, his voice was low, even, and controlled, belying the near-panic of a few moments before and the geeky exterior he put on.

"What else did he say? Did he literally say 'cut all ties with The Circle' or how did he word it?"

My, he was taking this much better than I thought he would. I was starting to see why they chose him for the head of security.

"He actually said, 'You are to end all contact with The Circle except to tell them that your contract with them is null.' He also told me I need to turn the belt over to him, but I can keep the other stuff. I'm supposed to keep my mouth shut about that little statue thing. He also wants me to sign papers."

"Good God, and you agreed to this? Willingly?"

"I had to!" I couldn't keep from raising my voice, and I jumped when Sara put a hand on my shoulder in a silent attempt to calm me down. It didn't work. "He's threatened to bring my family into this. I didn't want to do it, but I didn't have much choice at the time. I'm trying to do the best I can with what I've been given, so at least give me some credit for that. Besides, I've got a plan to deal with him anyway."

To his credit, he at least made an attempt at sounding sheepish. "Sorry. Under the circumstances, it just sounds a little extreme, even for a vamp. He must want something out of you to put you in that kind of position."

"No kidding."

"There's a bright side to this, though, since he didn't tell you to cut ties with all employees, just with 'The Circle.' That means I can still technically help you as long as I'm doing it as your friend instead of as part of the coven, under the corporation's cover. I'll waive any fees since I've got a personal stake in this anyway."

Well, fancy that. I hadn't even thought of Royce's terms that way. Maybe I did have more slack to work with than I thought, and I was really lucky Arnold was going to help me get through this pro bono. Getting a professionally trained mage to act as your metaphysical bodyguard generally was something only the very well-to-do could afford.

"Thank you." I felt like ten-pound weights had just lifted off my shoulders. "I'm really grateful for all your help. You've already done a lot for me."

"Don't thank me yet. Like I said, I've got personal reasons for doing this, it's not all for your sake. Oh, and where is this thing with your family? Are you leaving now? I'll just meet you there and stick with you until I can figure out a better solution to keep you safe."

Recalling the dice, the coke-bottle glasses, and the weird T-shirt, I couldn't help cringing at the idea of having him show up at my brother's birthday party. They'd probably think I was dating him, and I'd have to go along with it since I couldn't tell them what he was really doing there.

"This can't wait just a few more hours?"

He sounded less enthusiastic than I felt. "No. I don't want to take any chances at having another death hanging over my head. Especially a preventable one."

"Great." I sighed, steeling myself for the inevitable twenty questions from Sara, my brothers, and worst of all, my parents. What the heck could be so dangerous as to merit having a mage bodyguard at a family barbeque? "Then you're going to have to keep quiet around my relatives about what's going on. And be prepared to deal with my overprotective brothers." And politically incorrect parents. I sincerely hoped they wouldn't realize right off that he was a spark. And even more, that they wouldn't say something offensive.

"No sweat. Give me the address."

I did, feeling more and more uneasy by the minute. My family hated that I was a PI instead of doing something "safe" like nursing or waitressing or being a secretary somewhere and "letting a man take care of me." I briefly thought about asking him to pretend to be human, then realized resignedly that would make me even worse than my family for trying to make him be something he wasn't. Besides which, I doubt he had any way of tamping down the aura that followed in the wake of any actively practicing mage.

"Great, I'll meet you there in about an hour?" he said.

"Yeah, maybe an hour and a half." I made a face at Sara as she mimed being love-struck, clasping her hands over her heart and fluttering her lashes goofily. I smacked her in the arm, wincing when she hit me right back. "See you there."

As I ended the call, Sara once again kicked back in the chair, examining her nails. "You really think your dad isn't going to notice he's a mage?"

I shrugged, staring at the phone in my hand. "Maybe not at first. Eventually he'll figure it out."

"Guess you better get ready to face the music then."

"Yeah," I muttered, rising with a groan to head to the shower. "I guess so."

Chapter 18

After I was ready, Sara and I drove to my parents' place on Long Island, swinging by the mall so I could grab a latte and a gift. I felt especially cheesy for getting Damien a gift card and a movie, but I figured he'd get a laugh out of *Zombie Cheerleaders from Outer Space* and might forgive me if I gave him something cool later. Assuming I lived long enough to get the real gift I'd bought him, buried in a closet back at my apartment.

Though I wasn't comfortable about it, I stuffed the belt and perfume into my duffel and put on the necklace before I left. The bag was perched in my back seat, and I felt a little better knowing I had some manner of weapon with me, even though I didn't know how I'd ever bring myself to use it.

The street was shaded with old oaks and elms, the yards wide and deep, with lots of kids running around and riding bikes up and down the steep hill. I loved the view from up here; the balcony at the back of my parents' house looked out on the water less than a mile away. The smell of salt was thick in the air and the sky faintly overcast, but it was clear and warm enough that it wouldn't stop my dad from firing up the barbecue. It would probably rain tonight. Just what I needed to improve my mood.

Arnold was there already, though I almost overlooked him leaning against a high-end sports car, which probably had a monthly payment higher than most people's mortgages. He hadn't struck me as the type to drive something so flashy. Surprise, surprise, he was also wearing presentable jeans and a nicely unassuming black button-down shirt under a leather jacket, with the hint of a white T-shirt showing at his collar. Somewhere along the way he'd lost the glasses. He looked like a totally different person, and made me feel like a heel for thinking that someone that worked for a company as high profile as The Circle wouldn't know how to dress.

"Hey, you made it," I said. "How long have you been waiting?"

"Not long." He turned to Sara, who was eyeing him from my side. He extended his hand to her in greeting. "Hi, I'm Arnold."

"Sara." She shook his hand. "Nice to meet you, Arnold."

"She's my partner." I noted the strange look he was giving us and rolled my eyes. "My *business* partner."

From the way his expression immediately cleared up, I knew he had been thinking Sara and I were an item. Ugh. Moving right along.

"Do you want to tell me now what you couldn't say over the phone, or after you deal with my prying siblings?"

He frowned at me like I was foolish for asking. "I don't think this is a good place for it. Why don't we discuss it after we leave? In the car, maybe?"

"You planning on leaving your car here?" I asked, incredulous. I mean, not that there's tons of crime in this neighborhood, but you don't just leave a car like his sitting out in the middle of the street, even in suburbia.

He sighed, now obviously annoyed. "I thought I'd be driving, since I'm supposed to be watching over you, not the other way around. There are probably some people on the streets looking for you right now, which means they're also going to be watching for your car."

"Oh." Brilliant. And here I thought I knew what I was doing, being Miss Bad Ass PI and all. "Okay, you've got a point. I'll see if I can leave my car in my parents' garage for the week, but I'll need a cover story."

"That's easy enough," Sara chimed in. "Just tell them that we're all going to my place in the Hamptons for a week and you don't want to leave your car in the garage at the apartment. Didn't someone steal your radio a month ago?"

"More like three, but yeah. Good idea."

With that settled, I headed toward my parents' house. It was a fairly decent-sized two-story colonial with a vibrantly green front yard, whitewashed walls, and dark green trim. My mom likes traditional décor and my dad loves the rustic look, so along with antique furniture and plush carpeting, they have trophies and hunting equipment hung up all over the place.

Someone had left the front door open, and I could hear a football game on the big screen in the living room. The three of us walked up the wide steps and through the screen door. My mom, who was an older, shorter, curvier version of me, poked her head out of the kitchen to see who was in the hall. She brushed a few faded red curls out of her eyes and smiled, a reflection of my own amber eyes glinting back at me.

"Hey, honey, you're just in time. The potato skins and hot wings will be done in about five minutes. Who's this you've got with you?"

Arnold peered over my head, lifting his hand in a friendly wave and smiling. "Hi there, Mrs. Waynest. I'm Arnold, hope you don't mind my dropping in with Shiarra."

"Not at all."

She stepped into the hall to usher us in and give Arnold a warm handshake and a once-over. Not to mention shoot me a questioning look. There was something close to guilt behind it that made me instantly suspicious, though I couldn't exactly say anything about it in front of Arnold.

"Is Janine coming?" Mom asked.

"No, I'm afraid not," Sara said, amused.

My mom loved Sara and had taken her under her wing and wanted desperately to do the same with Janine. She invited her to everything and Janine always said no, except once when she unexpectedly showed up at a Superbowl party. Mom took the opportunity to try to pair her up with Damien, but it was a disaster and Janine never accepted another invitation again. Though we never knew whether it was her general fear of men or something about my brother (his horrible taste in movies, perhaps) that drove her off, I couldn't say I was sorry not to have her along today. My mom still persisted in cheerfully inviting her to every family shindig we had. She was nothing if not tenacious.

"I think she's still in London, but I'll tell her you asked after her the next time I see her."

"Oh, that's unfortunate. Well, the boys are all in the living room watching the game, why don't you go on in there and relax? I'll bring the finger food out in a few minutes, and I'm sure Rob will be firing up the barbecue soon."

"Sounds great," Arnold said, giving me a sidelong look and a smile that bordered on sly. I couldn't imagine why, and it made me even more uneasy.

"Thanks, Carol. Do you need help in the kitchen?" Sara asked.

"No, everything is just about ready. Go on inside, I'll join you kids in a few minutes." She hurried off into the kitchen, almost like she was trying to avoid further conversation. Usually she'd ask Sara and me to help or at least stand around and talk for a few minutes to see how we were doing. Weird. Especially since I'd brought Arnold. Every other time I brought a boy to the house, it always started with twenty questions, usually ending up with me embarrassed, if not the guy, too, so this was a nice change of pace.

Glad that we'd passed the first hurdle smoothly, I sincerely hoped my dad and brothers would be equally easy to deal with as I led the way to the living room. Damien and Mikey were avidly watching the game on the TV, and it looked like Mikey's girlfriend, Angela, had curled up on the couch next to him and fallen asleep on his shoulder. I glanced to the side as I walked in and almost tripped over my own feet at what I saw.

My dad was in the corner playing chess with my ex-boyfriend.

Chapter 19

"Hey love, nice to see you," Chaz said as I froze in horror in the doorway.

He looked just as good as ever, bright eyes as blue as the summer sky, blond hair sticking up in short, gelled spikes, and utterly oblivious to the cold spring winds outside, in a tight tank top that matched his eyes and did an admirable job of showing off his slightly hairy but firmly muscled arms and chest. Everyone but Angela looked up as Sara and Arnold came to a dead stop behind me, and I could almost feel the attention riveting on Arnold the second he appeared.

My dad rescued me by standing up. I know some gears must have been turning but he showed no sign as he wrapped one of his tree-trunk arms around my shoulders.

"Glad you made it, girls. And who's this?" He didn't let go of me as he extended his free hand to Arnold.

Arnold didn't flinch at putting his much smaller

hand in my dad's, and I tensed in anticipation of it getting crushed in Dad's grip. He used to play football, worked in construction for over twenty years, and was built like a truck. His thinning yellow-reddish hair was straight but almost as long as mine. He liked to tie it back at the nape of his neck, making him look like an aging heavy metal drummer or retired Hell's Angel or something. Thankfully, Dad generally isn't a "mutilate first, ask questions later" kind of guy, and he didn't destroy Arnold's hand when he shook it.

"Mr. Waynest? I'm Arnold. I'm a friend of Shia's."

"Nice to meet you, Arnold," he said, glancing down at me before hastening into introductions. "I'm Rob. That's Chaz at the chess table, and my boys Michael and Damien on the couch. That's Mike's girlfriend, Angela. Why don't you come on in and have a seat?"

They each gave a little wave, except for Chaz, who looked like he was fighting an inner battle not to launch himself across the room for Arnold's throat. He'd always been the jealous type.

Sara immediately headed to the far end of the room, plopping into one of the recliners and watching the rest of us with interest. I felt like a bug under a microscope as Mikey and Damien scooted over on the couch, making room for Arnold and me. Mostly it was Chaz making me nervous. What the hell was he doing here? I'd told my mom we'd broken up almost two months ago.

I sat down next to Damien and we hugged. "Happy b-day, little bro."

Damien grinned at me, a younger, thinner version of my dad with my mom's eyes and hair. He usually kept it cropped short and bleached it a little so it wasn't a shock of fire red ringlets like mine and Mom's. Mikey was the one who inherited the softer, straight coppery hair and green eyes of my dad, though both of them were built like him and took after him in the sports department.

"Thanks, sis. Hey, so, Arnold," he said, leaning forward to peer around me at the mage, "what do you do?"

My mom walked in with a tray of goodies, throwing me a pained, apologetic look as she set it down on the coffee table. That made me about ninety-nine percent sure that she was the one who invited Chaz.

Arnold reached out to grab a potato skin. "I'm in security. How about you? Oh, and happy birthday, man. I didn't realize or I would've brought something."

Damien chuckled and took a hot wing. "Don't worry about it. Security, huh? You and Shia must be like peas in a pod then. I'm a firefighter."

Mikey added, "I'm a lawyer. Angela here is a paralegal. She'll probably talk your ear off about it once she wakes up."

He and Damien shared a grin, and I couldn't help but add to it. Angela really is a chatterbox. A very blond, very cute, and very smart chatterbox. I hope the two of them get hitched soon; they've been dragging things out way too long.

Chaz made a move on the chessboard and got up,

heading for the snacks. His movements were even more sinuous and snakelike than I remembered. I guess when Weres thought someone was horning in on their territory, they started acting more predatory.

"Any of you boys want a drink?" my mom asked, edging away from the table.

A chorus of "yeahs" came up from around the room and my mom skittered off back to the kitchen.

Chaz didn't take any food but stood close, next to the couch, and kept his gaze riveted on Arnold. Even with his hands pocketed in his jeans, the air of suppressed violence made me glad I was sitting between two guys, even if there was nothing they could do against an angry werewolf anyway.

"So. How long have you two been together?"

Hoo boy. This didn't bode well.

Arnold answered before I could even open my mouth. "Not long." His tone of voice said "drop it" but it didn't look like Chaz was about to back down. I couldn't believe that Arnold was playing along with it like we were an item.

"Guess you two met and *sparks* flew, hmm?"

I started at that emphasis, wondering how Chaz could possibly know he was a mage. Arnold leaned back, putting one arm up on the back of the couch and the other over my shoulder. I shot him a horrified look, but I think the only person who saw it was Sara, who looked like she was trying hard not to laugh.

"Something like that," Arnold replied, his own

tones as casually biting as Chaz's. "That's why we're headed out of town after this. She mentioned being tired of being up at all hours, especially with the full moon coming. Wants to get away from all the *fur*balls and fanged things coming out of the woodwork for a few days. Can't say I blame her."

I could have just about died right there. I could not believe a werewolf and a mage were having a pissing contest in my parents' living room, veiled or not. Feeling this was getting way out of control, and far too fast, I cut in, a little desperately, "Um, Dad, how much longer before the barbeque? I'm starving."

My dad looked up absently from the chessboard, though I knew he had been paying close attention to everything being said. He was a smart cookie; it would be a small miracle if he hadn't realized what was going unsaid in the conversation just a few feet away. Mike was frowning and Damien just looked amused.

"I'll go fire it up now. Mikey, Damien, come give your ol' dad a hand."

The boys got up, Mike carefully dislodging Angela so she could curl up on the couch. She stirred a bit but didn't wake. Chaz stayed where he was, and I just sat stiffly next to Arnold, who was all too relaxed. The two Others sized each other up silently as my dad and brothers shuffled out of the room.

Once they were gone, Sara spoke up first. "Chaz, stop being a jerk. She broke it off with you two months ago. Why are you even here?"

As one, Arnold, and Chaz, and I all turned to

look at Sara. I think I was more surprised than either of them.

"Carol invited me. I wasn't about to turn down the chance to make things right with Shia." He turned back to look at me, his gaze softening and deep voice turning faintly pleading and cajoling with that hint of a growl to it that I'd once thought sexy as hell. Now realizing the guttural quality was due to his being an Other, it just gave me the shivers. "You know I never meant to scare you like that. I wouldn't hurt you for the world."

Chaz was adorable. He had a look of such contrite longing with that edge of question and desire that it was difficult to remember why I needed to say no.

Shifting while we were alone and postcoital was quite possibly the worst method imaginable he could have used to break the news. A few drinks and the afterglow did absolutely nothing to stifle my shock, not to mention my fear at having a monster straight out of a fairytale appear in my living room—even though said monster had not long before done such boyfriend-esque things as pick up tampons and watch *While You Were Sleeping* with me.

I don't know what got into his head that he decided to spring it on me at the time. We'd worked our schedules to align so that we had that night and the whole of the next day off together. I made dinner, we had some wine, and I put a movie on in the living room we didn't bother to watch. Afterward, he insisted he needed to tell me something that couldn't wait. There I was, getting excited and thinking he was about to pop The Question. Instead, he got up and stood next to the couch. Before I knew it, after a short series of sickening pops and creaks and a rush of fur, there was this big, gray wolf with Chaz's eyes staring at me.

I screamed bloody murder and had a fit. It took me a few minutes to get brave enough to grab one of the throw pillows to cover myself while I opened the door and booted him out. He didn't do anything but whine and put his tail between his legs, skittering out of my apartment like a kicked puppy. It was rather incongruous since as a wolf he was roughly the size and dimensions of an exceptionally buff Saint Bernard. None of my neighbors had called the cops or done more than peek into the hall before slamming their doors shut.

I mailed his clothes and a few of his things he'd left at my apartment back to him a week later, and wouldn't talk to him for over a month afterward, vowing I'd never date the lying furball again. What if there was something else he was hiding? If we were ever to sleep with each other again, I'd have to sign one of those freaky contracts binding me to him. It would leave me open to the possibility of him turning me Were—with or without my consent. His deceit throughout the entirety of our relationship made trusting him impossible.

He got off light under the circumstances. Me screaming at him and kicking him out was a cakewalk compared to being jailed and, in all likelihood, killed for his indiscretion. The justice system didn't take kindly to Others who ignored the legal requirement of Weres and vampires to contract anyone they got "intimate" with—in any sense of the word. I hadn't filed a formal complaint, but that didn't mean I was open to fooling around with him again. Bad enough I was about to be contracted to Royce; it was time to put my foot down.

Even though that look of his made me blush like a schoolgirl, I didn't turn away. Instead, I took a deep breath to steady myself, eventually managing to find my voice. "Doesn't matter. We're done. It's over. Move on."

Arnold seemed immeasurably pleased at my words, though he was wise enough to keep his mouth shut. Chaz's shoulders slumped and he trudged over to a recliner, sitting on the edge and leaning forward expectantly.

"I wish you'd reconsider. At the very least we can still be friends. It'll kill me to see you with a mage, but as long as I still get to see you now and then, I'll be happy."

Whoa, whoa, whoa. What the hell was this? Chaz was never the sentimental type. I was instantly suspicious, though unfortunately I couldn't seem to suppress the growing attraction I had for him.

He'd been a sweetheart (if a bit of an egotist) before we'd split up. Not so much in the flowers-and-chocolates kind of way as the hold-the-door-and-pick-up-the-tab way. And damn but did he ever look good; he had everything I liked. Muscles, intelligence, and a touch of the bad boy—a formidable combo when it came to my hormones. At least I knew now where the hint of danger in his personality came from. It didn't help said hormones any that he was eyeing me like he was wondering just how close Arnold and I had become and what his chances were of getting back in my pants. Yeah, I recognized that look.

Knowing he could probably smell the first stirrings of desire on me, I gave a little frustrated curse under my breath before shoving myself off the couch and walking toward the kitchen. If he'd been human, maybe, *maybe* I would have been able to sit there and bear his scrutiny, but knowing what I knew now about Others, I couldn't deal with it. Not this soon after Royce, and especially not on less than six hours of sleep in the last forty-eight.

"Chaz, I can't talk about this right now. Just stay here, I'll discuss it later." I could almost feel the three of them—Chaz, Arnold, and even Sara—starting to protest. "Don't even get me started. All of you stay here, I'll be back."

I had to talk to Mom about this.

Chapter 20

My mom was putting sodas and beer on a tray when I came in, her back to me as she rummaged in the fridge. She almost dropped the bottle in her hand when she turned around and saw me, her eyes widening with surprise and a measure of guilt.

"Oh, sweetie, you startled me. Help me carry this in to the boys." The words were rushed, and she started to bustle around like she was going to run out of there and avoid me some more.

"Mom, hold up a sec." I walked over and put a hand on the tray to keep her from grabbing it and rushing out. "Why did you invite Chaz over? I know I told you we broke up."

She sighed, leaning her hip against the counter and folding her arms. "I want grandkids, Shia. You and Chaz seemed to be getting along great, and frankly I don't see Mikey or Damien settling down before you do. Chaz is a nice boy. I can't understand why you didn't try to work things out with him."

A spot of red betrayed her embarrassment, but

she sounded firm and sure of herself. That was something we both shared; when backed into a corner, even if we were afraid or embarrassed, we usually came clean about what we were thinking.

"You were with him for almost five months, that's the longest I've seen you with anyone since high school."

Oh God, not this again. "So you thought by inviting him over today we'd just magically end up back together?"

I knew it came out snotty, but at that point I didn't care. I hated it when my mom tried to set me up with someone, more still when she was sneaky about it.

"Well, I didn't think you'd be bringing another boy over," she said defensively. "I was starting to worry about you. Spending all your time with Sara makes people wonder, honey. I just want the best for you."

It felt like my cheeks had suddenly caught fire. My face must have looked about as red as my hair. Even my mom thought I was into girls now? This was getting well and truly embarrassing, not to mention annoying.

"You've got to be kidding me. I *date*, Mom, I just don't usually bring men over! The minute you start talking grandkids, you know they're going to run for the hills."

She gave me a pitying look and I remembered again why I never brought boys over to the house. "It's okay, I believe you. Just remember, you're not getting any younger and neither are me or your dad. We want to see you safe and happy with a family of your own, that's all."

Safe? With a werewolf? I remembered guiltily that I hadn't told her that part about the breakup, and it made me feel even worse since I couldn't say anything about it now. She'd have conniptions if she found out there was a Were in the house. My parents aren't so déclassé as to be White Hats or part of the less vocal, but just as obnoxious, Concerned Human Citizens. However, they aren't exactly supportive of the equal rights movement for the Others either. As long as none of them moved into the neighborhood and they stayed out in the city, my parents would tolerate them, but that was about it.

"Yeah, well, Arnold's a great guy, too. He's looking out for me."

I truly hoped I wasn't digging myself a deeper hole by telling her this. If she somehow found out later that Arnold was a mage, she'd kill me. Probably not so much because he could do magic but because, even if we somehow ended up together, the chances of us having kids was slim to none. Not that I was considering *actually* dating him. Yikes.

"You should let him take care of you, then. Your line of work is dangerous, honey. Dealing with monsters should be left to the experts, like the police. That stunt last month almost gave your dad a heart attack."

That made me cringe. I hadn't realized they knew about the thing at the Embassy.

She continued, "The last thing we want is to see you or Sara get hurt."

I reached over to grab one of the beers, feeling more than shitty about having to hide what was really going on in my life. I just couldn't see a way around it; the truth really *would* give my parents a stroke. Especially if they found out about Royce and the papers. My dad would probably try to stake Royce himself if he found out. Who knows what my mom might do.

Keeping my gaze off her own, I held the cold beer to my forehead for a few seconds, hoping to cool the burning heat of embarrassment while I also tried to swallow down the guilt and think of something useful to say. That's when I remembered I was supposed to leave my car here and had a cover story to match.

"That's part of why I'm going out of town. We're going to take a vacation in the Hamptons for a week." God, I was so going to burn for this later, I just knew it. "Look, I know my job is dangerous but it *is* my job, and I can't just fob off the dangerous stuff on someone else. I won't ask Sara to take the dangerous stints for me."

She frowned, busying herself with the cans and bottles again. "I don't want you to give all the dangerous jobs to Sara either, I want you to give them to the cops where they belong."

I threw my free hand up, trying to convey my exasperation. "The cops won't take the jobs we take, Ma. That isn't what cops do. We track people down and do surveillance, not arrest them. Most of the time I never even talk to the people I'm tailing. It's not as bad as you think."

Most of the time. Except when dealing with magi, Weres, and vamps, it wasn't that dangerous at all.

"All right, all right. No need to get in a huff about it." Finally, she was backing down. "I only bug you about it because I care about you."

Twisting the cap off the beer, I took a swig and stared out the window. There was a fat squirrel on the bird feeder in the elm tree, stuffing itself silly on stolen birdseed.

"Can I leave my car here in the garage until I get back? I don't want someone breaking in again."

That much was true, at least. I had just spent a ridiculous sum fixing the broken window and replacing the stolen radio and would hate to have to go through that hassle again.

"Sure, that's fine. I just wish you'd think about a career change. You know your dad and I would be more than happy to help put you back through school if you want to do something different."

"I like my line of work, Ma. I'm going to stick with it." Turning my gaze back to her, I smiled to soften the blow I knew those words were trying to make light of it. "At least I'm not a cop, right?"

She laughed, obviously heartily amused by the thought. Yeah. Funny.

I felt really bad about hiding things from her, especially how dangerous my job had actually become in the last few days, but at least she was nodding agreement now instead of badgering me about my love life.

"You always were headstrong, doing things your own way." Her wry grin of amusement dragged one out of me in return. "Got it from me, you know."

I chuckled, feeling another pang of guilt, fear, and heartache that I wished more than ever I could share with her. Especially since, after next Monday night, I might never see her again. Tears stung in my eyes, and I turned away so she wouldn't see.

"Yeah, Mom, I know."

Chapter 21

Throughout the rest of the day, things settled down into an uneasy peace. Chaz and Arnold threw a few verbal salvos at each other, but never outright clashed or degenerated into anything physical. They were actually civil to each other over dinner on the deck, sitting across from one another at the picnic table. I wasn't sure if it was for my sake, or for the sake of blending in with my family. Probably the latter, since the survival of the Others had depended upon their ability to pass for human prior to their announcing their existence to the world. Hard to believe that happened less than ten years ago.

Once Angela woke up and joined us, she had, as predicted, chattered up a cheerful storm about the case her boss had won against Mikey. He groaned and complained and tried to get her to shut up about it, smiling the whole time. She also took a keen interest in Arnold and managed to glean some interesting tidbits from him, like the fact that he had graduated from a very upper-crusty institute of technology, was from a well-to-do family from Seattle, moved to New York just over a year ago, and was overly fond of cheese fries.

Fortunately, he didn't say anything about magic or dice or Dungeon Quest or whatever the heck it was he played.

Damien cracked up over the movie when he unwrapped it, and I promised to come over and watch it with him soon. Once the cake was eaten and the last of the presents unwrapped, I said it was time for us to go back to Sara's.

Chaz was the only one who protested, though only mildly. I think he knew he was pushing my buttons by hanging around tonight. The good-byes were quick and relatively painless, my dad making it a point to invite Arnold over to watch the game on the big screen the next Sunday with him and my brothers.

Weirded out by the strain and awkwardness of the day, I slid into the back seat of Arnold's car and shut my eyes, too tired and drained by two nights of almost no sleep to think anymore. Sara offered to put my car in the garage and grab my stuff, and I was quick to take her up on it.

A few minutes later, she tossed the bag into my lap, waking me from my stupor as she slid into the front passenger seat. Arnold had already started the car, and the faint sound of rock music drifted out of the speakers. I shifted around as much as I could to get comfortable, closing my eyes again as he pulled out.

"So, Shia," he said, "that was remarkably awkward. You dated a Were?"

I growled a curse under my breath before answering. "Yes, I did. Not that it's any of your business."

"Your life is my business right now. Anything else like that I'm going to have to field if I'm hanging around you the next few days?"

Sara cut me off before I could speak. "Of course there is. This is Shia we're talking about."

I flipped her off, not that she could see it. "There is a lot I need to tell you. But you promised to tell me something once we got in the car. You go first. Spill it."

His grip tightened on the wheel so hard I could hear the leather squeak. Touchy.

"Okay. Veronica asked you to find an object called a focus, which grants powers to the holder. Depending on what type of creature is using it, the powers it grants are different. It's never been in the hands of magi so far as I know, but when a Were uses it, he can summon and force the transformation on other Weres around them. It augments the strength of the pack in possession of it, and can actually bind other packs temporarily into one much larger force, all working toward whatever the holder's goal may be. When a vampire uses it, he or she can also summon, control, and force transformation on a Were. However, it doesn't do much else for vamps and they have a harder time calling more than a few Weres at a time.

"This thing was supposedly destroyed before

World War One. I have no idea how Royce found it, but we got a tip that he was using it about four months ago. Veronica was in Acquisitions. She was assigned to get it from Royce at any cost, but quietly and discreetly. Before she got in touch with you, she had tried contacting Royce directly. When he refused to sell, she sent someone in to steal it."

He muttered a faint curse, coming to a smooth stop at a light and once more throwing me a quick glance.

"The focus was hidden and the mage who tried to get it was killed. It was hushed up and a directive came down that Veronica needed to find a way to smooth things over with Royce and a different method of locating it and getting her hands on it without any more losses to the coven. Hence her hiring you. I'm assuming Royce found out somehow that you were working for us, and that he's the one responsible for Vero's death."

Though I'd been on the verge of falling asleep when he started speaking, by the end of his little speech I was bolt upright in the cramped back seat. What he'd just said meant that spilling my guts to Royce about working for The Circle effectively sealed Veronica's death warrant. I don't think it was possible for me to feel more heartsick or guilty than I did at that moment.

Knowing it would come out sooner or later, I gritted my teeth and just said it. "I was the one who told him I was working for The Circle. He knew about it before I said anything, but I confirmed it. Some girl named Allison came in, the one who works reception at your office. She told him about the belt you gave me and after that he thought I was sent by The Circle to kill him. I didn't go in there intending to tell him anything, but when he looked like he was about to go for my throat, I couldn't help it. I spilled and told him what I was really there for."

Arnold didn't move and didn't look back at me. His gaze seemed faraway and his attention elsewhere, because the light had turned green and he hadn't taken his foot off the brake. Since we were still in the 'burbs, no one was behind him honking for him to get a move on yet. Eventually he came back to the present, flooring it and jolting me back.

"He knew before you even came to his office? That you were working for us? You just confirmed it for him."

"Yeah. And let us not forget Miss Bitchy Receptionist of the Year who came in and blew my cover story out of the water."

Irritation cut through his voice. "I heard what you said. I knew Allison was up to something with Royce's business, but I didn't think she had a direct line in to him. Two-timing corporate whore. I told the CEO to fire her months ago."

Sara actually laughed at that, though it was more incredulous than amused. "You knew she was a mole?"

"Well, yeah. She was kind of hard to miss. For some reason people don't listen to me in that place. I mean, I told them we needed a better screening process ages ago, but that never went anywhere. I was lucky to get them to update the security system on our vaults. They never do anything until something actually happens and they have no choice."

Recalling that "security system," I shivered and pressed on. "Anyway, you need to hear the rest of this. I already told you I'm banned from working with The Circle now. Royce wants me to sign papers and get them to him by Monday night."

He cursed, eyes glued to the road and thoughts obviously racing. "And turn over the belt, right? Well, you know what, he has to purchase it from you. It was gifted, so it belongs to you. And if you put it on, he can't take it from you anyway."

"What does that mean, exactly?" Sara asked, quicker than I to ask the question.

"Once the belt is put on, the wearer can't remove it until the next sunrise. It also gives the hunter an edge, granting things like strength, speed, stamina, and heightened senses to put the wearer on par with the things they're hunting. We've since lost the spelling instructions on how to make them, but The Circle was gifted with a couple of them a few years ago in payment from another coven for services rendered. Courtesy of a very pissed-off mage who lost a family member to a vamp ages ago."

I couldn't see her expression from this angle, but Sara sounded pleased. "Really? That's handy. Especially since I doctored the papers to read that Shia will be able to hurt or kill Royce, too, not just the other way around."

"Smart, I like it," he said, grinning at her as he gunned the engine and pulled onto the expressway. Once he'd merged into traffic, he turned to me.

"Looks like you get to be the fearless vampire hunter after all."

Chapter 22

When we got back to Sara's place, I took her up on the offer of a comfy guest bedroom. Arnold, very kindly, had decided to take a week of vacation time to work with us, and he and Sara were going to stay up and work on the contract. Comforted by the fact that I had some friends solidly at my back, I was finally able to get a good night's sleep.

The next morning, feeling much refreshed if a bit groggy without my coffee, I stumbled down the stairs to find Arnold sprawled on the couch snoring away. He really took his guard duty seriously. Smiling at that, I tiptoed by into the kitchen to make coffee and breakfast for the three of us.

The smell must have roused them both, since Arnold soon came in rubbing his eyes and yawning, followed a few minutes later by Sara, and we sat down at the table to toasted English muffins and coffee.

"So, Sara," I asked, taking a bite of muffin. "Are we actually going into the office, or are we really playing this out like we're leaving town? If we are, we need to tell Jenny."

If our receptionist was even still working for us. After our meeting on Friday afternoon, I was willing to bet she'd gone job hunting over the weekend. Yet another reminder to talk to Sara—later, privately—about our finances.

"Yeah, I'll take care of it. I'll tell her to come in to answer the phones and that we'll be out this week."

I nodded. "I guess I should find a notary. ETA on the contract?"

"It's done," she said, sipping her coffee. "I just have to print it, and you should manhandle it a little so it looks like the same one you walked out of his office with."

Sighing, I looked to Arnold next. "You going to play chauffeur so I can get this done?"

"Sure. I can't go with you to see Royce tonight, but I'll drop you off and stay close in case you need help."

That was a relief. I smiled at him, grateful that he was willing to come save the day. My good cheer faded when I remembered what he'd said yesterday—he was doing this for his own reasons. I had to wonder what was on his agenda.

"What about me?" Sara asked.

Arnold and I stared at her like she'd grown two heads. "You can't be serious," he said at the same time I sputtered out, "Are you nuts?!"

With a scowl, she leaned forward on the table and pointed at me. "You shouldn't be going in there alone. I haven't signed anything and he doesn't have any leverage against me, so there isn't much he can do to hurt me. You, on the other hand, could use all the help you can get if you expect to get out of this alive."

In a sudden panic, I shook my head, curls flying wildly before I pushed them out of my face. "Sara, no! You don't want to do this, trust me. I didn't think he had anything on me either, but he still put me in this spot. He told me I should tell you to consider signing a contract with him, too, and believe me, you don't want that!"

Her eyes narrowed and I wanted to throttle her, knowing she was thinking about doing just that. I held my breath, waiting for her to answer. Arnold looked like he was biting his tongue to keep from adding his own thoughts to the conversation, though I don't know why he chose to stay out of it. After a moment she relaxed and slumped back in the chair.

"You're right, I don't want to get involved. Not yet. Royce would get suspicious if I showed up with you now, ready and willing to sign."

That was not exactly why I didn't want her involved, but hey, at least she wasn't going to try to face him head on.

We all got quiet for a few minutes. I stared at the table, Sara sipped her coffee and looked thoughtful, like she was planning something, and Arnold just cleared his throat and scuffed his feet a little. It was an awkward silence, and I really didn't want to be the first to break it.

Eventually, Arnold stood up, the sound of the chair scraping over the linoleum sounding overly loud. "I'm going to shower and get dressed. Shia, you might want to think about what you want to do with the rest of your day. We can't be seen by anyone you know if we're going to stick to the cover story that you're out of town. I only hope that ex of yours carries the word back to any packs looking for you."

I gaped at him, realizing all of a sudden what his behavior of yesterday was all about. "You really wanted them to think I was out of town so they wouldn't come after me? Or know where to look?"

He nodded, a wry grin slowly suffusing his lips. "Of course. I told you that you have a tail. That should throw them off the scent for a little while at least."

I felt about a thousand times more stupid than I had a moment ago for not realizing it sooner. Here I'd thought he might actually be trying to save me from Chaz's affections, not his pack.

That thought made me frown. I was hesitant about sounding dumb or egotistical, but I needed to know what was going on if I was going to save my skin. So I asked the question.

"You really think Chaz was there because of something to do with this mess I've gotten into? Not because of me?"

"I don't have any doubts about it." The touch of sympathy in his tone made me want to sock him. He didn't have to rub it in. "He might want you, but he must have known he was taking a risk contacting you after revealing himself. He hid what he was, didn't he? Never gave you a contract before . . ."

"No."

I knew where he was going with his question and wasn't interested in hearing him finish it. I didn't think I could bring myself to press charges against Chaz for initiating a relationship with me without a contract, but if he persisted, I sure as hell wouldn't stick around to see what other laws he was willing to break. Vamps and werewolves, considered too dangerous to interact with people without some kind of safety net, were required to keep *any* physical contact to a minimum until their partners signed contracts. Embarrassing as it was to look back on, Chaz and I had been intimate plenty of times without my spotting any signs of danger. It didn't mean they weren't there—only that I hadn't seen them.

Arnold nodded, giving a helpless shrug. "That just leads me straight to the conclusion that he was sticking his neck out in the hopes of getting close to you again in case you might have a lead on the focus."

So much for my thoughts of Chaz having a heretofore-unknown romantic streak.

He continued, apparently unaware of, or ignoring, my sudden sour expression. "Anyway, I'm going to go take that shower. Let me know if there is anything else you need to get done or pick up before tonight."

Once he was out of earshot, Sara turned to me,

brows raised and expression wry. "You really believe that?"

I slouched back in the chair, folding my arms across my chest and glaring with helpless rage at the cheerful, sunny day shining through the kitchen window.

"I don't know what to believe. Chaz could be a dick, but he was never that slick or conniving before. I have a hard time believing he wasn't just there to see me again."

He wouldn't have given me all those flowers, sent all those cards, or left all those messages if he hadn't truly wanted to get back together. Right? Of course, it didn't matter since I wasn't exactly planning to jump in the sack with him. As far as I knew, he'd been honest with me about everything except what he was. Even now, thinking about how he'd looked and felt in those moments before he shattered that perfect image with fur and fangs sent a pang of regret through me for kicking him out. That had been an act of necessity and self-preservation, though. I wouldn't have changed my actions if he'd been Don Juan incarnate. At this point, it was nothing more than an ego boost to think he still cared.

"Well," Sara said, slathering some jam on her English muffin, "you can always call him and ask. Maybe he'll play it straight with you this time."

I couldn't help but laugh. "Yeah, and maybe tonight Royce will say this whole mess was just a mistake, so sorry for the inconvenience."

She grinned at that, blue eyes glinting with mirth. "You never know."

Oh well. At least we could make light of the situation.

Taking a bite out of her muffin, she mumbled at me through her mouthful, "So what's the plan for today? I'm going to work some more on the missing persons case, that Borowsky kid, while you guys are out. What about you and Arnold?"

I rubbed my chin, thinking about it. What exactly did one do on (probably) one's last day alive?

Chapter 23

On one's (probably) last day alive, one apparently stood around for almost an hour waiting for a notary to stumble over the clauses in a contract before signing it.

The man was in his mid-forties, balding, lisping, and had glasses thicker than Arnold's that he used to squint at the fine print. Arnold had driven me to a place not far from Sara's, a little copy and print shop that had a sign reading CHEAP NOTARY! in the window. *Cheap* being the operative word.

The notary finally looked up at me across the counter, lips pursed in disapproval.

"It's not my place, miss, but are you sure you want to sign this? It's not too late to back out, you know."

I fought back the urge to rub at my aching temples. "Yes, I'm sure. Can we get on with it, please?"

Looking even more displeased than before, the guy handed me a pen. I scrawled my signature on the *Human Notice of Willing Consent and Agreement to*

Binding Contract with Other Citizen page and shoved the pen and paper in his direction. He picked up the pen and put his own neat, professional signature under mine, dated it, and stamped his seal on the page.

God save me, I'd just signed myself over to Royce.

I had a copy of the contract made and paid the guy. Taking my receipt and the contract with me, I devoutly hoped that Sara was right and Royce wouldn't bother reading the contract over or examine it for anything but my signature before taking it down to the courthouse for filing. Arnold opened the car door for me once we got to the tiny parking lot, putting a hand on my shoulder before I got in.

"Try not to worry. We'll figure out a way to get you out of this."

Irritated, I shrugged his hand off my shoulder and slid into the seat, staring down at the papers clutched in my lap.

"It's too late for me to get out of it. Once this gets lodged with the court, that's it. Until one or both of us are dead, Royce can make whatever is left of my life miserable."

"You can do the same to him, you know."

Arnold shut the door and went around to the driver's side. Once he got in and revved up the engine, he looked at me again, his green eyes bright but narrowed in seriousness.

"Vampires, even more than humans, hate when things don't go the way they plan them to. Especially ones as old as Royce. They pride themselves on their ability to predict what others will do and keep the odds in their favor. It's something of a survival instinct. As soon as he knows the contract is different, he'll probably try to weasel out of it. Particularly if you show up with that belt on."

I frowned at that, brushing my fingers over my temples. "I'm not sure how I can show up in his office pretending to have given in while wearing a bunch of stakes at my hip. It's just not going to match the image of me meekly handing over a contract."

The grin that suddenly curved his lips was alarmingly sly. "I know. I thought of that. We're going shopping."

Shopping. I was going to be branded a vampire's toy tonight and he wanted to go shopping?

"It'll be cold tonight, so you can wear a long jacket to hide the belt. I want to make sure you have the right look—you need to look like you intend to hurt him back if he tries to hurt you. It might make all the difference in whether he stands down or tries attacking you anyway."

It took a minute to digest that. "You're saying I need to look the part of the 'fearless vampire hunter' so he thinks twice before trying to bite me? But I have to hide it long enough to get close to him so he knows I'm actually a threat?"

He nodded, not taking his eyes off the road. "You got it."

What exactly did a "fearless vampire hunter" wear? Combat boots? A trench coat? Reflective shades at night?

Thinking about that, as well as what I'd inevitably have to face tonight, I shifted around uncomfortably and stared out, unseeing, at passing buildings.

"Royce has been at least ten steps ahead of me every time I've dealt with him so far. Did I tell you I had some White Hats break into my place the other night? They tried to bully me into joining their cause. He knew they had come before I'd told anyone. Now here I am, doing their work, and not even getting a nifty white hat to wear while I'm at it."

That startled him. He looked at me, horrified, before quickly focusing back on the road. "Don't for a second even think that the White Hats are on your side. They'll happily gut you and burn you at the stake for signing those papers, no matter what your intentions really are."

"I know that. Jeez. I was just being facetious. Though it would be nice to go in with backup, I'm sure as soon as they finished up with Royce, they'd gun for me next."

"Not necessarily in that order. They hate donors almost as much as they hate the vamps themselves."

"Yeah, I know."

"On another note, you should still be on the lookout for the focus while you're with Royce tonight."

I grimaced, wishing mightily that I didn't have to worry about that stupid thing, too. I had enough of my own problems.

"Are you sure I really need to look for this thing? I mean, not that I like the idea of Royce having more power over anyone, but why not just let him keep it?"

Arnold frowned and tightened his grip on the steering wheel. "It's too dangerous to leave it in a vampire's hands."

Oh really? And a power-hungry coven of magi are better guardians of this thing, huh? What actually made it out of my mouth sounded a lot more civil than what was going through my head.

"I remember what you said to me over the phone yesterday. You said something about the end of the world as we know it. I take it that wasn't just a lame reference to a song?"

His thin lips briefly quirked in a smirk, his grip on the wheel relaxing a tad. "No. You're right, I did say that."

The silence dragged on. I helped him along with an "And?"

"This thing is really, truly dangerous." Brows lowered in thought, he stole a glance at me, then looked straight ahead again. "You heard about what Veronica's body looked like when the cops found her, right?"

With a sudden chill of foreboding, I nodded. "Royce used that thing to do that to her?"

"I think so. There isn't any other logical explanation for it. Like I told you before, that thing lets a vampire have a measure of control over Weres."

I remembered the description in the newspaper. "So Royce drained her, and used the focus to make a Were savage the body?" Ew.

"Best as I can figure it out, yeah. I don't have any solid proof, but it fits."

"Okay, not that it isn't bad enough, but what does that have to do with the end of the world?"

He didn't say anything for a long moment, and I watched the emotions flitting across his face. He had a good poker face, but I could see that he was fighting an internal battle. When he finally spoke, the words were careful and measured, which meant he was likely hiding something else beside whatever he was about to tell me.

"Certain people have more will and finesse in using arcane objects than others. Royce is one of the oldest known vampires, and he's not averse to stepping out into the public eye. He flaunts it, actually, which you may have already noticed, considering he was one of the first Others to use the legal system and the press to win over human support for things like equal rights for vampires. While what you may have already seen of his work is impressive, he is capable of a lot more than he lets on.

"Since it is in his hands, I'm assuming, based on what's known of this thing, that he is perfectly capable of using it to start a war. While it might not serve his interests yet, I don't think it's too far-fetched to assume he might use it for that purpose sometime soon."

Arnold paused and drove in silence for a minute. I had the feeling there was something else underlying what he was telling me, something he wasn't saying and that I was just missing.

He continued. "He's not happy with The Circle.

What intelligence we have on him indicates he's been gathering up similar artifacts and actually making some deals with the local Were packs. The newshounds weren't too far off Sunday morning. He can use that thing to turn Other against Other in an all-out war, weakening the power bases of magi and Weres to a point where he can step in and take over.

"If he accumulates too much power, or creates too many other vampires, he can use it to overtake the city and spread outward from there. Remember, he's been around at least long enough to have seen the rise and fall of Rome, the burning of the Holy Land in the Crusades, and learned firsthand from the triumphs and mistakes of some of the greatest military minds in our history. He knows what he's doing, and I for one am not interested in seeing vampires overrun the planet."

I listened to all that with a growing sense of unease, trying to picture the charismatic vampire as some kind of warlord or dictator. It didn't fit with what I'd seen of Royce so far, but there was no doubt that Arnold was right about his growing power base. However, even if Royce did make it to the top of the Other food chain, there weren't nearly enough vampires, Weres or magi combined to be able to overthrow any major government or country. What did Royce need with a dictatorship anyway? He already had most of New York under his thumb as it was.

I couldn't figure it out. I guessed I'd just roll with the punches for now.

"You're right, I'm not interested in seeing vampires take over everything either," I said. "I'll keep an eye out for the focus."

I was careful to keep my voice from betraying any doubts or hesitation. What I didn't tell him was that if, by some miracle, an opportunity presented itself to snatch this thing from the vampire, I sure as hell wasn't going to be handing it over to The Circle.

Chapter 24

Arnold took me to a specialty shop near Central Park. From the display in the window, it looked like some kind of tattoo parlor and leather fetish shop. I was leery of going inside, but once Arnold finally persuaded me to follow one of the heavily pierced and tattooed assistants through the "Staff Only" door in the back of the shop, I saw why he had brought me here.

The assistant led the way down a rickety flight of wooden stairs and unlocked a nondescript door marked STORAGE, half-hidden by piles of boxes and crates. We then entered the obviously less than legal part of the business, a large, well-lit room with an admittedly impressive array of body armor and weaponry on display in glass cases, hanging from racks and tacked on the walls. I was reasonably certain they didn't have permits for any of that stuff, particularly the heavy caliber minigun under a lighted display or the neatly stacked boxes of incendiary grenades next to the register cheerily marked ON SALE—30% OFF WHILE THEY LAST!

I noted the back wall had a section with a carefully hand-crafted wooden sign over it declaring HUNTER'S PLAYGROUND: FOR THE EXPERT EXTERMINATOR. From what I could see, it consisted mostly of wooden stakes with faux-leather grips, fragile-looking vials of holy water probably meant to shatter on contact, crucifixes, crossbow bolts and arrows that ranged in size from a bit thicker and longer than a pencil to as long as my arm, UV flashlights, and some other odds and ends I couldn't quite make out.

Arnold headed toward a fairly normal-looking guy perched on a stool behind the register, leaning against the counter and reading a paperback. Unlike the assistant who showed us down, this one had no piercings or visible tattoos, and was wearing a plain white button-down and slacks instead of ripped jeans and a T-shirt with some obscure band's logo on it. He looked vaguely familiar, but I couldn't figure out where I'd seen him before. His features were nondescript, neither handsome nor ugly, and he didn't seem to recognize me either once he looked up. I dismissed the nagging sense of familiarity as nothing more than my imagination.

"Arnold," the guy said, a smile slowly curving his thin lips, "haven't seen you around here in a long time. How are you, man?"

"Could be better." The mage smiled back, though it was a grim, cheerless thing. He reached over the counter to shake the guy's hand, tilting his head toward me. "Jack, this is a friend of mine. She needs some extermination equipment."

Jack came out from behind the counter, leaving the paperback behind and extending a hand in greeting. When we shook, I had to make an effort not to withdraw immediately, as his hands were dry and calloused, sandpaper rough. His gaze was as empty as his smile, but he led the way without comment over to the portion of the wall I'd been admiring from afar. I was shocked-but-not to see there was also a decent selection of cutlery on display in a glass case below the more mundane stakes and holy waters.

"We need some body armor and some decent cover-up. What do you have in her size?"

Jack looked me up and down, his gaze and expression reminding me of someone looking over fruit in the grocery store for bad spots. It wasn't pleasant being under his scrutiny, but I stood there and took it and inwardly vowed to get back at Arnold for putting me in this position.

"Well, we don't have much on short notice. I might be able to trim something down, but I need to know what kind of weapons she'll be using so I can work with it."

"Stakes," I said sourly, figuring I could do some of this myself.

"What else?"

I must have looked blank, because he turned to Arnold after a couple of seconds and raised a brow, his expression hinting that I'd said something rude or stupid.

Arnold shrugged and turned to me. "What weapons do you know how to use? Guns? Knives?"

Irritated, I gestured at the rows of guns on the walls. "Do I look like the kind of girl who carries hardware like that in her purse? I don't use this stuff, Arnold. The most I've ever done was pop a few shots in a shooting range with my dad when I was a teenager."

Jack grinned at that, his expression finally betraying some amusement. "A novice? Interesting choice of hunter, Arnold."

We both shot him a look that had him holding up his hands and backing down, still amused despite our glares.

"Take a look around and see what catches your eye. I'm going to see what we have in the back in the way of body armor."

Once he stepped away, disappearing through a curtained alcove, I put my hands on my hips and turned to look at Arnold. "This was not what I thought you had in mind when you said we were going shopping."

His look was all too calm, even bland. "Where did you think we were going to go? The mall?"

"I don't know. I thought whatever it was would at least be street legal."

He shrugged, spreading his hands in a helpless gesture. "Not much help for it, I'm afraid. There isn't enough time or any kind of easy way for me to take anything else from the vaults. It's either this or go somewhere that will broadcast your presence to every side that's looking for you right now, including any tail Royce put on you. Or go in with no protection at all."

I muttered darkly at the injustice, but chose to keep most of my thoughts to myself. I picked up a set of bolts, read the hand-lettered label that proclaimed GUARANTEED TO EXPLODE ON CONTACT! and quickly put them back where I found them. Sidling a little down the aisle to the handguns on display, along with a series of different caliber silver bullets, I tried to figure out exactly what kind of hardware I wanted to carry around with me. I'd already decided on a handgun, since I had no intention of getting close enough to use a sword, stakes, or daggers, nor the know-how to use those or a bow or crossbow. A rifle or shotgun would be too big and unwieldy, and there was no way I was even going to think about carrying grenades in my pockets.

After some internal debate, I pointed out a matching pair of silver pistols with tiny, built-in laser sights and black grips that appeared to be small enough to fit my hands comfortably. Probably expensive as anything, but I figured I could deduct it as a business expense. Arnold nodded his approval, and while we waited for Jack to come back out, I started poking around the UV flashlights.

Jack came out a few minutes later with some folded-up material in his arms, setting it on the counter of the gun case. "Decide what you want?"

I pointed out the guns and he unlocked and opened up the case, placing the twin pistols in my hands. They were a bit heavier than they looked, but the grips were comfortable and the laser sights were a huge plus. If I had to hit a moving target, I'd probably miss by a mile since I was never much of a shot to begin with. However, I was fairly confident these looked badass enough to make even the hungriest Other think about finding its meal elsewhere.

"I'll take them," I told Jack, "and some clips with speedloaders if you've got them."

He nodded assent, but held up a hand in caution. "Don't fire these anyplace where cops might be able to see you do it. The bore was altered so the bullets won't be traceable, but if you don't have a permit and since there's no serial numbers on these, you won't be able to sweet-talk your way out of jail if you're caught with them. Or out of the hands of their maker if he finds out the cops got their hands on some of his work."

Oh, that was comforting. With more than a little trepidation, I nodded agreement before asking, "What did you find in the back?"

His lips quirked in a secretive smile, like he knew something I didn't. He probably did. Carefully unfolding and laying out the black clothing he'd pulled out, I frowned on noting that they just seemed like a normal pair of black tights and a turtleneck save that the material was a bit thicker than usual.

"Ever see one of those nature shows where some divers go swimming with sharks?" His crystalline blue eyes betrayed nothing.

"Sure, maybe once or twice." I eyed the clothing speculatively.

He placed his hand over the shirt, showing

pearly white teeth in something approaching a predatory grin. I had an urge to step back, but fought it down and listened.

"Then I'm sure you've seen that they wear a different type of diving suit, one that's meant to keep the sharks from taking a bite out of them. Same principle with this, only a tighter weave and different material. It's a bit more flexible, too. Feel it, tug at it, you'll see what I mean."

Miniature chainmail? I reached out to finger the sleeve of the sweater-looking part, getting the feel of it. It was pretty thick, and I could feel another layer of something hard but somewhat flexible underneath the slick, silk-like black cloth. I did as he suggested, taking part of the sleeve in each hand and tugging at it to see how much it gave. It barely stretched, and I kept pulling as hard as I could until I was reasonably reassured that he was right—the material wouldn't tear easily. Feeling a little uneasy still, I gestured at the case of knives and swords a little farther down.

"What about something sharp? Will it stop those?"

He shook his head. "Depends. This isn't meant to stop bullets or knives, it's meant to slow down or stop an Other from being able to claw at or bite the protected areas. If they slash at you with claws or a knife, it should protect you. With the strength of an Other behind a knife stab? Probably won't save you. They won't be able to bite through, though, and I believe that's what you were most worried about, yes?"

Considering the vamp and Were viruses were usually transmitted through bites, yes, it was. I nodded, trying not to feel sick with worry and not succeeding well at all. He gathered up the clothing and guns, taking everything over to the register to ring it up. I reached for my purse, cringing internally at how much this would probably cost me. Arnold put a staying hand on my arm and stepped forward with a thick bundle of cash, handing Jack a few bills off the top. I glanced at him in surprise, and he answered me with a sly grin.

"Call it a bonus. The Circle owes you for this."

Jack placed the cash in the register and handed a handwritten receipt over to Arnold. He placed the guns in small wooden cases lined with red cloth, along with a clip for each. Then he threw that, more ammo, and a shoulder holster for an easy cross-draw along with a little tissue paper on top into a plain white paper bag on top of the neatly refolded clothes, handing it over to me. Once I took the handles, he walked us over to the door leading back to the storage area. He gave me a grim half-smile and spoke a few cryptic words before shutting and bolting the door behind us.

"Pleasure doing business with you. Glad to see you made the right choice."

I glanced at Arnold as we started up the rickety stairs. "Any idea what that was about?"

He shrugged in an uninterested way. "No. Maybe he just meant you picked a good gun or something."

We left and headed for his car. While he unlocked the doors, I peered into the bag, poking through the boxes to take a closer look at the clothes beneath, hoping they would fit. Then I slid into the leather seat and fiddled with the radio. Since the day was fairly warm, he put the top down, then slapped my hand away from the knobs and tuned to a preset station playing some kind of techno rock.

"Let's hit the mall, get you a jacket, then grab some food and head on back to Sara's."

He eased the car into traffic. I tilted my head back against the headrest, closing my eyes and just trying to enjoy the fact that I was in a convertible with a reasonably good-looking guy who'd just paid for a bunch of stuff that would probably help save my life.

All I could think about was that, in less than eight hours, I would have to face Royce and put those signed, notarized papers in his hands.

Chapter 25

It didn't take long to find a suitable jacket in the mall. I needed something that would hide the weaponry well enough for me to get my foot in the door and, hopefully, add a little protection while still allowing for freedom of movement. Especially when it came time to draw down, if it came to that.

One of the stores actually had a nice selection of leather trench coats, and I was lucky enough to find an ankle-length black one in my size. I also swung by the shoe store and bought some combat boots. I didn't normally wear those, but they seemed suitably badass and like they would fit with the jacket and the clothes and the guns. I think. Come on, I've never seen a fashion guide that tells you how to accessorize your shoes with your stakes and guns, have you?

We picked up a pizza and sodas on the way back to Sara's. Once Arnold had parked at Sara's place and I started to get out, he put a hand on my arm. I paused with one foot resting on the curb.

"Is Sara single?"

I blinked. That was unexpected. "Maybe. She mentioned something yesterday about this cop she'd been seeing. They're usually on and off. I thought they were off but now I guess they're on again."

He nodded before getting out of the car. I watched him for a moment, trying to decide if he was asking me for security reasons or something more personal. Since Veronica was out of the picture, I wondered if that was why he was suddenly interested, and I felt an irrational twinge of jealousy.

Whatever, it wasn't my problem and he was *not* my type. I don't knowingly date Others. Not after what happened with Chaz. I hadn't particularly gone out of my way *not* to before, but I wasn't one of those thrill seekers that spent all my free time at the bars and restaurants frequented by the local supernaturals either. Plus, even the thought of being contracted gives me the willies. The extent of my experience with Others has led me to believe that the majority of them are deceptive, conniving, and occasionally violent assholes. No offense to any assholes out there.

I held the dogs back while Arnold hustled inside with the food and shopping bags. They barked up a storm as usual and tried to squeeze past me when I hopped up the porch steps and ducked inside.

Sara had set out the pizza and soda, and we all grabbed paper plates, poured some drinks, and settled around the kitchen table. Arnold watched Sara and me with an odd expression as we folded our pizza slices in half before eating them. After a minute or two of this, Sara grinned at him. "What, you've never eaten pizza with a New Yorker before?"

I picked a piece of pepperoni off my slice, popping it in my mouth before turning to Sara. "Are you going to use the rabbit ears or should I just carry my cell with me tonight?"

She shrugged, getting up to grab the garlic salt from one of the cabinets. "Probably just your cell. We don't know what Royce can and can't hear or sense, so it might be best if you limit the electronics. Just make sure you have me set in your speed dial this time."

I nodded sheepishly, and Arnold looked mystified. "Rabbit ears?"

"Yeah. Just a nickname for a bug we wear when we speak to someone and think the conversation may require recording or turn ugly. It lets someone else listen in, and that's mostly what we use it for, in case we need someone to bail us out in a hurry."

"Ah."

"What?"

"We use similar tactics at The Circle, except we use charms or familiars, not electronics."

Oh, that was comforting. At my sudden wary look, he laughed and shook his head. "Don't worry, none were used with you except during your initial meeting with Veronica."

He took a big bite out of the pizza, all too cheerful about that. It gave me the willies, which decreased my appetite, though not enough to stop me from finishing off the slice I was working on.

"Hey, Shia, no luck on the Borowsky kid," Sara said. "All I got was a tip from one of his friends that he's into the Goth and vamp scene, way more than his parents knew. Nothing surprising, nothing helpful. Anyway, you've got a few hours 'til sundown. Do you know what you want to do for the rest of the day?"

"Hiding under a rock somewhere sounds good to me."

Arnold nudged the bags beside the table with his foot. "You should probably put everything on and practice moving in it. If it's been a while, I'd suggest taking a few practice shots with the gun, too."

"You really think I'm going to need to use it?" I felt the blood drain from my face. God, I hoped it wouldn't come to that.

His lips curved downward, gaze sliding away from mine. "I don't know. I hope not."

Well, worrying about it hadn't helped anything yet. I resolved to start thinking about what I *could* do instead of how everything could go wrong. At the very least, I could do what he said and try on the clothes, get used to moving in them, and make sure the whole ensemble wouldn't look too ridiculous when I showed up at Royce's office.

Wiping my greasy fingers on a crumpled napkin, I got up and gathered the bags, belt, and vial of Amber Kiss perfume.

"I'm heading upstairs to change. Be back in a few minutes."

They both gave me the thumbs-up, munching on their pizza. I wasn't hungry, but I'd probably make myself eat another piece later when I was feeling a little more secure. Like after I had some stakes and guns on my person.

It took a minute for me to pull on the new clothes. At first, the turtleneck shirt and pants seemed uncomfortably tight. You could see the slightest bump under the shirt where the charm necklace that let me see through vamp and magi illusions rested against my skin, plastered in my cleavage. I hadn't removed it since the meeting with Royce, and wasn't planning on willingly taking it off for as long as I lived.

The shirt covered almost my whole neck, but I noticed that the slick material made it difficult to slide my fingers under it and yank it down lower. After getting over the initial irritation, I realized this was a good thing. It meant Royce would also have a tough time pulling it down enough to reach anything vital. Same with the wrists and ankles, though the pants were just a touch too long and I had to figure out a way to fold the material under so it wouldn't bunch up in the shoes and irritate my skin.

I took a little time to stretch, reaching down to touch the floor, squat, split, and basically just make sure my freedom of movement wouldn't be too restricted. Thankfully, the stuff clung like a second skin and wasn't so stiff that I lost any flexibility. The burning ache in my muscles was a reminder that I'd missed my normal exercise over the weekend and would have to figure out some time to make it up—if I survived tonight's ordeal.

With the pants tucked into my new combat boots and the silver cross at my neck gleaming against the flat black of the shirt, I had to admit as I examined myself in the full-length mirror, that I did indeed look the part of a vampire hunter. Or maybe a thief. Or a Goth? Yeah, I didn't like where this train of thought was going.

The shoulder holster was next. I had to fiddle with the straps to adjust them. Then readjust them when I realized I had put it on wrong. Then fiddle with and adjust it a little more so it didn't dig into my boobs quite so much. What a pain. It would make for an easy cross-draw, though, and the weapons wouldn't be too conspicuous under the jacket.

The belt came last. I stared at it for a minute, laid out on the guest bed, looking utterly innocuous except for the big-ass silver stakes in their sheaths on one side. The trio of silver stakes had leather grips, worn and stained a dull gray from the sweat of many palms. The belt itself was a dull black that hadn't yet been bleached by time. On the inside, where it would lay against cloth or skin, I knew it had glyphs branded into it, though I didn't understand what they were for or what they meant. Putting it on meant it would adhere to me until the next sunrise. It meant I would be knowingly, willingly dipping my fingers into a magic melting pot.

Taking a deep breath to steady myself, I reached out a trembling hand, praying that the choices I'd made were right and that this thing really would help see me through 'til tomorrow's sunrise.

Chapter 26

There was no flash of light, crackle of magic, or thunder of epic orchestral music from an unseen band in the background when I put the belt on. I half expected something, maybe even just *feeling* a little different.

Absolutely nothing changed once I settled it around my waist, adjusting it so the buckle and a couple of clips of extra rounds hung off one hip and the stakes off the other. I was both relieved and a little disappointed.

If not for the stakes, the outfit wouldn't look half-bad. A little dark for my taste, definitely not something to wear around the office, but to a club? Maybe. I tied my hair back in a loose ponytail to make sure it would stay out of my face. Then I picked up the duster, figuring I might as well give it a try though it was too hot to wear for long and I certainly wasn't interested in parading around the house like I'd just stepped off the set of the latest sci-fi action movie.

I reached into the bag and pulled out the pair of wooden boxes that held the guns so I could holster them and see how they "fit" with the outfit. When I lifted the lid of one of the boxes, the first thing that caught my eye was something gleaming white against the red velvet lining.

It was a pin of a tiny white cowboy hat. A White Hat pin. The symbol of their little clique of vigilante vampire and Were hunters.

I stared at it for a minute, trying to figure out why in God's name it would even be there. The guy, Jack, must have slipped it into the box while he was putting the guns away.

Suddenly I recalled where I had seen him before. The bastard looked a bit different in plain clothes and under bright lights where I could see his features clearly. He was the one who had politely let himself into my bedroom to "ask" me to join the White Hat cause—at knifepoint.

Crap, he must think I'd tracked him down and taken him up on his offer. Did that make me a card-carrying, pin-wearing member now? How did this development fit in with all my other troubles? Were Jack and his buddy planning on coming back?

Ugh. I'd just have to deal with that worry later. I only hoped it didn't come back to bite me in the ass once that "later" eventually rolled around.

The trench coat worked admirably to hide the weapons. It didn't do much for my figure when it was buttoned up, but I practiced doing a quick draw of the guns, then the stakes. Everything went almost too smoothly.

With the addition of the jacket on top of the body armor, it was quickly becoming stiflingly hot. Before long I shrugged it off and gathered it up in my arms, leaving the rest of the outfit on so I could get approval from my posse downstairs. On my way down, I debated whether or not to mention the pin to either Sara or Arnold, and decided against it. Things were complicated enough already, and I was reasonably certain I could figure out a way to get the White Hats to leave me alone on my own. Eventually.

The two were in the living room, heads close as they leaned over the contract I'd already signed. I couldn't hear what they were muttering to each other, but they looked up when I cleared my throat.

Sara grinned and Arnold simply nodded, his brows raised. "It came together better than I thought it would. Can you draw the guns easily?"

I tossed the duster to a chair, then demonstrated the quick draw I'd been practicing upstairs. They both jerked back in surprise, and I laughed.

"Hey, I'm just fooling. But just so you know, they're not loaded yet *and* the safety's on. The trench hides everything well, too. I think this might actually work."

Sara rose with a languorous stretch. She walked over to me and lightly ran her fingertips along my sleeve. "What is this stuff?"

I shrugged. "Some kind of body armor that protects against Were claws and vamp bites apparently. Won't stop a bullet or a knife thrust, but it should do the trick if Royce goes for my throat." Or something else. Yikes.

She regarded me thoughtfully for a moment. "And have you decided exactly what your plan of action is once you get into his office? Or what you'll do if he does attack you?"

"Yes," I said with more confidence than I felt, "I have. I'm going to show up, try to sweet-talk him into forgetting about the contract. When he refuses, I'll reluctantly hand the papers over. Then, if he tries anything, I'll tell him about the changes in the contract and give him a chance to rethink his actions."

"And if he persists?" Arnold asked. "What then?"

I sighed, rubbing the bridge of my nose with the tips of my fingers. "Then I'll hit the speed dial on my phone to call you guys and open up the jacket so he knows I'm prepared for and will retaliate against whatever he wants to dish out. Tit for tat."

"Okay. I'll wait in the car with Arnold then," Sara said. Turning to him, she spread her hands in a helpless gesture. "Not that there's much I can do if we need to go in shooting, but I imagine that's where you come in."

He cracked his scrawny knuckles and assumed a menacing look that was more comical than intimidating on his features. His green eyes sparkled with mischief, which didn't help make him look any more menacing, more like a kid in a candy store.

"Fortunately, unlike you ladies, I won't have to worry about legal backlash if I go in with guns blazing, so to speak. Other-to-Other battles are still for the most part left up to us to work out amongst ourselves."

I had to admit to curiosity. "How come you didn't just do that in the first place? I mean, couldn't you just, you know . . . magic missile him or something and save you and The Circle—and me—a lot of trouble?"

"Sadly, no. The political backlash would be more than even The Circle could handle. Aside from which, singly, I'm not really a match for him. However, with you there wearing the belt, the two of us together should be able to handle him. Plus, I won't have to worry about the stir it would cause since we have witnesses who think you and I are an item. If it looks like I just went in to protect my girlfriend, I won't have to worry as much about being canned for it later."

Lovely. I sighed again, folded my arms, realized how uncomfortable that was with the holster on, and unfolded them to leave my hands dangling at my sides. "That's just peachy keen."

Turning to Sara, I put my hands on my hips and looked at her questioningly. Usually she thinks of something I haven't when it comes to planning, so it felt a little odd that she hadn't added much to the conversation. "Got any other bright ideas about tonight?"

She shook her head, folding her own arms and rocking back on her heels. "You've thought up about as much as I have. I can't think of anything else to do or any other way to handle it."

My jaw dropped open in shock. I'd thought everything out as much as she had? Now *that* was scary.

Chapter 27

We waited until past sunset to leave Sara's place. I didn't think it would be a good idea to keep Royce waiting, but Arnold and Sara disagreed, telling me it would put him on edge and make him think I was having thoughts of running instead of facing him tonight. It would be more convincing if I acted well and truly reluctant to hand over the papers.

I had slid some ammo clips into the pockets of the jacket along with my cell phone. When they dropped me off in front of Royce's office building, Arnold promised to park close enough to come to the rescue or make a fast getaway if needed.

Now, I stood in front of the office tower, staring up at the building while clinging to the closed edge of my trench coat with my free hand and taking a few deep breaths to steady myself. I glanced at the documents in my other hand, feeling my stomach flip-flop in queasy reaction. "This is it," I breathed, knowing that everything in my life was about to change.

Keeping my head bowed, I tucked the stack under my arm and affected as wooden and reluctant a stance as I could manage as I walked in through the revolving doors. I didn't know if there were cameras or security guards, and I didn't want to take the chance that Royce might have some other kind of sentry watching for anything suspicious. There was a guard at the desk, a different one this time. He barely glanced up as I headed to the elevators, the coat flaps slapping softly against my legs with each step I took.

I felt my palms starting to sweat, my heart creeping up into my throat as I entered the elevator and hit the button for the eighth floor. This was it. This was really it. I hoped and prayed the Amber Kiss perfume I was wearing would dull the scent of my fear, that he wouldn't realize what I'd done, that he wouldn't think to look over the papers before filing them with the courts.

When the elevator "pinged," I took another deep, steadying breath, stepped out, and clumped slowly to his office. When I opened the door, I was surprised to be greeted by a receptionist and a bunch of other people sitting at the desks and in the offices that had been empty before.

"Can I help you, miss?"

I stared for a second, that deer-in-headlights look of complete shock at being confronted by an actual human being written across my face. People really worked here at night? "Yes—uh . . ." I stammered, "Mr. Royce is expecting me?" Why in God's name were there people here?

She nodded, gesturing for me to take a seat in one of three chairs lined up against the wall, near a small table with restaurant and fine dining magazines scattered across it. I moved over to a chair and slumped into it, trying to get around my shock at seeing people working so late. They probably kept odd hours due to working for a vampire. It made sense once I thought about it. After all, he couldn't be here to supervise them during the day, and someone with an empire (so to speak) as diverse and widespread as Royce's would need support staff. Funny, I hadn't given it any thought until confronted with it, except maybe to assume the empty desks and offices were for show.

In an agony of suppressed terror and fading adrenaline, I sat and fidgeted for close to an hour. It was getting unbearably hot in my jacket, but I didn't dare take it off or even unbutton it, not with the chance of someone seeing the guns, ammo clips, and stakes. I don't know if he was trying to irritate me or heighten the sense of anticipation with the wait. Either way, it was driving me crazy.

Finally, an eternity or so later, a young man who, in his slightly-too-big suit and crooked tie, looked like an earnest intern trying hard to fit in with the big boys came around the receptionist's desk to greet me. "Ms. Waynest? Come with me, please."

I did as he bade, rising slowly from the chair, clutching the papers to my chest. He led me down a long hallway to a small conference room. On the way, we passed Allison, The Circle's receptionist, going in the other direction. She gave me a scathing look as we approached. What bug crawled up her ass? Her obvious and intense hatred had no ready source that I could see. She whacked me with her purse when we passed, and didn't look back. I stared at her over my shoulder until I bumped my shin on a desk, cursing softly in pain before hurrying to catch up with the little intern. He was watching me with a mixture of confusion and amusement, but politely said nothing.

Once inside, he indicated I should take a seat. A pencil-skirted older lady was arranging a dish of pastries, coffee, and tea at a sideboard, and as soon as she saw us, she hurried out. After I sat down, the kid cocked his skinny wrist to look at his watch and then stood at one side of the door, eyeing the painting on one wall with studied disinterest. I soon found myself doing the same, wondering what this was all about.

Royce entered a few minutes later, sporting an elegant navy blue suit and striped tie, his gleaming hair tied back at the nape of his neck. He nodded to the young man and approached me, holding out his hand expectantly. "Shiarra, I'm glad to see you did as you were told. The papers?"

I tightened my grip on them, twisting around in the chair a little and shrinking back. I knew I was gaping at him, but it took a second for me to regain enough of my poise to stammer out an answer. "I—Mr. Royce, can we maybe talk about this first?"

The vampire exchanged a look with the guy by the door, who grinned widely enough to show fully extended fanged incisors. Oh shit.

Unthinking, I jerked back from the table, stumbling to my feet and backing away to put some distance between us. Royce and the other vampire stayed where they were, seeming no more than vaguely amused by my panicked reaction.

"Look, you can't—this—it doesn't work like that. You can't touch me until they're filed!" I babbled. "Whatever it is you want from me, there has to be another way. Please just tell me what you want from me, you don't need the papers for that."

"Shiarra, we've already had this discussion. My terms are simple, and you've already done the difficult part." He sighed, sounding a trifle annoyed. "Just give me the contract and let's get this over with. I'd rather we not be here all night. I'm a busy man."

Stalling, I looked back and forth between Royce and the other vamp. "Why is he here?"

"To take the papers to the courthouse. He won't touch you. Isn't that right, John?" The other vampire nodded, though that fiendish, toothy grin remained prevalent. I think he was enjoying my frightened reaction a little too much. "There, you see? Come on now," Royce continued, his voice soft and pleasantly cajoling. "You'll make this much easier on all of us if you just hand them over."

I looked down at the documents I was holding, feeling my heart rate rev up another notch. Here goes nothing.

I hesitantly sidled around the table and held out the papers, keeping as much distance between us as I could. I didn't have to fake the tremors making the papers shake. He took the stack out of my hands, doing just as Sara had thought he would and immediately skimming to the last couple of pages just to note my signature and the notary's stamp. Turning his back to me, he passed the papers over to the other vamp.

"Make a copy of this for our files and then run it down to the court. Call my cell once you've paid the fees and filed it."

John nodded, took the papers in hand, and left, closing the door. I wanted to breathe a sigh of relief, knowing he'd bought it, but I couldn't relax just yet.

My stomach about dropped down to my shoes when he turned back to me, those depthless black eyes boring into mine with a hunger so primal and dark, I knew for a certainty that he would gladly drink every last drop of blood in my body and not regret it for an instant. The social veneer had been stripped away, leaving the monster beneath bare to view.

"Now," he said softly, his pace slow, measured, and as predatory as a stalking jungle cat, "we can get down to business."

Chapter 28

"Do try to make a run for it," he snarled, my heart skipping a beat at the soft promise in his tone. "It's been so long since anyone's been afraid . . ."

Afraid? Try terrified. I staggered back a step, one hand behind me to keep from backing into something, the other held out in front of me to ward him off. "Whoa, whoa, whoa, wait a minute! No, we're *not* doing this!" I desperately tried to think of a convincing reason to make him wait. "It's not filed," I squeaked, "not yet, you can't do anything to me yet!"

"Oh," he murmured, easing the rolling chair I'd been sitting in back under the table as he matched me, step for step, "but I can. John will be in the courthouse in about twenty minutes. After that, none of your laws apply to us anymore. Until then, I can still push every button you have to make the first drop of blood on my tongue worth every bit of trouble you've caused me."

"Trouble? Trouble I caused *you*!" I felt a sudden

surge of anger. Good, much better than quivering terror. "I told you I wasn't out to hurt you, and now the stupid focus and the stupid contract with The Circle probably don't matter anyway since Veronica is dead! If not for you and Veronica, I would probably be home in bed watching TV right now. Instead I've got every Other and White Hat on both sides of the river gunning for me. Don't even *start* with me about trouble!"

He grinned without any real humor at my outburst. "You underestimate yourself. And your worth. It doesn't matter anymore. The contract makes you mine."

I was clearheaded enough to pull out the rolling chairs to try to slow him down, anything to block his way and keep him from getting his hands on me that much sooner. He calmly pushed them aside, inexorably closing the distance.

"What do you *want* from me?" I asked, ticked that he wouldn't just say it already and get it over with.

"I want," he said, his arm snaking out lightning quick to close tight as a vise on my upper arm before I could stumble out of his reach, "you to save me."

"What?" I choked out, trying to writhe out of his grasp. His fingers tightened until I cried out in pain, tears squeezing unbidden from the corners of my eyes.

He didn't draw me closer, only held my arm still, that glimmer of hunger still shining evilly in his black eyes. His voice took on a low, guttural quality, as though coming from some beast below the surface of his hardened, all-too-human features. "Stop struggling. I can't control the hunger *and* fight the focus. Stay still."

I tried, honestly, but there was a part of me screaming "OH-MY-GOD-THAT'S-A-HUNGRY-VAMPIRE-HOLDING-YOUR-ARM" that made it awfully hard to just sit still and listen.

"I'm bound to someone, just like you will be to me. Listen to me, because I can't fight this forever. I don't have the focus. I'm not able to tell you who does." He paused, and his jaw clenched tight, fangs bared fully in a grimace as he turned away from me. I prayed whatever it was he was fighting internally lasted long enough for me to figure out a way out of this. He started speaking again, all in a rush, and I noticed that his voice sounded slightly different from when he was talking about what a pain in the ass I was. There was an urgency behind it, and he sounded a lot more like he had when I had met him back in The Underground. "Don't fight the binding, and don't fight me, or the one who has the focus may be able to force my hand into killing you. You need to find it and take it from the holder."

His fingers spasmed, tightening around my arm, his other hand reaching out to steady himself on the table. It took everything I had not to scream in pain, but somehow I managed. God, he was strong, probably strong enough to snap my arm if he put just a little more effort into it.

"Not interested," I panted, using my free hand to slide under my jacket and grab one of the guns.

"But thanks for the offer," I said as I shoved the muzzle under his chin.

He abruptly shoved me away from him, sending me sprawling back on my ass. It was a good thing the safety was still on, or the gun would've gone off and he'd be missing a good portion of his face.

"You conniving little bitch!"

"Alive and whole conniving little bitch," I shot back, using one hand to grab on to the sideboard next to me to pull myself up. I knocked a bunch of cookies or something to the floor in the process, but didn't bother to look. My eyes stayed firmly focused on the vampire just a few feet away, who looked like he was having a tough time deciding whether or not to rush me. My other hand kept the gun trained on him, though technically I couldn't do anything to him with it just yet.

"You can't fight back," he growled, taking one menacing step forward. "Are you crazy or stupid or both? There is no provision in that contract that can save you from your own people if you shoot me."

Levering up to my feet, ignoring the twinge in my back, I brandished the gun at him and gestured for him to back up. Panting a little from fear and pain, I narrowed my eyes and deliberately flicked the safety off the gun.

"*Au contraire,*" I said, feeling particularly high and mighty right at that second for having gotten the better of a vampire as old as he was. "It's been doctored. You touch me, and I swear to all that is holy I will use this gun to shoot those pearly white fangs of yours into the back of your skull. Want to try me?"

His face twisted into an angry, silent snarl, but he backed up a couple of steps. Thank the Lord, it was working. The plan was working! I unbuttoned my trench coat very deliberately, very slowly, revealing the other gun and the stakes. His eyes widened at the sight of the belt, and his fists clenched at his sides. "I told you to give that to me!"

"Tough shit. It was a gift. It's mine, not The Circle's, and doesn't come with buying out their contract." After a moment's thought, I added, "Aside from which, you don't own me. We have a binding agreement that we can legally hurt or kill each other with impunity. That doesn't mean we should act on it."

He growled, low and deep, rumbling in his throat and sending a shiver through me. I really needed to reconsider baiting the already very pissed off vampire.

"Check," he said, his tones resuming that honey-sweet lull that made it hard to decide whether or not to be frightened of him. The fangs made it easier to stay scared. "But not mate. I'll let the contract stand as is, then. You've caught me off guard this time, it's true. But you can't hide from me forever, and the minute you let your guard down, you're mine."

"Is that Royce speaking, or the one holding the focus?" I asked snidely, cocking my hip to look a lot more relaxed and arrogant than I was. "You're starting to sound a little like a bad B-movie."

He snarled and narrowed his eyes, leaning forward threateningly. "You're speaking to the holder of the focus. I know who you are, Shiarra Waynest. Do you know me?"

I paused. What the heck was this? "No." I let a bit of my own glare come out. "I don't care who you are or what you're after, I just want you to leave me alone. Can we make a deal, you go your separate way and leave me out of whatever it is you're up to?"

"No," he said, the scowl easing into a dark, dangerous smile, the kind that would melt your insides if you didn't know there were fangs hidden behind those velveteen lips. "Maybe, if you'd been less intuitive, if you hadn't worked for The Circle. Maybe. Not now. I'll find a way to hunt you down, whether I have to use Royce or another means of reaching you. Your little pet mage can't keep you safe from me."

Okay, this was just getting creepy. "That's nice. I'm leaving now. You stay right where you are or so help me I will use your teeth for shooting targets." I cautiously backed around the table, never taking the gun or my eyes off him and some part of me intuitively knowing where to step so as not to bump into any of the scattered chairs.

He did what I said, seething, something dark and menacing moving behind his eyes. Alien thoughts, not his own. I could almost see him fighting to regain some measure of control of himself, clawing toward but never quite reaching the surface. Like a part of him wanted to spring at me and another wanted to stay put. It was hard to tell which side was winning out.

Just in case he lost his mind and decided to jump me, I slid my other hand into my pocket, fingering my cell phone to turn off the key lock, and pressed until I heard the reassuring beep that said my pre-prepared text message had been sent to Sara. If I wasn't downstairs in the next five minutes, she and Arnold would come looking for me.

"Shiarra." Royce's voice was faint, slick with unspoken promise, hissing out between his clenched teeth. "I know where your parents live. I know you've been staying with that rich little cunt. I know you're still working with someone from The Circle. Walk out that door, and I will personally see that every Other in the state makes it their business to destroy everything, everyone you've ever known."

Chilled, I paused with one hand on the doorjamb. What was *with* this guy? "What did I ever do to you? I already said I don't want any part of this."

He took a slow step forward, creeping closer to me. There was still a healthy distance between us, but no more table or chairs to bar his way. "You interfered. You forced my hand." Anger started creeping into that not-quite-Royce's voice. "You made me have to take it before I was ready. But you know what?"

"What?" I asked, unnerved. He wasn't making any sudden movements, but I didn't like that surreal gleam to his eye as his snarl turned into a dark, nasty grin.

"Seeing you bleed will make it all worth it." With those few words, he sprang at me, faster than I would have thought possible.

Chapter 29

I screamed and jerked back as he came at me, moving with a boneless grace, his fingers curled into grasping claws. My finger tightened on the trigger and he twisted to one side, hissing a spitting mixture of pain and epithets as he fell just short of me when I pressed my back flat up against the door. The bullet barely slowed him down, since he gathered his feet up under him and leapt up almost as soon as he'd fallen, black blood oozing sluggishly out of the wound in his shoulder.

I seemed to have acquired a sixth sense, knowing exactly what he was going to do before he did it. As he sprang forward again, I ducked, twisting my body around to get in another shot to his torso as he came at me. There was little room to maneuver, and he was driving me back from the only exit, but I wasn't so interested in that as in avoiding having him sink his fangs into me or crush my arm again.

His eyes had shifted to glowing red pools of hot hatred, his fangs nearly cutting into his lower lip as he came at me. There was no room for thought as he reached grasping fingers for my wrist, capturing the one that held the gun and forcing the third shot to go wild. I could hear shouts and pounding on the door as we fought, but they were distant, somewhere outside myself. As he crashed into me, I fell back, digging a knee into his stomach and forcing him to flip over my head and land painfully on his back. Whoa. Where'd I learn to do that?

His grip loosened as he hit the floor, and the two of us twisted and shifted like snakes, coming back to our feet in seconds and warily facing off just a few feet apart.

As I reached for the other gun, he came silently forward once again, lips peeling back from his fangs as he slid one arm around my waist in mockery of a lover's touch. The other came up to grab my wrist again, forcing my arm back and to the side as he drove his fangs against my neck, trying to bite through the material.

I could feel the pressure of the bite, but the fangs never penetrated. I'd probably have one heck of a weird-looking bruise at the crook of my neck later on. Enraged, he scraped his fangs over the material as he kept trying and failing to pierce the shirt, which I was more than thankful for right at that moment. His grip on my wrist was painfully tight, but my other arm was still free. I slid my free hand up and under his jaw and shoved, hoping to at least get him off my shoulder.

The result was a little more than either of us were expecting. His jaw audibly snapped shut and he staggered back unsteadily, like I'd given him one mother of an uppercut. His fingers at my back slipped and slid against the slick material of my shirt and finally lost their grip entirely. He had wrapped the fingers of his other hand entirely around my small wrist, and didn't let go, almost jerking me off my feet as he pulled back.

Unthinking, quick as a whip, I closed the newfound distance between us with a stake in my free hand, just barely piercing his chest right above where I somehow knew, just *knew*, a blackened husk of a heart rested. He went very still, the hatred frothing behind those black eyes turning into an abrupt kind of panic and fear. I was willing to bet it had been a very, very long time, if ever, since he'd had to worry about an untimely end to his existence. He hadn't had a doubt in his mind when he attacked that he would win. I knew for a certainty that it was the "real" Royce looking so afraid. After all, what did the holder of the focus have to worry about other than losing a valuable pawn? If not for the fact that I knew he had been trying to kill me a few seconds ago, I might have felt sorry for him right at that moment.

"Look," I said quietly, realizing dimly and with a vague sense of horror that there was a part of me that *wanted* to push that stake home, *wanted* to end his existence, and that I had to put effort into *not* destroying him then and there. "I don't want to kill you. I don't want to fight you. I just want to get out of here. So you're going to back the fuck up, give me some space, and let me walk. *Capeesh?*"

He nodded, and I watched in morbid fascination as something twisted and swam behind his eyes even as his fingers slowly released their vise grip on my wrist. Though I didn't really want to show weakness in front of him just then, as soon as he let go, I shook my wrist out and grimaced just a little. Man, he had a tight grip.

Fortunately, I had never lost my hold on the gun, so once I'd worked a little circulation back into my wrist, I lifted the weapon until it was aimed square at his nose. Next I tucked the stake that had magically found its way into my hand back into its sheath as I slowly backed toward the door again. He stayed right where he was, fists clenching and unclenching at his sides, but otherwise unmoving. It looked like the holder of the focus was trying to goad him into doing something stupid, and he was gamely fighting against it. That, and, oddly, the blood that had been trickling out of the bullet holes in his shoulder and stomach had ceased flowing. Creepy.

Once I put my hand on the door handle, he spoke, voice low and uneven, like his control was wavering. "*La Petite Boisson* tomorrow night. Bring the mage."

His eyes were closed, his expression contorting like he was in pain. When his eyes opened again, that feral glitter had come back to them, and he took a step toward me. His voice was once again that sickeningly sweet lull, promising all sorts of things that I really, really didn't want anything to do with. "When I get my hands on you, you will beg to die. But I won't let you. I am going to drag out your death for days, weeks, years. You could only wish you had gone the easy route and given yourself over to Royce."

"That's nice. Here's how it's actually going to play out," I said with far more brashness than I felt. My insides felt like they'd turned to iced jelly, but I kept talking smooth and bored like I was going over my grocery list instead of threatening the obviously psychotic holder of the focus. "When I find you, and you stop hiding behind your big bad vampire flunky"—Wow, did I really just call Royce a flunky?—"I am going to kick your sorry, cowardly ass from here to the Mississippi. And trust me, I will find you."

He snarled and took another threatening step, so I shot him in the knee. He fell, howling and cradling his injured leg, and I stared in stupid shock. I hadn't even thought about pulling the trigger, hadn't even really tried to take aim. The laser sight wasn't on. How could I have managed to hit him? I'm not *that* good a shot.

Yet somehow I'd just felled him with no real effort, knowing instinctively that it would take him too long to recover from the knee injury for him to follow me. *Go in for the kill. He's easy prey now,* a soft voice whispered in the back of my mind. *He can't run or fight back as well wounded like that. All it will take is one quick thrust and it will all be over.* Chilled, I shook my head violently to stop the thoughts prodding at me, holstered the gun, and yanked the door open.

The people who had been gathered outside the door backed up immediately, all of them looking frightened and shocked. I threw one last, pitying look over my shoulder to the vampire who was glaring at me with someone else's hatred in his eyes. There was some part of me that was hating back, not Royce, but the one who was making him lash out against me. Sure, he was a manipulative bastard, probably worthy of some loathing, too, but I knew what it was like being under someone else's thumb. It couldn't have been easy for someone who was so used to being in control to be subjected to something like the hold of the focus. He was suffering from that indignity a lot more than I was just now.

He was a vampire, but he had also been human at one time. While he'd been a manipulative asshole in the short time I'd known him, he hadn't done anything to physically harm me exactly, only use me. The holder was something else. Whoever it was seemed out for blood. Royce was smart enough to have let me go once he knew the papers had been doctored; it was the holder forcing him into acting like such an unconscionable, unreasoning shithead.

That made it much easier to make my next decision.

"I'll save you," I promised before turning on a booted heel and rushing past the people and through the offices, faster than I'd ever run in my life. The cubicles and doorways were a blur, and once out the door, I barely paused in my rush to the gleaming exit sign down the hallway. I'd take the stairs and meet Arnold and Sara outside so we could make a quick getaway.

But who will save you? asked that mocking voice in the back of my mind.

Chapter 30

Arnold and Sara were in the lobby, having a shouting match with the security guard, who was also shouting orders into a walkie-talkie and waving a gun at them. When my friends saw me burst out of the stairwell, they started shouting in relief at me instead. I couldn't make out a single thing anyone was saying, and even though I was nearly shot by the skittish security guard, who trained his gun on me the instant I appeared, I didn't stop running for the doors leading out into the street.

"Let's get out of here!" I cried on my way past the guard desk.

They followed quickly enough, and I glanced back just long enough to see Arnold pointing in the direction of the car. Three blocks away, I finally spotted it, and only then turned to see what happened to Arnold and Sara.

They were trailing gamely behind, but a block and a half away. A New York City block is pretty dang long, and it surprised me to see how much distance I'd put between us. Strange. Just like my newfound strength and Annie Oakley shooting skills, it seemed I'd picked up some peculiar latent talents in the last half an hour or so. The sound of police sirens in the distance was getting louder, but I couldn't see where they were. There was a part of me that simply *knew* that the cops were roughly half a mile away, coming toward Royce's office building from a different direction than we'd been running. Weirded out, I started pacing, only then noticing I wasn't even winded once Sara and Arnold joined me, huffing and puffing, a minute or so later.

"Go, speed racer." Sara grinned at me weakly, taking a few quick breaths. "When did you turn into a marathon runner?"

"When . . . she . . ." Arnold gasped, wheezing more than I would've expected considering it was only a couple of blocks. Maybe he was a heavy smoker? ". . . put on . . . the . . . belt . . ."

Horrified, I looked down at the plain black leather circling my waist. "This did *that*?"

He nodded, braced his hands on his knees for a moment before clicking the car open. We all slid inside, me in the back, Sara in the front, and I cringed as something that sounded like faint, mocking laughter bounced around in my skull. *I can do a lot more than that if you let me,* that strange, whispery voice said.

"What the blue flying *fuck*!" I exclaimed, scrabbling at the belt buckle. Arnold and Sara twisted around in their seats, eyes wide as they stared at me having a fit over the buckle. It seemed like the tongue had adhered with superglue to the rest of the belt and wasn't about to be pried loose by my frantic fingers.

That won't help anything, it said, that edge of mocking laughter grating on what few nerves I had left. *You're stuck with me until sunrise. Relax.*

"I won't relax! Get out of my head!" I cried, redoubling my efforts. Sara and Arnold exchanged a look and I glared at them. "Snide looks aren't helping me get this thing off any faster!"

"Uh, Shia, you do realize you were just talking to yourself, right?" Sara said, amused.

"She was talking to the belt," Arnold said, though he was still staring at me like I'd grown two heads. I finally folded my arms across my chest and growled in frustration, quickly unfolding them when the guns started digging into my ribs again. Damn it, I had to remember how uncomfortable it was to do that. "It's . . . uhh . . . It's sentient. A dead hunter's spirit inhabits it and gives it its power." He had the grace to look sheepish, I'll give him that.

Seething, I reached out and grabbed the collar of his shirt, practically dragging him into the back seat with me. He yelped and grabbed at my wrist, but wisely didn't fight back. The way I was feeling just then, I probably would've punched his teeth in if he had. "Why didn't you tell me this sooner?!"

"Would you have put it on if you'd known?" he shot back. That gave me pause. Knowing that some dead guy would be talking to me through a fashion accessory all night? No, no, I most definitely would not have put it on or even touched it with a ten-foot pole. However, I had to admit that it had saved my skin in the fight with Royce.

I gradually relaxed my grip on Arnold's shirt so he could settle back in his own seat. Looking a trifle offended, he straightened his collar and started the car, quickly pulling out into the street. Probably so I wouldn't pull that stunt of dragging him into the back with me again.

"It's most likely been dying for someone to talk to. According to the logs, we've had it in the vault for over fifteen years, and I don't think the coven that had it before The Circle used it more than a handful of times prior to giving it to us."

"Great." I was just thrilled to hear about the sordid—okay, boring—past of the talking inanimate object around my waist. "So when the sun comes up, I can take it off again, right?"

"Yes," he said at the same time that weird voice started chattering at me. *You heard the vampire, he wants you to return tomorrow night. You'll need me as much as I need you. This is freedom for me. Wear me, let me out, and I will reward you with strength and knowledge beyond your wildest dreams. You don't have to hunt if you don't want to, just let me out, wear me, use me, LET ME GO LET ME OUT LET—*

Sara had been saying something, but the droning of the belt kind of drowned her out. "Fine, whatever, just shut up already!" I said, relieved when it did as I said. I hastily turned to Sara. "Not you. Sorry, repeat that?"

"I said," she replied dryly, "that you might want to consider wearing it until the current crisis is over.

I take it by the way you were booking it out of there that things with Royce went south?"

Cringing at the thought of it, I nodded, wondering if the belt had anything to do with the fact that I wasn't shaking in terror or suffering any kind of adrenaline rush. Especially after that battle royal in the conference room. I felt an odd sense of smugness just then, as if it read my thoughts and agreed with them. Creepy thing.

"Yeah. Apparently he doesn't have the focus."

Arnold almost snapped his own neck with whiplash when he looked back over his shoulder at me. "What?!"

Yelping, I pointed back at the road, and he turned his attention back just in time to keep from plowing into a cab cutting into our lane. Once he'd straightened out of fishtailing from braking so hard and my pulse resumed something resembling a normal pace, I continued my explanation.

"Someone was controlling him with it. I don't think he really wanted to attack me, but it didn't seem like he had a choice. We fought, I won, and I promised I'd try to bail him out."

Arnold made a choking sound that sounded suspiciously like laughter. Sara, who was rigidly holding on to the oh-shit-handle on her door with one hand and the dashboard with the other, was staring at me over her shoulder. "You're joking, right? Seriously, *you*, saving a vampire?"

I glared at her. "Oh, can it. I felt sorry for him. Besides, whoever was controlling him is seriously pissed off at me right now and is out for blood.

Royce is my only lead to the one who actually has the stupid thing."

"Check your forehead. Do you have a fever?"

"For God's sake, Sara!" I smacked her shoulder, eliciting a pained "Ow!" out of her. "If I don't meet him tomorrow at his restaurant, I might as well throw in the towel. Whoever it is had some kind of evil master plan that I spoiled, and now they want me to pay for it. If I don't go, I might never get another chance to find out who's behind Veronica's murder and trying to kill *me* now."

"All right, all right." She let go of her death grip on the door so she could rub her bruised shoulder. "Tomorrow night, though? What are we going to do until then?"

"Hide," Arnold cut in before I could speak. "We'll find a place to bed down for the day, a hotel or something out of town, and come back tomorrow night to find Royce. Maybe there's something I can do in the meantime to track down the holder. Get some clues or something."

"Why should I hide?" I asked, irritated. "I was safe enough at Sara's before."

"Because Royce has the resources to have tracked her down, and if you aren't at your apartment, that's the next logical place to look. After that fight, aren't you worried whoever it is might try to find you to finish things off?"

Recalling the alien hatred blazing in those black-and-crimson eyes, I shuddered and nodded. "Yeah, but I shot his knee out. He's not going to be finishing anything tonight."

Arnold sighed at that, sounding tired and beaten. "I didn't say Royce. I was talking about the holder. He'll probably start using another vamp tonight, or switch to a Were to fight you during the day when the belt won't protect you. Assuming the holder isn't another vampire, who would probably rest during the day."

"Oh, that's just great. Peachy keen," I grumped, settling back in the seat and wishing mightily I could cross my arms but having to make due with putting my clenched hands on my thighs.

"Honestly, I'm kind of surprised he didn't gang up a bunch on you up there. It was just you and Royce?"

"Yeah," I said, recalling how Royce had balked more than once against the one speaking through him to me. "He was trying not to fight me. A couple of times he managed to hold back when I think he was being ordered to attack."

Arnold laughed, and I frowned at him. Laughter didn't seem like a very appropriate response. "We're in luck!"

I gave a very unladylike snort, followed by Sara's own incredulous laughter. "Luck? You've got to be kidding me."

"No, we are," he said, grinning wolfishly. I'd have been worried if he was a vamp or a Were with a look like that. "That means that the holder is weak-willed. Can't control more than one Were or vamp at the same time. Not of Royce's age and strength. Maybe a couple of younger ones, but at the very least, it's an advantage in our favor."

Wow. Maybe that explained why the holder was so bitchy and pissed off.

Sara threw in her own two cents. "Then we actually have a chance at beating this thing?"

Arnold nodded, and I breathed a deep sigh of relief. That was some of the best news I'd heard all week.

Chapter 31

Later that night, the three of us sat around a cheap, scarred table in a remarkably seedy hotel a few blocks down from Times Square. It was the only one we could find on short notice that would take cash and didn't check ID against the names of their guests. That was primarily mine and Sara's idea, not Arnold's. Credit cards and everything else could be traced, and I was still pretty sure that, in addition to Royce, my ex, and the holder of the focus, the cops were probably looking for me in connection with Veronica's death.

So we'd gotten two rooms, though so far the three of us hadn't been interested in separating. Especially with roaches the size of Godzilla skittering around the floors and walls. Ugh.

"Remind me again why we're doing this?" I propped my feet on the edge of my chair and wrapped my arms around my legs so I wouldn't chance a bug running across my foot.

Arnold looked as grossed out as I felt, watching

with morbid fascination as the shadowed outline of a roach sedately marched across the TV screen, right across the news anchor's face. "I thought it would be safer than waiting around for a vamp or a Were to find you. I'm starting to think we should take our chances somewhere else."

Sara curled her lip, staring at the TV, too. "Yeah, Roachzilla over there is big enough to be a Were-bug. Screw this. Why don't I just ask Janine if we can crash at her place for the night? She might even be out of the country so, if we're lucky, we won't have to deal with her face to face."

"Who's Janine?" Arnold asked.

"Janine's? Are you sure?" I'm pretty sure my face showed about as much distaste for that idea as Sara and Arnold's did for the roach.

"Uh, guys? Who's Janine?" Arnold asked again, ignored by Sara and me.

She shrugged, not looking overly pleased. "Got any better ideas? I personally don't want to wake up with bugs in my hair or crawling around on me while I sleep."

Oh God. "Call her."

She did. I heard Janine's high, panic-frantic voice from across the room, and rubbed my temples. Guess she was in town. The belt was adding its own muted background noise somewhere in the back of my skull, twittering laughter that mocked the tinny, high-pitched tones coming out of Sara's cell phone. Deciding to drown them both out, I finally answered Arnold's question, talking a little louder than was strictly necessary. "Janine is Sara's younger sister. She's a bit of a pill. Nice enough, but very flighty and scared of everything."

"Oh. Great. She going to have a problem with me being a spark?"

I started, and he cracked a goofy smile. Guess he thought it was funny to call himself a spark the way some minorities thought it was funny to refer to themselves in derogatory terms. "Probably. Just don't do anything flashy, and we may not have to take her to the ER with a heart attack."

He chuckled and nodded. "I can do that much."

"You know," I said, "you don't act anything like I thought a mage would. I haven't even really seen you *do* anything, except light those candles and make the wall disappear. You just said a word and poof, it happened. No grand gestures, no bolts of lightning from the sky or flashes of light. Is all magic like that?"

"No, not really. The only reason it was like that is because those spells were set to certain key words. The actual preparation work beforehand is where you get the sparkly lights and cracks of thunder in the background." He grinned and I stared at him, trying to figure out if he was being serious or just pulling my leg.

"Want to see something cool?"

"Uhm," I said, not sure I did. The belt chose that moment to interject a snide *You know you're curious.* I wished mightily that it would just shut up. "Okay, I'm curious," I said.

He cupped his hands together, whispering a few words so quietly I couldn't hear them over the sound of Sara and Janine in the background. When he opened his hands, a tiny black mouse poked its head out between his fingers and I jerked back in surprise and fright.

"Oh my God, that's a *mouse*! Get it out of here!" I might've jumped up on top of the bed if I wasn't afraid there would be roaches under the covers.

He seemed disappointed at my reaction, and cradled the mouse up to his chest, lightly stroking its head with the tip of one finger as he frowned at me. "Bob's my familiar, he won't hurt you."

"Stop being a baby, Shia," Sara said across the room, covering the mouthpiece of the phone with one hand.

Reluctantly, I settled down a little more in my chair, taking a closer look—but that's it. No *way* was I going to touch a mouse. "His name is Bob? You named your mouse Bob?" I asked, hearing the touch of a frightened whine in my voice and hating it. I hated the sound of mocking laughter from the belt even more.

"I didn't name him, he named himself. He's a familiar, not a normal mouse," Arnold explained, putting his hand down on the table so the mouse could scamper down and start twitching his whiskers at me a little too close for comfort.

Making sure my legs were tucked very close to my chest so no part of me was near enough to the table to touch it, I shot a look at Sara, who was listening to Janine jabbering and shrugging at me helplessly. "Um. What's a familiar?"

"Kind of like an extra helping hand. Different

types of animals do different things. Bob, like most rodents, is good at collecting information for me." When he put his hand on the table, the mouse quickly ran over to it and leaned against it. His thumb absently ran along the slick black fur as he talked, and the mouse seemed happy enough to stay where it was, so I gradually started relaxing a little more. "Some magi like using birds to carry messages for them. It's a little old-fashioned, especially considering most everyone has e-mail or a cell phone these days, so it's mostly the backwoods Europeans still doing it. Some magi use cats, as they're an excellent way to focus and channel energy between the world of the living and the dead. The Egyptians were particularly fond of them."

"Why would anyone want to deal with the dead?" I asked him, not sure if I was actually curious or just trying to keep my attention on something other than the furball at his fingertips.

He pointed with his free hand in the general direction of my waist. "Things like that are made with the use of energy from where the dead linger. Different magi specialize in different forms of magic. That's one of the benefits to working with a coven instead of going solo. When you have magi like me who specialize in information and security, it works well when you also have magi who specialize in defensive spellcasting, offensive spellcasting, with the occasional crafter to make artifacts like the belt to augment the intangible stuff the rest of us do. Even an illusionist has a place and purpose along with the rest of us. It just depends on what our clients want, or what the coven as a whole is striving to do. Our flexibility is part of what made The Circle's services so in demand, and such a great place to work."

"Yeah," I said dryly. "Sounds like a dream come true. Where do I sign up?"

He chuckled, shaking his head. "Wow, I did sound like a walking, talking advertisement for a second there. Sorry."

"Hey, so Janine says we can stay at her place," Sara said as she flipped the phone shut, walking back over to resume a similar crouched posture as mine on her seat. Guess she was afraid of having Roachzilla crush her foot, too. "However, she doesn't want to have to play hostess and said we're on our own as far as food and entertainment. I don't know about you guys, but that's fine with me."

Arnold and I nodded, rising to pick up our things. I watched in fascination as Arnold closed his hands over the mouse and it once again disappeared to parts unknown. He wasn't wearing long sleeves, so there really was no other explanation than magic for why it wasn't there when he moved his hands off the table. While it raised his creepy factor a few points, it was admittedly kind of cool to see him do some real magic.

When he saw me watching, he grinned and gave me one word in explanation. "Conjuration."

Whatever that means.

Chapter 32

Janine was waiting on the wide marble steps in front of her building when we pulled up, and she did not look happy to see us. A shorter, skinnier, more nervous version of Sara, her blue-as-the-summer-sky eyes never quite managed to meet anyone else's, and her hands never stopped fluttering over something, smoothing the bright golden strands of her hair or fussing with her clothes, fingering a piece of jewelry, that sort of thing. She was very pretty and scared of her own shadow.

If looks could kill, the one she shot to Sara when she saw Arnold with us would've turned her into a crispy critter. Though I hadn't been paying much attention to their arguing on the phone, I figured out easily enough that Sara had left out the small detail that we'd be bringing someone else with us.

After we introduced Arnold, we followed Janine up the steps. Arnold was polite enough not to remark on the fact that Janine was visibly reluctant to shake his hand and carefully kept as much distance between them as possible. We passed through the automatic glass doors, which slid open with a soft hiss to grant us entrance, and into the elegant foyer of the apartment building.

Unlike Sara, Janine chose to live in one of the pieces of property her parents had left to them on their death. The apartment was very close to Central Park, and while it was far from a penthouse suite, being on the first floor, there was no doubt that it was very costly to stay here. The foyer was quiet, decorated in gold leaf and marble pillars with a few tasteful pieces of artwork. The soft burble of water trickling over the fountain in the center of the room masked the hiss and crackle of static of the security guard's radio.

Despite the serious atmosphere of the lobby, it was reassuring having the security guy there, even if it was highly unlikely anyone would think to look for me or Sara here. The guard didn't do much more than crack a thin, polite smile and give a short wave to Janine, passing a curious look over the rest of us filing behind her.

"Make yourselves at home, guys," Janine said as she unlocked her front door. Rather than stick around to give the guided tour, she tossed her keys on a delicate end table next to the door and promptly headed toward her bedroom, not looking back. "I've still got some work to do, so if you want to watch a movie and order in pizza or Chinese or something, there are menus in the drawer next to the fridge."

"Thanks, spaz," Sara said, not without a touch of affection. "I owe you one."

Janine flashed a quick half-smile before disappearing into the back. Arnold folded his arms and checked out the living room, one brow arching in surprise at the size of the place and the obviously expensive furnishings.

Sara and I tossed our duffels and purses on one of the oversized couches. I settled into one and flipped on the big screen, channel surfing while Sara went to the kitchen to order some food. Arnold went to the bookcases and started examining the titles, brushing his fingertips along the spines as he read them.

"So," Arnold asked me, keeping his voice fairly low, "what's with Janine? She doesn't seem so bad."

I smirked, turning up the volume on the tube just a little to make sure she wouldn't overhear. "She's not. Yet. Once you're around her a little, you'll see. She ran out of here like her ass was on fire because we brought you with us."

"Why? Am I that scary?" He turned with a grin, looking about as dangerous as a kitten.

I smiled back and shook my head. "She has trouble dealing with new people and new situations. She's never talked about it to me, and Sara's never told me anything, but I suspect it may have to do with her parents' sudden death or maybe something else bad happened to her in her past. She's been that way as long as I've known her, almost five years. It's nothing personal, don't worry about it."

He frowned, looking speculatively off in the

direction Janine had gone. Hmm. Was he interested, or just covering his bases?

Sara came in a moment later with a grab bag of menus, and every one blessedly delivered, even at that late hour. We all threw some cash on the table and decided on Italian, ordering far too much food for the three of us.

We fell on the food when it arrived, a marathon of old Japanese monster movies playing in the background. Then, in a blissful, carbohydrate-induced stupor, we spent the rest of the evening watching downtown Tokyo get destroyed over and over again.

Janine must have turned the TV off, cleared the food off the coffee table, and thrown blankets on us sometime during the night. We'd fallen asleep on the couch, all sprawled against each other. When I woke up, Sara had her legs in Arnold's lap, and my head was on her shoulder. One of my legs dangled over the arm of the couch, the other tucked up until my knee was almost against my chest.

My back screamed a protest when I got up, and I groaned when one or two of the stakes jabbed me in the ribs as I twisted up to a sitting position. Arnold was already awake, but unmoving, blinking blearily at me as I sat up.

"G'mornin'," he managed to say, sounding like he needed coffee almost as badly as I did. "Sleep well?"

"Sort of. A bit cramped up, though. We must have been exhausted to crash out here."

I stood with a stretch and a yawn. The belt didn't feel quite so snug this morning despite the heavy meal, and I tentatively pulled at the buckle. It worked! I yanked it off, immeasurably relieved now that it was daylight and I could remove the silly thing.

"I'm going to shower and get dressed, I'll be out in a little bit," I said, grabbing my duffel and heading toward a bathroom.

He nodded, closing his eyes and tilting his head back against the couch. He looked pretty wiped out. I figured I'd do the nice thing and make breakfast for everyone, including our absent hostess, once I was ready to face the day.

Peeling off the body armor I'd slept in was no easy feat. It felt like a contortionist act just to get the shirt off. Once I did, I almost wished I'd just left it on.

Beneath the shirt I was a mass of bruises. None of them really hurt too badly, but overall it looked like I'd had a ton of bricks dropped on me. The ones at my neck were the only ones that were painful, sending little sparks of agony through my shoulder when I gingerly pressed a fingertip to them. Wincing, I cut that out soon enough, and with a sigh started up the shower, not having to wait long for the water to be almost hotter than I could stand.

As I washed my hair and scrubbed myself off, I reflected on what had come of having a full-out physical fight with a vamp. On the bright side, I was alive. On the brighter side, I still had all my bodily fluids. I could deal with some bruises if it meant survival. Still, I could see little indentations inside the bruises around my collarbone where Royce must have come pretty close to actually breaking the skin even through the body armor. There were impressions of fingerprints in black and blue on my arm, and sickly greenish-yellow spots around my legs and butt from when I'd fallen and, no doubt, from when I'd flipped the vampire onto his back.

All in all, not too shabby. I'd come out on top, if a bit worse for wear.

Oh, well. So no bikinis for a few weeks. It was spring anyway—I'd live.

Chapter 33

Later, feeling clean and refreshed, the three of us were walking down the street in search of good bialys and coffee. Janine had recommended a bakery a few blocks from the apartment. Unfortunately, I hadn't thought I'd need a turtleneck when I'd packed my emergency bag of clothes, and kept flipping my jacket collar up in a vain attempt to hide the bruises around my neck. Janine had fluttered around a little when she saw the discolorations, her concern actually making me feel kind of bad and awkward. Especially since she was obviously afraid but too well mannered to ask outright if we'd dragged some of that trouble back to her place and just hadn't told her about it.

Sara and Arnold had politely declined to say anything, but I felt their eyes slide over to my neck every few minutes. Finally sick of the scrutiny, I tried arranging my hair so the fiery curls might hide the marks. Mostly they just ended up flying into my face and getting caught in my mouth when I tried to talk.

"How could you?" I heard a bitter, growling voice behind us and whirled, surprised. "How could you have signed for *him* but not for *me*? You lying little slut!"

"Chaz!" I exclaimed, taking an involuntary step back as he jumped out of a car stopped in the middle of the street with a snarl on his lips and fists clenched at his sides. He ignored the irate honks and curses from other drivers as another two guys got out of the car after him. More Weres from the looks of them. Great. "What are you talking about?"

He pointed accusingly at my neck. "Look at you! You let him bite you already, didn't you? You never went out of town, you went straight to *him*."

He was coming closer, his packmates following hot on his heels and seeming to get hopped up on the scent of anger and fear thick on the air.

"Chaz, what the fuck? She doesn't belong to you, back off!" Sara, arms folded, glared up at him. Was she crazy? None of us had weapons and tonight was the full moon. You don't get in the way of an angry Were-anything during the full moon!

"Shut up, he wasn't talking to you," one of the others told her. I saw part of the pack tattoo visible under his short-sleeved T-shirt, the spear and sun for the Sunstriker pack. His eyes were a feral ice blue, the glittering gaze of a wolf on the hunt staring back at Sara from under a sweep of artfully emo dyed black bangs. The rest of his hair was short, except for the strands arranged to fall across his brow and hide one of his eyes.

Looking at the third Were grinning savagely at Chaz's side, also tattooed and wearing a more nondescript T-shirt and loose-fitting jeans with practically half his boxers sticking out of the top, I suddenly realized how right that cab driver from the other day had been. The Sunstrikers really were just a bunch of posers. Bullies, yes, but posers nonetheless.

My attention was abruptly brought back to Chaz, who was looking more than a little miffed. Was that a hint of fang showing in that snarl? "He hurt you, didn't he? I'll kill him!"

"Chaz, for God's sake, calm down!" I backed away as he advanced toward me and Arnold tugged on Sara's arm, pulling her back with us. "It's not as bad as it looks, and you don't need to do anything. Just stop a minute, will you?" Finally he listened and stopped trying to close the distance between us. I stopped when he did, and Sara and Arnold moved behind me to get my back. Or hide behind me. Whatever.

Chaz's companions stopped, too, looking to him for direction. I guessed Chaz must be the pack leader or something. I'd never really bothered to ask him anything about it after I'd screamed bloody murder for him to trot his hairy ass out of my living room and stay out of my life. To this day I still don't know why the neighbors never called the cops. I sure was loud enough for them to have heard me.

"Listen," I said, finding a little of that old anger

burning deep down, fanning into flames at the sheer *gall* of him, accosting me on the street like a jealous boyfriend. "You and I are *done,* finished, over. You burned your bridges with me when you hid what you were, you insufferable ass. Then, bringing your goons with you to try to scare me and my friends? Who the hell do you think you are? I've got I don't know how many people after my ass trying to *kill* me in the last few days, and you think this show of bravado is going to win my affection? I broke up with you because you *lied* to me, and you *hid* things from me, and you were a *dick,* not because you're a Were! Get over yourself!"

Everyone was staring at me; I even saw a touch of awe on Sara's face. Chaz was speechless, opening and closing his mouth as he started to say something and then thought better of it. He looked both chagrined and angry, wavering in between as though he *wanted* to be offended but wasn't sure if he *should* be. I folded my arms across my chest (no holsters to jab me in the ribs this time) and tapped my foot, waiting for him to spit out a reply or rebuttal.

He slowly lowered his head, spreading his hands and deflating somewhat as the anger was finally overtaken by his embarrassment. "Shia, I'm sorry. It's just, I know how you feel about Others and the thought of a vamp's hands on you makes me mad enough to lose my head." He sighed and stood up straighter, resuming that effortlessly strong, body-builder's pose he knew I liked so much. Playing me like a fiddle, that's what he was doing. Of course, knowing that didn't make it any easier to resist those gym-made washboard abs or sad puppy dog eyes. "Will you at least let me help you? Give me a chance to show you I'm not that bad?"

I glanced back and forth between Sara and Arnold, wondering what they thought. Both of them had stony expressions, looking about as moved as a pair of boulders. I fidgeted, trying to think rationally but already knowing the battle was lost. True, the holder might be able to make him turn on me, but what if they didn't know about him? Arnold had said the holder was weak willed. Maybe that meant I could still count on Chaz, since the holder wouldn't be able to control him and Royce at the same time.

Chaz didn't have that strained look about him that Royce had when he was being forced into doing something he didn't want to. His gaze was clear, and his voice sounded exactly the same as I remembered it, with no hint of poisoned honey sweetness to it. He would've attacked me already if that was his intent. And what he'd said at my parents' place was true: he'd never hurt me, and I don't think he really ever meant to scare me like he did. I could admit to myself now that I had overreacted a little when I saw him shift. He'd been putting trust in me to accept him as he was, all of him, and I'd given him the boot. How I'd reacted—that I'd been a bigoted, racist moron—did not sit well. Having now seen firsthand that vampires and Weres and magi had feelings to hurt, just like me, I suddenly felt like the bad guy for having thrown him out instead of the other way around.

The past couple of days had well and truly skewed my once plainly black-and-white views on Others. Maybe Chaz really wasn't the Big Bad Wolf. After all, if I'd been in his place, I probably would've hesitated to tell me I was a Were, too. Grimacing, remembering my reaction and some of the unthinking things I had said in the past about Others, I could see why I might have neglected to *ever* say anything about it. He was braver and maybe stupider for showing himself to me than I had previously given him credit for.

Not to mention I didn't like the idea of him possibly going Rambo on me and trying to take down Royce on his own. I'd much rather keep an eye on him.

I figured I could risk giving him one more chance. I threw up my hands and tried to keep my voice as brisk as it had been, rather than letting any sheepish note creep into it. "Fine, whatever. But leave the Three Stooges behind." I pointed to the two dorks at his side and the driver who was idling at the curb.

One of the Weres growled softly at that, showing a little bit of upper and lower fang. They weren't too pronounced, as he wasn't shifted, but it was more than enough to make all three of us non-Weres take a quick step back. Chaz casually smacked emo-boy in the chest with a closed fist, sending him stumbling back with a yelp. "Done."

The other Weres shook their heads, exchanging the universal well-that's-the-boss-for-ya-what-can-you-do look before shuffling off to their car. I overheard one of them say something about "alpha my ass" to the others, though they silenced themselves quick enough when Chaz gave them a menacing look and a growl from deep in his chest. The hairs on the back of my neck rose at the sound, nothing that should come out of a human throat, and the other Weres continued on their way a little more speedily. Chaz turned back to us with an expectant look, all innocence, as if he hadn't just acted completely inhuman a moment ago.

A bit nonplussed, I gestured for everyone to follow me. I took a quick look around my ex to make sure that the other Weres weren't coming back. The tall, skinny one who Chaz had smacked threw a black look at me over his shoulder. Annoyed, I flipped him off before turning on my heel and continuing down the street, figuring it would do me a world of good to at least *act* like I was a bigger badass than the werewolf at my heels. One thing I'd noticed over the last couple of days was that every Other I'd dealt with so far, even Arnold, stopped treating me like a pushover when I acted sure of myself. Because of that, I kept my head high and didn't look back, acting like I expected everyone else to follow, including my ass-kissing ex.

Despite the cool façade, I still had doubts and worries. The moon was going to be full after dark. How the heck was I going to keep Chaz from killing Royce tonight?

Chapter 34

Sara and Arnold were *not* pleased with my decision. I wasn't too happy about it either, but that wasn't going to change anything. My mind was made up as far as Chaz was concerned. His help could prove invaluable to us later.

"So, I came up with a theory this morning," I said to Sara as we walked along looking for the bakery.

She arched a brow, glancing over at me before returning her gaze to the sidewalk. Arnold and Chaz were both watching me with interest. "Do tell."

I shrugged the jacket up a little more on my shoulders, eyes narrowing in thought. "When I went to go see Royce the last two times, there was a girl there with him."

"Allison Darling," Arnold said.

"Yeah, her. I already know she doesn't like me. Don't know why, but there's something there."

Arnold glanced at Chaz, then me. Chaz looked curious and had a touch of an eye twitch when I mentioned Royce's name but wisely kept his mouth shut. "You think it's her?"

I nodded, ticking off the points on my fingers. "She's the most likely suspect. She was there both times I've gone to Royce's office. She's pissed at me for some reason, I haven't quite put my finger on that yet. She told him when I had the belt. And whoever it was making Royce go schizo on me obviously wants me dead, or at least hurting. It makes sense as much as anything else I can come up with that she's the one." I was careful not to mention the focus. I was trusting Chaz, but not *that* far, not yet.

"Someone wants you dead?" Chaz asked, the first touch of anger coloring his voice. We all ignored him. Better not to get him too riled up at this point. Not this close to the full moon.

Sara frowned. "That doesn't make any sense, though. Why would she want you dead? Do you know her from somewhere else?"

"No, but since when did any of this shit make sense? These are Others. No offense," I quickly added as Chaz and Arnold looked over at me, irritated.

Sara said, "I don't know. Arnold, what do you know about her?"

We all turned our attention to him as we waited in a crowd of people to cross the street. He rubbed the back of his neck, looking straight ahead instead of focusing on any one of us. "I don't know. It's a possibility. I know she was funneling information to Royce as early as last November. But I can't imagine what she'd hope to gain with you dead, especially since Veronica is out of the picture now."

"No witnesses, maybe?" It came out a little more archly than I meant, but hey, this was my potential murderer we were talking about here.

He glanced warily at Chaz before answering. "Maybe. I don't know. If I swing by my place later, I can log on to the server at the office and pull up her address. We can go ask her in person."

Chaz looked just as confused and left out as ever. I guess he really didn't know anything about what was going on and wasn't on the side of the bad guys after all. If that's what Arnold was suspicious of.

"Hey, look, guys," Sara pointed up the street.

We had finally arrived at the little bakery. It had a scrumptious-looking selection of freshly baked goods and delicious-smelling coffee. The four of us ordered bialys and coffee from a man behind the counter absorbed in the morning paper, which he reluctantly set aside to serve us.

Chaz pulled out some cash from his wallet. "Want me to get yours?"

I shook my head, smiling. Trust Chaz to be the gentleman.

Sara peered around Chaz to me, an odd look on her face. "Shia, what was that girl's name again?"

Arnold answered for me. "Allison Darling. Why?"

Giving the guy who was ringing up her stuff an apologetic look, she grabbed the paper off the counter, ignoring his "Hey!"

She held up the cover story, one eerily similar to the one we'd stared at a lifetime or so ago back in

Sara's kitchen. ANOTHER MAGE MURDERED! COVEN VOWS VENGEANCE! I snatched the paper out of her hand, scanning the story below the grainy photo of Allison. The other three crowded to read over my shoulder while the guy at the register impatiently tapped his fingers on the counter.

The story was similar to Veronica's in that the body looked like both a Were and a vampire had gotten to it. Last night the body was spotted floating in the East River. The cops dragged her out, or what was left of her anyway, and apparently someone at the paper had made an early call to the CEO and coven leader of The Circle to get her opinion. Alexandra Peterson was horrified and saddened, and promised the help of The Circle in any way they could to find and stop the madman behind the murders.

So much for my theory.

Chapter 35

Okay. So my number one suspect was obviously not the right one, since she was just as dead as Veronica.

This was awfully coincidental, but there wasn't a whole heck of a lot I could do about it. It all put me back at square one.

We had bought our breakfast and decided to find a place to sit down outside to eat. Not that any of us had much appetite after reading about the new murder. We wandered into Central Park looking for a bench that all four of us could sit on with enough personal space between us to fit ten or so more people.

Chaz remained remarkably placid, almost servile in how he treated me. It was odd having him hover, offering to pay for my food, carrying the bag for me, holding doors open, all the things he used to do. When I made a suggestion, he deferred to my idea more often than not. It was a little unnerving how eager he was to please.

Sara and Arnold weren't buying it. When he held the door for Sara, she stood there and waited until he went out first. When he offered to carry the bag of bialys, Arnold casually plucked it out of my hands and walked right past him. It was a little embarrassing how they were treating him, but I understood their caution.

Eventually, we found a big-enough, empty park bench. Sara and Arnold sat on one side of me, Chaz the other. I could almost taste the fear in the air, the way they said vamps and Weres could, coming off Sara and Arnold. Their nervousness around Chaz wasn't rubbing off on me, for some reason.

I almost pitied Chaz for having to deal with this, knowing that anytime a non-Were knew what he was, they'd have that touch of fear in the backs of their minds that he'd shift and tear them apart, no matter how civilized he appeared at the outset. Truth is, most Weres are not very violent except when provoked. They earned their reputation simply because once the beast was unleashed, it was well and truly deserving of some fear. A vampire's strength usually pales in comparison, unless they're ancient, and an enraged Were is fully capable of tearing even the hardiest vampire apart.

Chaz was watching the rest of us thoughtfully as we ate. Sara and Arnold were giving him the silent treatment. After taking a sip of coffee to steady myself, I twisted around on the bench to turn my back to them and talk to Chaz without straining my neck.

"You know, I don't mind spending time with you,

but today's really not the best day. Maybe we can just go catch a movie in a few days, after this job is done."

He frowned. "Shia, you signed a contract with a vampire. If someone doesn't protect you, you may not be alive in a few days."

The truth of those words made the rest of my bialy look entirely unappetizing. I took another chunk off it and stuffed it in my mouth anyway, knowing I'd need my strength tonight. Mumbling around the bread, I shifted my gaze away from his. The concern in those baby blue eyes was just too much.

"I know. I've got some tricks up my sleeve. Don't write me off just yet."

"I don't want to see anything bad happen to you. Why were you getting involved with Royce anyway?" He glanced around me at Arnold. "Magi, too? I don't understand why you're doing all of this. It could get you killed if you're not careful."

Wow. Did this mean he didn't know about the focus? I peeked over my shoulder at Arnold, ignoring the twinge of pain it caused. Fortunately, Arnold seemed willing to answer, though he looked wary enough that I guessed he was being careful how he worded things. He had reason to be careful, too. If a Were knew a mage was trying to one-up or control them with magic, there were no laws on the books that could protect that mage from being splattered all over the street.

Finally, Arnold said, "My coven hired her to do some work recovering something from Royce. When he found out who she was working for, he basically blackmailed her into signing the contract. I'm helping her because, like you said, she needs assistance or she's going to die. Personally, I don't want that kind of karma on my shoulders. That simple."

How sweet. If only it were true.

Sara piped up. "She's not completely helpless. We've reworded the contract so that she can hurt or kill him with no legal ramifications. The door swings both ways this time."

Chaz nodded, looking surprised and maybe even a little pleased. "That was a smart move." Turning his attention back to me, he lightly placed his hand over mine on the back of the bench. I think it was to my credit that I didn't pull away or even flinch at the touch, and he seemed relieved by that. "I'll take care of you, if you'll let me. My pack can help keep you safe."

"Thanks," I said, finally letting a bit of a smile through. "You don't have to do that. Tonight we're going to have our little showdown, and after that, everything should be smooth sailing."

He nodded, then pushed off the bench to stand, clenching his fists tightly at his sides. I could hear his knuckles popping from here. "I'll come with you. I'll help keep you safe."

"Um," I said, turning to Arnold and Sara for help. Arnold didn't seem to know what to say, but Sara cut in.

"Won't you be . . . uh . . . furry tonight?"

He grinned, a bit of elongated canine visible on both top and bottom. They were so tiny, you wouldn't notice it unless you were looking for it, like we were. "Yep."

"So doesn't that mean you need to go hunt or run with your pack or something?"

"No." He folded his arms and looked off in the distance. His tone and manner took on a measure of seriousness I wasn't used to seeing in him. "We're not unthinking beasts when we shift. We are primarily driven by instinct, true, but there is a part of us that knows and remembers what it is to be human." He looked at Sara, and the intensity of his gaze drove her to pull back. Just a little, not very much, but it was enough. Confidence crept into his voice, an easy command, something else I hadn't ever seen in him before. Not like that. "You all smell like food, but for the most part we remember enough of ourselves to keep from doing harm."

For the most part. Great. Clearing my throat to break the growing tension, I said, "I need you to remember something else, too. You can't kill Royce tonight."

"Why?" Chaz demanded, sounding puzzled and angry.

"Because . . ." I took a deep breath, glancing at Arnold and Sara, trying to think of something to say that would sound convincing enough. If I was going to have a Were with me tonight, it would only be fair if he knew about everything. Including the focus. Keeping my gaze steady on Chaz, I decided to go with the truth. "I promised to save him."

Chaz's mouth dropped open in surprise, his arms unfolding as the shock of what I'd just said hit and sank in. His mouth worked for a second, trying to wrap his wits around the fact that I, the one who was terrified of everything Other, now wanted to save one. A very, very dangerous one.

"Someone's using magic to control him. They might try the same thing on you. It may be better if you just let me handle things tonight."

He took a couple of unsteady steps to sit down heavily on the bench again, confusion soon twisting into a horrified understanding. "The *Dominari* Focus. Someone has it? *Here?*"

Arnold answered for me. "Yes. Unfortunately, we don't know who. They're using it to control Royce, but not very well. Our only hope at this point is that the one using it doesn't have the strength of will to control more than one Other at the same time."

Chaz reached out, fast, too fast, his hands on my shoulders and worry glinting in suddenly feral eyes. I didn't even have enough time to jerk back or gasp in shock before his hands were on me. Arnold and Sara jumped to their feet as he spoke, fright and concern making his usually calm, stoic voice waver. "Shia, you can't involve yourself in this! I can't—I don't want to end up hurting you . . ."

I put my hands up to rest on his cheeks, lightly rubbing my thumbs over the coarse hairs as I met his eyes, unflinching. "It's too late for that, Chaz. I'm already involved. I have to do this, and it would be better if you stay back so the holder doesn't try to use you, too."

A low growl rumbled in his throat, soft but infinitely more frightening for the helpless rage that dragged it out of him. I hoped and prayed he'd keep calm enough not to shift right here in the park. After a very long, tense moment, he slowly withdrew his hands, turning away and pulling back from my touch. His brows had lowered in a scowl as he glared at nothing in particular somewhere in the trees. "Then you'll go. But I'm coming with you. It's pack business now anyway if someone is using that thing. There's got to be something I can do to help."

Arnold expelled a shaky breath, and I looked at him in some surprise. He was truly frightened, pale-faced and his hands shaking. Was he afraid for me? Or afraid Chaz was going to turn on him? "Are you sure you can fight the focus if the holder tries to use you?"

Chaz slowly turned to look at Arnold, who took an involuntary step back, bumping into Sara. Even I felt myself contract a little at the force behind that gaze. "No. I'm not." His soft conviction didn't brook any further discussion or argument on the matter.

I felt a touch of pity for him. I hadn't meant to drag him into this, but his pride and concern for me, as well as the responsibility for ensuring the safety of his pack, meant he had an obligation to see this through. Rising off the bench to stand, I extended my hand to him, unable to keep myself from smiling slightly when he took it without hesitation.

"Then let's work together, and make a plan," I said. "No matter what happens, this is ending tonight."

Chapter 36

Sara went back to Janine's to pick up our stuff. None of us, despite my change of heart, thought it prudent to let Chaz know about Janine or where she lived. Chaz offered to let us wait out the rest of the day at his place, but that didn't seem particularly wise either. Arnold didn't like the idea of going back to his place, my place, *or* Sara's, so I finally made a snide remark about spending the day in the park.

"Actually," Arnold said thoughtfully, "that's not a bad idea. Central Park is big, and I doubt anybody would come looking for any of us here." He turned to Chaz, who did not appear pleased at the prospect. "What do you think?"

He shook his head, lip lifting briefly in a touch of disgust as he glanced around. "Depends on how long we stay. The Moonwalkers might take it wrong if I stick around here too long, especially since tonight's the first night of the full moon."

I recalled how the cabbie that had driven me

back to my car from Royce's building the other day had dissed the Sunstrikers. Seemed there was no love lost between the two packs. After a moment of thought, I said, "I'd rather not stir up another pack or bring them into this. What about the zoo?"

"The Central Park Zoo? Since it isn't technically part of the Moonwalkers' territory, I suppose that could work," Chaz said. Then he grinned in a way I didn't like; it was far too predatory. "Though the animals won't care for me much."

"Whatever." I rolled my eyes. "We'll just have to leave with enough time for me to get ready. The park closes before sunset anyway."

We waited for a while for Sara to come back. I found a sunny spot to lie down on, folding my hands behind my head and closing my eyes. It would be nice to relax and not think about my possible impending demise for a few hours, but there was way too much on my mind for any hope of that.

Arnold parked his skinny butt on a big rock next to me, keeping an eye out for anybody or anything suspicious. Chaz leaned up against a tree and watched people pass by on the path; joggers, mothers pushing strollers, people walking dogs.

I thought about everything I had seen and learned and done in the last few days. Somewhere in this mess there had to be a solution, or at least a hint to what might lead me to figuring out who had the focus. There seemed to be something there, an idea hovering just out of my reach, the glimmer of a thought that seemed to become less and less substantial the harder I tried to grasp it.

My phone started buzzing, startling me into a yelp. Arnold and Chaz both looked alarmed, then gradually relaxed, smirking at each other at my reaction. Muttering in irritation, I dug into my jeans and pulled it out, picking up the call from Sara.

"Hey, where are you?"

Low, masculine laughter answered me. I stiffened, looking down at the phone in shock for a second before putting it back to my ear. "Who is this?" I demanded, wondering what in God's name had gone wrong this time.

"*La Petite Boisson.* Tonight. Leave the mage at home, or your little friend is dead," an unfamiliar man's voice said. I could hear muffled sounds in the background, what I sorely hoped were not muted screams, which abruptly ended when the guy hung up on me. I lowered the phone from my ear and stupidly stared at it, trying to get my wits around what just happened.

Arnold reached down and put a hand on my shoulder. "What happened? Is everything all right?"

"Fuck!" I exclaimed, loud enough to startle both men and cause a mother with her two toddlers on the path below us to shoot me a dirty look and hurry the kids along. "Somebody has her. The fucker kidnapped Sara!"

Arnold swore and Chaz leaped to his feet.

"We never should have sent her alone . . ." Arnold said.

"Yeah, well, it's too late for that now," Chaz replied, irritation clear in his voice. "You didn't trust me alone with Shia and you didn't trust me enough to show me your daytime hiding spot. So now we pay the price for separating."

"Don't start that shit, you two," I said, rolling up to my feet and starting off at a run back in the direction of Janine's apartment. "Fuck, fuck, *fuck!* I hope they haven't hurt Janine, too . . ."

This changed everything. Oh God, Sara might end up hurt or even killed if I didn't play my cards right. It was one thing for me to get tied up in this craziness—it was quite another for this psycho to drag my friends into it, too.

Even though I wasn't wearing the belt, I seemed to have retained some strength from it, and as I bolted along, I suddenly realized Arnold wasn't keeping up. I slowed my pace for the mage's sake, though it was difficult not to burst into a full-out run. He was having a tough time of it, blowing and huffing like a bellows and lagging a bit behind. Chaz, on the other hand, was barely breaking a sweat by the time we'd run from the park to Janine's building.

Everything looked okay when we got there. The security guard at his station recognized Arnold and me, giving us a nod. That gave me some hope for Sara's sister, at least. We hustled past him to Janine's door, which fortunately wasn't locked.

Janine was sitting on a couch with the remote in her hand, glancing up from channel surfing when the three of us stumbled in. She sat up abruptly, confusion and fright contorting her pale china doll features. "Shiarra? What's going on? Who's this?" She gestured at Chaz.

I paused to steady my breathing, and watched poor Arnold brace his hands on his knees and lower his head. That Janine was okay, at least, was a blessing, and he seemed almost as relieved as I did. "Something's happened. Did Sara come back here?"

She shook her head, her panic rising. "What happened? Where is she?"

I closed my eyes, cursing the stupidity that led to us splitting up. From everything that happened the last couple of days, I thought *I* was the target. Stupid as it was, I never would've credited a bad guy with trying to use Sara to get to me. Not like this.

Janine really wasn't going to like this. Steeling myself to the inevitable breakdown, I swallowed my grief and anger to explain, "Sara's been kidnapped. I'll—I don't know exactly who did it, but I'll find out. Tonight. I'll get her back." Before she can get torn apart like Veronica and Allison. Please, God.

Janine jumped about three feet in the air. "Oh, God! We have to do something! Call the police, the . . . somebody—you have to do something!" Her hysteria made Chaz and Arnold shift uncomfortably, looking anywhere but at her.

I moved closer and placed a hand on her shoulder, urging her to sit back down. "Don't worry, we'll save her." I prayed I wasn't just mouthing platitudes. God, how I hoped. "Don't drag the police into this. Whoever took her might kill her out of hand if I don't do what they asked me to. We'll figure out a way to get her out of there."

"Oh, no," she moaned, wringing her hands and

gradually, tensely lowering back down to the couch. She shot a fearful look at the men, tears glimmering in her eyes making me vow not to let mine fall. One of us had to be strong here, and it sure as hell wasn't going to be Janine. I could dissolve into a puddle of misery later, after I saved Sara. For now, I focused on the anger, clinging to it, using it to keep from driving myself into despair over increasingly overwhelming odds. Those responsible would pay dearly for causing so much pain and misery.

"How could this have happened?" Janine said, wiping at her tears.

I shared a helpless look with Arnold before shaking my head and running my hands through my curls, getting some of the sweat-plastered strings off my forehead and out of my eyes. I wanted to shake my fist at the sky, shout and scream against the holder of that thrice-damned focus, throw and destroy things and beat them into submission. I wanted to hunt them down like the cowardly curs they were, let *them* know what it felt like to be hounded and hunted and harassed. When I got my hands on them, I would make sure they felt every last indignity, bruise, cut, and abrasion they put Sara and me through.

If they didn't keep their word, if they did the unthinkable and killed her, I don't know what I would do. Whatever it was wouldn't be pretty.

But it would all have to wait until after sunset.

"I'll let Arnold and Chaz fill you in. I need to get ready to fight this thing."

With that, I turned and stomped off to the guest bedroom. I'd be damned if whoever was doing this caught me unprepared again. The next minion I met was going to get a bullet between the eyes, contract or no contract.

Chapter 37

Chaz let out a low whistle when I strode back into the living room in the armor, belt, and holster. The guns weren't going to be out of easy reach until the holder of the focus was dead, no matter how many times I forgot and jabbed myself in the ribs by folding my arms. The sweet scent of cloves and cinnamon also clung to me, as I'd applied some more of the Amber Kiss perfume, just in case. I put the trench coat on, slung the duffel over my shoulder, and headed for the door.

"Let's go, guys."

Chaz and Arnold stood and started to follow me, but I paused at the door and looked back over my shoulder. "Janine, I'm sorry, but I'd recommend you go lay low somewhere else for a couple of days."

She looked up when I spoke, her eyes red from her tears. What surprised me was the anger there, glinting in the icy blue depths so like Sara's. I'd never seen her anything but a neurotic, nervous wreck before, so the sudden intense animosity was unexpected.

"You find her. You get her out of this mess. If you don't, I'll—I'll do something. Something bad. You won't like it."

"Janine." I hesitated in the face of her anger. "You know I don't want anything bad to happen to her. She's my best friend. I swear, I'll do everything in my power to save her, to get her back."

She continued to glare at me from her seat. The two men were awkwardly shuffling their feet and trying to back away as inconspicuously as possible. "Do it. I swear to God, Shiarra, if she gets hurt because of this mess you dragged her into, I *will* do everything I can to make your life miserable." I might have taken offense if the angry look hadn't suddenly crumbled into helpless despair. She lowered her head into her hands, hiding her tears.

"Janine, I promise, I'll do everything I can to get her back."

She didn't turn in my direction when I spoke, not that I could blame her. All she did was nod in response.

I felt bad, but with everything else going on, I didn't have any time to sit and hold her hand. There was too much work to do. I had come up with the semblance of a plan while getting dressed and scrubbing the worst of the sweat off my face. My hair needed a wash, but I didn't have time, finger combing it instead and using water to slick the curls back out of my face as much as possible.

As the three of us stepped out into the noonday

sun, I waited until there were no pedestrians nearby and then said, "Arnold, you were talking about familiars last night. Mage familiars."

"Yeah. What about them?"

"Does every mage have one?"

"No."

Crap. That was disappointing. But he wasn't finished.

"Newer magi fresh out of the Academy generally don't. Neither do some of the less well off or not very powerful ones. Generally any practicing mage has one, though, particularly if you're part of a coven and expected to be casting on a regular basis. Why?"

I grinned. Maybe something was finally going right after all. "Does that mean Veronica had a familiar?"

After a moment, recognition dawned and he started grinning right back at me. Chaz was looking at us like we were crazy. Maybe we were. "Yes. Yes, she did. A cat."

Somehow I wasn't surprised. "Excellent. Do you think there's any way we can get into her apartment to find it? Without alerting the cops?"

He looked thoughtfully at me, then frowned as his gaze slid to Chaz. "No." An awkward, hesitant expression crossed his face, which reminded me of what he was like when I first met him. All he would need to complete the look were the coke-bottle lenses. "I guess we can go back to my place and I can summon it. I'd need equipment anyway to be able to speak with it and see what it knows."

Chaz's brows rose. "Summon it? You can do that?"

"Yeah. Familiars are planar beings. Technically, it's considered rude to call someone else's familiar uninvited, but since Veronica is dead, I don't have to worry about the consequences quite so much."

"And you can talk to it, right? Find out what it knows, the way you do with . . . uhh . . ." I asked, fumbling for the name of the mouse he'd shown me. "Bob?"

"Sort of. Enough that I can maybe figure out who was there when she died. If we're lucky, maybe the holder of the focus was there and the familiar saw it."

Chaz's brows finally unfurrowed as understanding dawned. "You think somehow the person who had the focus was using Others to kill a mage?"

Guess he didn't read the Sunday paper.

"Yeah. It's kind of a long story," Arnold said. "Let's get going, I'll explain in the car."

We hurried to Arnold's car, parked in a guest spot at Janine's building. I let Chaz sit shotgun since the tiny sports car would have forced him to tuck his knees under his chin just to fit in the back.

Arnold efficiently wove through traffic heading downtown. Finally he turned onto a side street in the Village and pulled into a gated garage below a small, new-but-made-to-look-old, red brick apartment building. The majority of the cars parked down there were trendy sports models like his. No minivans or broken-down junkers here. He pulled into a numbered parking space and Chaz, ever the gentleman, helped me clamber out of the back and shouldered my duffel.

Arnold led us to his apartment, which was open and spacious, with large windows offering a great view of the street and a park down the block. The floors were a clean, shiny hardwood, and rather than the expected geekdom or magic paraphernalia, he had some nice electronics and plush, comfortable-looking furniture. There was a stereo, a large flatscreen TV, and a bank of four computers lined up against one wall, along with more movies than you could watch in a year shelved in floor-to-ceiling bookcases.

I left my duffel next to the door and shrugged out of my jacket, tossing it over the back of a couch as Arnold led the way down a short hall. I managed to catch a peek into his bedroom, a bunch of bookshelves lining the walls and a laptop sitting open on the rumpled blue and white sheets. Arnold shut the door before I could get a good look at all the figurines and gaming books on the shelves, but I still saw enough to be amused.

We moved on to the next room, and as Arnold flicked on the light switch, it only took one look for me to know without a doubt that this was where the magic was done.

Chapter 38

My first thought was that his landlord probably wasn't going to like it that he'd etched—no, on closer inspection, *burned*—a very large pentagram into the center of the room, right into the nice hardwood floor. It wasn't the usual star and circle that I'd seen a thousand times in movies and on book covers and magazines. There were dozens of other symbols inside the circle, mostly outside of the star, none of them familiar to me.

There were white candles set at each of the five points of the star, just inside the line that made up the circle. I noticed a number of bookshelves here, too, though none with gaming manuals. Nothing but arcane texts, spellbooks, books on herbs, and surprisingly, a couple of shelves devoted to books on physics, languages, and history. Tucked away in a corner was an altar holding dried flowers, crystals and stones, a small silver knife, a mirror, and a chalice.

It smelled mostly like dusty books and dried flowers, but there was an undertone of ozone or something that made the air positively crackle with energy. I noted distantly that Chaz's nostrils were flared and the hair on his arms had risen. Guess he didn't like the feeling any more than I did.

Arnold waved us back to the door, heading over to a chest of drawers beneath heavily draped windows. "You guys can stay if you want, but it might be better if you waited outside. I need quiet and concentration for this."

"No," I said, "I'd like to see what you do. I'll stay."

"Me, too," Chaz said, folding his arms and leaning against the wall. I sat on the floor facing the windows, carefully adjusting the holster and belt so I wouldn't jab myself in the process.

Arnold pulled some things out of the dresser and set them on top. I watched with interest as he flicked through some files, selecting a small packet out of one, then pulling out and neatly arranging on a silver tray a piece of quartz, a plain wooden disk, two silver bowls, a few pieces of twine braided into a circle, a bottle of spring water, and a lump of what looked like sculptor's clay.

One by one, he moved the items into the circle. He put one of the bowls in the center of the star. The quartz, twine, clay, remaining bowl, and disk were each put inside one of the triangles that made up the points of the star. Next he poured some of the water into the bowl that was in a point. Lastly, with two deft fingers he plucked something too small for me to make out from the packet and dropped it into the bowl in the center, resealing the packet and returning it to its file in the drawer.

After that, he walked over to the shelves, perused the titles briefly, then took down a thin, unlabeled volume. Skimming through the pages, he moved around the outside of the circle, plucking up the small dagger and moving back to the center. Without looking up from the book, he absently pricked his finger with the dagger, letting a couple of drops of blood drip into the bowl before moving to stand before one of the points.

Chaz and I exchanged mystified looks. It was odd seeing Arnold, the nerd in jeans and a rumpled button-down, performing this arcane ritual and muttering over the pages of an ancient book.

Eventually he found what he was searching for and looked up, holding the book open with one hand, the dagger in front of him with the other. "*Luminare. Jungere!*" he said, and Chaz and I jerked back slightly as the candles all simultaneously lit themselves and a haze shimmered in the air, enclosing the circle in a huge sphere.

Arnold started in on a rapid, fluid litany of unintelligible words. Every now and then he threw in a word that sounded almost, but not quite, familiar. Maybe it was Latin or Greek, or some heretofore-unknown tongue. I couldn't put my finger on it.

"Speak to us. Do you know what happened to your mistress?" he finally said, in such a normal tone of voice that I almost missed it. I glanced in the circle, surprised to see that a small black cat was now sitting on its haunches in the center, next to the bowl. The clay and water from the points of the star were now gone.

The cat pricked its ears forward, bright yellow eyes drifting over to look at Chaz, tail twitching slightly as it did so. My jaw dropped open as it turned back to Arnold and spoke in a soft, hissing voice. "A vampire and a werewolf worked together to kill Veronica Wright. I take it I was summoned for information rather than a new binding?"

"That's right," he said, snapping the book shut and regarding the cat with a touch of wariness. I wondered why. Despite the fact that it was talking, in all other ways it looked like a normal cat to me. "You will not be bound as a familiar; I only ask for your assistance to find the ones responsible for Veronica Wright's death, and in return will call any hold you have on this plane by The Circle void. You will never be summoned by one of us again."

"Spare me the platitudes," the creature hissed, flexing its claws. "You cannot enforce that trade. I have another offer."

A slight twitch like a nervous tic started under one of Arnold's eyes, and I watched in fascination as he spoke, his voice carefully controlled in a way I'd never heard out of him before. "What do you want in return?"

It looked directly at me. "I want information. A piece of data or insight from each person in this room. No more."

A chill washed over me for no reason I could readily put my finger on. What was so bad about that? Arnold didn't seem to like the idea. "Three pieces of information from me. I am your summoner, not them."

"You called me in the presence of witnesses, mage." It yawned as though bored, rising to walk slowly around the inside perimeter of the circle, never quite touching the edges of the haze. "Take it or leave it."

"I can't speak for them." He shot a look at me out of the corner of his eye. I knew he didn't want us to talk to it, but at this point I didn't see much of a choice.

"Will you tell us everything you know about Veronica's death, who killed her and who was involved if we agree?" I asked it. Arnold looked like he wanted to throttle me.

The cat made an eerie sound that was half-laugh, half-purr. "Of course."

"I agree, then," I said, looking to Chaz.

After a brief hesitation, he shrugged and nodded. "Me, too."

Arnold swore softly under his breath before agreeing as well. "Information only. What do you want to know?"

It looked all too pleased. "No time limit was imposed. I reserve my question for the girl and the wolf for another time."

"No!" Arnold cried, desperate. "That was not part of the agreement. I'm not resummoning you later just so you can ask them questions."

"I didn't ask to be resummoned, mage. I will collect from them when I am ready." It lifted a paw to delicately lick at it, carefully splaying razor-sharp claws before making a big production out of cleaning its face. "My question for you is a simple one.

What do you think to gain by taking control of the focus when you know full well that any who wield it are destined to have its power turned against them?"

My gaze shot from the cat to Arnold, who was very carefully avoiding my gaze. The cat was asking the very question I'd been pondering since he'd mentioned that he was helping me for his own reasons. Not that I hadn't figured out by then that he wanted the focus for himself, but it was still a bit disturbing to hear it from a talking cat instead of straight from him.

"I want to restore balance to the—"

"No!" it hissed. "Information, I said. Not, as you might say, 'PR' bullshit."

He took a deep breath, his fingers tightening around the dagger and book at his sides. His green eyes narrowed to thin slivers, anger filtering through his voice. "Like I was saying, I want to restore balance to the Other community. If I can accomplish that, my standing in the coven will rise, and open the way for me to lead when Alexandra steps down."

The cat tilted its head to one side, thoughtful. "Your logic has two flaws. First, magi currently outnumber vampires and Weres. Particularly in this city, the ratio is almost four magi to one vampire or Were-creature. It does not make sense that you would want to bring more power to those not of your species. Second, Alexandra is unlikely to step down. You would need to fight her, and if you won, fend off many other aspiring, grasping magi for the reins of your coven. And therein lies the fault in your plan. You are not stupid, though I suppose avarice could make a fool of anyone. No. What is it *really*? Remember our deal, or I shall call it null and exact immediate payment on the penalties."

I could swear I saw him tremble at that. What the hell was this thing? "I wanted to use the focus to fuel a spell that grants me permanent power over vampires and Weres," he ground out between his teeth. A trickle of nervous sweat slid down his temple as he glanced at Chaz, who had pushed off the bookshelves to stand with his hands clenched at his sides, blue eyes glinting with suppressed rage. "I wanted to take its power into myself so that no one else could use it."

"Ahhh," the cat breathed, leaning forward on its paws. "This answer I accept. I will tell you what I know of my former master's death."

Despite my own intense fury with Arnold at that moment, I shifted my attention back to the cat. This was really what we needed. Maybe it knew something I could use to track down whoever had taken Sara.

"She was in the middle of preparing her usual vanity charms," it said, a touch of disgust in its voice, "when a knock came at the apartment door. As she was mid-preparations, I could not leave the circle and so could not follow when she went to answer. Before she could set a defensive ward, I heard the voice of a man speak the spell command for silence.

"Almost immediately, a female vampire, not long

turned, pushed Veronica back into my line of sight. The vampire was already drinking from her as she screamed with no sound. As she was under the male's spell, I formed my own circle and watched as the vampire took from her."

Arnold quietly cut in. "Do you know the identity of the vampire?"

The cat's ears lowered and its eyes narrowed faintly. "No. It was not of a bloodline that I have experience with. Though once the vampire took its fill and backed away, I did see and recognize the werewolf that took her place when the male ordered it forward. Reluctant as it was, I imagine because she was still alive, it obeyed the order to shift and ravaged the body as I watched. The alpha of the Moonwalkers was not pleased to be ordered, but he could not withstand the command of the focus."

Chaz swore, stepping forward. "Rohrik Donovan was being controlled by that thing?"

The cat slowly turned an infinitely contemptuous gaze upon Chaz, the kind of look only cats can truly manage. "Of course. No matter how strong the will of the victim, the focus grants the holder the power to overcome any resistance and come to full physical control of the Other over which they seek dominance."

"Did you see the focus, or the mage?" I asked, though at this point I didn't have much hope of it.

The cat turned to look at me, and I had to suppress another shiver. "I did not see the focus, but I felt its presence. Also, though I did not see his face,

I do know this—the male was not a mage. It was a sorcerer."

"Oh crap," Arnold whispered, his eyes widening.

I looked back and forth between the two, confused. "What's the difference?"

"The difference," the cat said in a voice so flatly bored that it frightened me more than Arnold's loss of composure, "is that magi use the energy that composes matter to bend, break, or otherwise manipulate the laws of nature. They learn how to control their abilities by study and apprenticeship with other magi. A sorcerer, also known as a 'wild' mage, uses a mix of his own life energies and the life energies of others as his fuel, and generally consorts with demons to learn, cast spells, or gain power. They do not rely on covens or other magi to assist them, rather on sacrifice and the tutelage of demonic forces to fuel their more powerful spells."

"Holy shit," I breathed, rising so unsteadily that Chaz had to reach out and take my arm so I wouldn't fall over. "You mean whatever thing has Sara might use her as a sacrifice to fuel a spell?"

"Perhaps," it said, cocking its head to one side as it regarded me. "Though I do believe the intention behind her kidnapping was to force your compliance in some matter. It does appear to be working."

"Son of a bitch," I swore, hating the tremor in my voice. "We've got to find her. Do you know where they are?"

"No," it said, rising to all four paws and arching its back with a stretch and a yawn. "Frankly, I'm not sure that any of you have anything of enough value to offer me in return for the information even if I had it. Though," and here it turned to Arnold, baring its tiny fangs in a semblance of a rictus grin, "I might be persuaded to find out for you with another slight concession . . ."

"Partire!" he demanded, his voice cracking in a mix of rage and fear. The candles immediately extinguished themselves, the cat and sphere over the circle disappearing to the sound of faint, mocking laughter.

Chapter 39

"What the hell was that thing?" I asked Arnold, shaking slightly as I thought about what the cat had said, that Veronica had been torn apart while still alive. There was a real possibility that neither Sara nor I would make it whole out of this fight. For some reason, knowing it hadn't been Royce who killed her didn't make me feel any better about facing him and whatever else was out there tonight. My confidence had been shaken, and I desperately needed something to focus on other than the mindless brutality of this thing. That way I could at least pretend Sara would still be alive when I went to rescue her later that night.

So far as I knew, I would only have one shot at saving her. I needed to make every action count.

"That," Arnold replied, seeming as nervous as me as he stumbled to the dresser and dropped the book and dagger with dull, muted thuds, "was a planar being. They are devious little shits. I was worried he might try to con a way out of the circle."

"What would be so bad about that?" Chaz asked, even as he drew me closer to wrap a protective arm around my waist. Any other time I might have resisted, but right now I was thankful for the supportive touch.

Arnold started picking up the items in the circle, and I noted with a bit of dull curiosity that the bowls were both empty and the lump of clay was vaguely cat-shaped, settled right where I had last seen the thing crouched. "It wouldn't necessarily do any direct harm to us, but unbound it would be free to act however it wanted. Since they dislike being summoned, it wouldn't be far-fetched to think it might try to do us some mischief. I remember one of my teacher's former apprentices summoning one once. He let it out of a circle unbound, and it promptly turned around and trapped him in a circle of its own making. Then it started using him like a familiar to channel energy through while it cast some spells. My teacher heard the screams. All of us did. He came in and banished it, but it burned the guy out so badly he couldn't talk for days and still couldn't cast even the simplest of spells when my teacher sent him home three weeks later."

"Nasty," I muttered, fighting the shivers and closing my eyes for the space of a breath before sliding my own arm around Chaz's waist. Werewolf or not, it was comforting to have his solid warmth there to lean against just now. For the time being, he looked human, and that was enough for me. "Arnold, will you do me a favor tonight?"

He looked up from the floor, where he was crouching over the silver tray and picking up his magical items. "What kind of favor?"

"Stay back and out of the fight. Whoever nabbed Sara told me to leave you behind tonight, and at this point, I won't do anything else to jeopardize her life. Maybe they'll take me instead, if I offer to take her place."

Chaz growled, a low rumbling that I felt more than heard as he twisted around to place both hands on my shoulders, looking down into my eyes. The worry in his gaze tugged at my heartstrings, and I steeled myself against having to argue the point. "Shia, you're upset. You're not thinking straight, you can't just give yourself over to this thing!"

"I'm thinking perfectly straight. Sara's in the hands of a killer. The killer wants Arnold to stay away tonight. They took Sara and are doing all of this because they're trying to get to me. I think it's perfectly logical." Especially since I planned on wearing the belt, and completely destroying anyone who so much as looked funny at me.

Arnold rose from the floor. He looked grim and frightened. "You're right. I'll stay here. But I won't stay out of it entirely. There are things I can do with your help. And to help you."

"Then do them. But don't follow me down there." I returned my gaze to Chaz and placed a hand on his cheek to bring his attention off Arnold and back to me. "I know there's a possibility that the holder might try to use you. But I will be eternally grateful if you'll come with me. If you can keep the alpha of the Moonwalkers busy—what did you say his name was? Donovan?"

I noted with fascination that his pupils dilated, something like fear passing behind his eyes even while his expression hardened in resolve. "Rohrik Donovan," he said softly, his voice flat and betraying none of the emotion I thought I'd seen a moment before. "He's the strongest alpha male I've ever seen. I don't know anyone that's fought him and lived."

My heart skipped a beat at that. I had no alternatives and this was the most solid plan I'd come up with. But could I rely on Chaz to guard my back? For an instant, my newfound conviction wavered and I felt myself on the edge of some black abyss waiting to swallow me up.

"I'll come. My pack will come. I don't know if I can fight the focus, but I'll try. We all will."

My breath came out of me in a swift rush of relief at that. The Moonwalkers would have another reason to hate the Sunstrikers now, but nonetheless I was still grateful beyond words that he would back me up tonight. I'm sure it must have showed in my face, but I still felt I needed to tell him I didn't expect him to play the hero tonight. "All I want you to do is keep any Weres he has guarding him off my back, and give me a chance to get close enough to try to get the focus. I don't know who else will be there tonight, but I'm assuming Royce, the vamp that killed Veronica and Allison, and maybe some of Rohrik's people, plus the sorcerer who has the focus."

He nodded, leaning forward to brush his lips in

a featherlight kiss over my forehead. "Don't worry. I know what to do."

Throwing caution, and every reservation I had, to the wind, I reached up with both hands and pulled him down into a kiss. It seemed to surprise him almost as much as I surprised myself, as he briefly drew back in shock at the touch. Before long, though, he slid his arms tightly around me, drawing me up against him and tilting his head to deepen the kiss, quickly shifting from soft and gentle to demanding and possessive. Feeling heat and electric desire rising in me, I wondered dimly why I ever let him go. His touch was just the way I remembered and loved it.

He drew back with a sharply indrawn breath at Arnold's loud "Ahem!" I fought back a mixture of disappointment and sudden keen embarrassment, looking away as I raggedly brushed a few stray crimson tendrils out of my eyes. "If you're finished, can we continue planning here?"

Chaz and I stared at each other for a heartbeat, too, before he slowly released me and turned to look at Arnold with a pleased, lazy grin. Answer enough.

"Yeah," I muttered, running a hand over my flushed face and looking anywhere but at the two of them. I don't know what got into me. I was never that forward.

"Good," he said, both of us pointedly ignoring the smug, heated look on Chaz's face. I wondered guiltily if my lips were as red and swollen from the kiss as his. "Here's what I can do . . ."

Chapter 40

The rest of the day felt interminable and too short at the same time. Chaz and Arnold left me to my own devices for a while as Arnold worked out protection spells to keep the focus from dragging Chaz under its influence immediately. Frankly, I was surprised Chaz agreed, considering what Arnold told the cat he wanted to do with the focus if he got his hands on it. Since what they were doing required concentration and zero distractions, I wasn't allowed in the room during their little experiment.

Actually, I'm pretty sure the reason they kicked me out was to put their heads together and figure out a way to keep me from handing myself over to the bad guys later.

As for me, I pulled the rolling chair by the computers over to the living room window and sat staring at the park down the street. Maybe I should have been planning or using those computers to try to hack into the floor plans for *La Petite Boisson* or something, but I felt completely empty of thoughts and emotions, blank as I watched the treetops outside swaying in a breeze I couldn't feel.

No, that's not quite right. Not entirely empty. I felt a distant ache, a touch of loss and fear for Sara.

She'd defended me, supported me, gone along with my crazy ideas even when she knew they were nuts or wouldn't work. She'd been there for some of the best and worst times of my life, helped keep H&W from going under even when we both knew the whole thing was just a crazy dream we clung to, to prove to ourselves and our families that it could be done. She was one of the smartest, bravest, and most supportive people I'd ever known.

And it was all my fault that she'd been taken.

"You're crying," I heard quietly from behind me. Without thinking, I reached up and touched wetness on my cheeks as I turned to see Chaz standing in the doorway.

I tried putting on a brave face, though I was pretty sure it failed. Smiling weakly around the tears, I turned my unfocused gaze out the window again. "I was thinking about Sara."

He moved close to me, placing a hand on my shoulder as he looked outside, too. It was too beautiful a day, with a few cotton-ball clouds scattered across the pale blue spring sky, the sun now hanging low but still shining down on the children playing in the street.

"If you sit here and dwell on it, all you'll do is upset yourself. We'll make it through tonight, don't worry. We'll save her."

"I know," I said, absently rubbing my fingertips under my eyes to wipe the tears away. "I just can't help but feel it's all my fault."

He took hold of the arms of the chair, twisting it around to make me face him as he knelt in front of me, taking my hands up in his own. "Don't torture yourself, Shia. It's not your fault Sara's gone. We'll get her back."

He looked so earnest and concerned, I nearly burst right back into tears. Never had I felt like a more horrible, wretched person than right at that second. His words were soothing and may have been true, but a part of me couldn't let go of the fact that I'd dragged Sara along for the ride, and that I'd been terribly, horribly wrong about Chaz all this time. He was patient, caring, and understanding, all the things I wasn't. I'd been a fool.

"Thank you," I whispered, knowing it wasn't enough, knowing it would have to be, even as I pulled my hands out of his and wrapped my arms around the back of his neck, leaning in to rest my forehead in his hair. He smelled like shampoo, sweat, and musk—male and alive. The musk scent was strong, and I knew it would only get stronger yet as the day waned and the sun finally set. His arms slid around my waist, just holding me, and I was grateful for his silence.

We stayed that way for a long time, though it must have been uncomfortable for him to remain in that kneeling position. Eventually he shifted under my arms and pulled away. He lifted a hand to sweep the curls back from my face and delicately run a thumb under one eye to brush away any remaining hint of my crying.

"I've got to call the pack to tell them what's going on. Are you going to be okay?"

"Yeah," I said, a tremulous smile curving my lips as I carefully brushed my own fingers through his hair to fix it back into spikes after my cheek had flattened it against his head. Funny, I think I actually meant it. I really would be okay, I just needed someone to hold my hand through the grief to the point where I could actually think straight again.

He stared up at me for a few more moments, concern bringing a few lines to light around his eyes. Then he nodded and rose, reaching into a pocket of his jeans and pulling out a cell phone. He wandered to a sofa and sat down. I twisted around in the chair so I could watch him, curious.

Most of the calls he made were about the same, mostly, "Meet at *La Petite Boisson* tonight. Yes, I know what tonight is. No, I'm not joking. Be ready for a fight. Tell so-and-so, too."

I got bored with listening after a while. Instead, I ran my fingertips over the handle of one of the stakes and pulled it out of its holder. Regarding the silver gleaming in the fading sunlight, I asked myself if I would really, truly be able to drive this piece of metal into another living (or perhaps unliving?) being.

My thoughts skittered back to Veronica's murder, the flat, bored tone of the cat speaking of her being ripped apart while still alive. To Royce asking me to save him, even as he visibly fought the control of the focus so he wouldn't kill me. Allison's picture in the paper this morning. To the sounds of muffled screams when Sara's kidnapper called me.

Yes, I decided. I would.

Eventually, Chaz made his last call. "It's done. They'll meet us there tonight. Though we'll have to figure out a way to get in without being seen."

"Either the service entrance in the back, or through the sewer or ventilation systems underground," I said, flicking a nail against the silver to make it thrum out a soft chime. "It's Royce's building, which means he's probably made about a million secret passageways to get out if something goes wrong." Even as I wondered how I could know such a thing, I knew without a doubt it was true. Royce was old, very old. One didn't survive as long as he had without having backup plans, contingencies, and more than one way out if things got too hairy.

Arnold came in cleaning some blue-gray dust or ash off his hands onto a rag as he peered at us. "You guys about ready to go? It's getting late." His gaze flicked over to Chaz, and I knew what he was thinking. He was worried he'd turn furry either here or in his car on the way to the restaurant.

I put the stake away and rose to stretch, pulling my hair back into a ponytail and picking up my duffel and duster. Time to face the music.

"Let's go."

Chapter 41

There was a line in front of *La Petite Boisson* when we got there, but this place was nothing like The Underground. People standing outside here were dressed in eveningwear: fur coats, tuxedos, silk dresses, business suits. Diamonds and other precious gems glittered from throats, ears, and fingers, not silver chains, studs, and leather collars. There were no handcuffs hanging from the red velvet rope cordoning off the line from the rest of the sidewalk. A large red awning shaded the smoked glass double doors, and down the street, marquees advertised plays and musicals, not the latest skin flick or strip shows.

The guards out front were wearing sharp black business suits and little twirls of plastic trailing from their ears to their collars. Security would be much tighter here than it was at either Royce's downtown office or The Underground. Not that it wasn't expected, but still, the sight was a little unnerving.

Arnold had driven us past the restaurant and dropped Chaz and me off in an alley a few blocks down. I didn't want him to be seen, and he promised to do whatever he was going to do to help far away from the actual battle. I wasn't entirely sure I believed he'd stay away, but he knew as well as I did that Sara's life depended on it. Maybe he would. God, I hoped he would.

Though I knew I was woefully underdressed and would stick out like a sore thumb in the crowd, I didn't care. I had the belt on, and my guns, all hidden under the trench coat again. As I adjusted the holsters for the umpteenth time and Chaz exchanged a last few words with Arnold through the open window, I looked up as I heard Arnold call my name.

I took Chaz's place in the window, leaning over to meet Arnold's gaze squarely. "You're going to stay away tonight, right? For Sara's sake?"

His eyes narrowed and his cheek twitched. That tic again. "Of course. Listen, I want you to take Bob with you."

I blinked. Of all the things I was expecting to hear from him, that wasn't one of them. "Your familiar? Are you sure?"

He nodded, extending his closed hand toward me. I flinched as he opened his hand and revealed the same little black mouse, beady eyes staring up at me behind twitching whiskers. "Bob will keep me in the loop on what's happening so I can step in if I need to. I can also channel some things through him. He'll help keep you safe."

As much as I was hesitant to touch the little beast, particularly now that I knew what planar beings were all about, I didn't want to offend either it or Arnold. I tentatively reached out my hand and it skittered up my arm to my shoulder, where it huddled against my neck between the turtleneck of the armor and my jacket. I could feel whiskers twitching against my ear and had to fight the urge to dance around and scream like a girl, instead making do with a shudder and a glare at Arnold for not warning me what Bob was going to do.

"He can't speak, but he'll understand if you talk to him. He can relay information, too." He grinned. "Just don't forget he's there and crush him or something."

I laughed despite myself. "Sure thing." I glanced at him as best I could with him on my shoulder. "Just . . . uhh . . . squeak if you need something, Bob."

He chattered softly at me, almost like he was laughing. Weird.

Chaz lightly brushed my arm as he backed farther into the alley. "The others are coming now."

"Others?" Even as I said it, I could see the hint of glowing eyes—many glowing eyes—farther back in the alley. The sun hadn't quite set, but it was too dark for me to make out more than vague shapes amid the rubbish and Dumpsters. Where had they all come from so quickly and quietly? It gave me the willies, but no more than anything else I'd faced so far. I could handle it.

Arnold cleared his throat. "I'm going to get going. Remember, just tell Bob if you think you need me. He'll relay the message. Good luck."

"All right. I'll see you later tonight."

He nodded and waved, taking off out of sight, and I turned to see who had come to join Chaz and me in the alley.

There were at least thirty of them. Mostly men, ranging from teenagers to thirty-somethings. At first all I could do was stare blankly, wondering where the heck they'd all found parking spaces in this part of the city. That, and why their eyes had that weird luminescence, reflective like a cat's in the oppressive shadows of the alleyway.

"Everyone, listen up!" Chaz immediately drew the attention of most of them, though I could feel the gaze of a few lingering on me, making my skin crawl. It was a hungry stare, and not in a sexual sense. I might've been able to shrug that off, but this was the hunger for food, for a hunt. For two-legged prey. "The Moonwalker tribe has been attacked, and we may be next if we don't do something about it tonight. This human"—and his hand swept back to indicate me, though I didn't particularly like being referred to as "this human," kind of like how I said "this Other," or "that spark," I realized guiltily—"is going to help us. We need to keep her alive to fight the mage responsible. The rest of us are going to keep the vampires and Moonwalkers off of her long enough to deal with the mage."

"I thought you said the Moonwalkers were attacked? What's going on?" one of the Weres asked, a young man I recognized from earlier this afternoon. He was the driver who had been carting around Chaz and his buddies.

Chaz took a deep breath, glancing at me before

speaking, keeping his voice low. "Someone is using the *Dominari* Focus."

A horrified murmur spread through the crowd, a panicked voice calling out, "How can that be? It was destroyed years ago!"

Another said, "That thing is a myth! No way someone really has it . . ."

"What if it takes control of us?" from another. "What then?"

"I don't know how. But Rohrik Donovan has fallen under its sway." The low hum of the crowd grew louder, astonished, frightened. "That's why we're fighting the Moonwalkers tonight. Try not to kill them; they aren't doing anything under their own power anymore. Not until the holder is destroyed. Together, as a pack, we'll overcome any of them under its power."

The murmuring and whispering flowed and I could feel the tension gripping them like a palpable thing. Fear drifted almost immediately into anger and hatred, growls and hisses becoming more prominent than fearful whispers, the abrupt mood swing catching me by surprise.

"Obey me in this. No killing unless you can't avoid it!" Chaz sensed the change as I did. There was a hint of resentment, a brief brush of defiance before Chaz growled softly. Almost immediately, any rebellion festering in the crowd died away into nothing. His eyes swept the crowd, each and every one of the strangers lowering their eyes and backing down in silent, not-quite-respectful agreement to his commands.

I noticed, when he glanced back at me one more time, that his eyes had taken on that odd luminescence, too. He grinned at me, full of promise of something unnamable, as a gleam I recognized as primal predatory hunger drifted into view.

"Remember, protect her!" I gasped when I saw the finger he pointed at me was now tipped with a claw, hair thickening into fur growing darker and longer on the back of his hand even as I watched.

A number of howls and yips answered those last words, soon joined by Chaz as he threw his head back, adding his own deep cry to the chorus around us. I threw my hands up to cover my ears, and some of the people on the street a few yards away cried out and started running away from the sounds drifting out of the alleyway.

I had just enough time to worry that someone might call the cops before I was surrounded by a pack of furred, clawed bodies, all of them hungry and staring at me with feral, inhuman eyes.

Chapter 42

"Oh my God," I whispered, my eyes widening at the mass of furred bodies pressing in around me in the alley.

Werewolves don't look much like men or wolves when under the influence of the full moon. Most of them can shift fully into wolf or human form, but when under the sway of the moon, they are something in between. The ones surrounding me either crouched on their hind legs, clawed "hands" resting against the walls or the ground and long, bushy tails sweeping behind them, or they stood completely upright, even the shortest towering well over my head. Their muzzles were long, dog-like, with pointed ears perked or flattened against their skulls. When they lifted their lips to snarl or snap at each other, they revealed elongated canines up to three inches long.

Their clothes for the most part lay in tatters on the ground around them, revealing sleek muscles overlaid by thick, just as sleek fur. Like any creature, their coloration varied; some had reddish pelts, others were brown or gray or black, some were salt-and-pepper, and one or two were a solid white.

I was startled when I realized I could see in such detail even in the alley, lit only by dim streetlight from around the corner. Then I remembered the belt, my fingers dropping to my waist as that odd awareness of another "self" drifted into my consciousness.

Even shifted, Chaz was easy to recognize. While the majority of the wolves had green or yellow eyes, his were a solid ice blue like a husky's. His fur was the same steel gray color I remembered from when he changed in my living room. None of the others had his color, or his massive, muscular bulk. He was a hunk as a human, and he made most of his money as a personal trainer; as a Were, he could bench-press a car.

One of the other Weres started creeping toward me, black fur bristling, green eyes wide and staring like a cat that just realized a bird was trapped in a room with it. My heart started creeping up into my throat and I took an involuntary step back, before Chaz suddenly slid between us with a kind of sinuous grace you wouldn't expect from a creature so large. As the black Were jerked back, Chaz snarled, baring fangs long enough to cleave through flesh and bone as he crouched down on all fours in front of me. The other Were turned away, snapping at the air before slinking back to cower behind some of the others nearby.

"Thanks," I muttered, though I found myself

pressing back against the dingy brick wall when those icy predator eyes turned to me. I stiffened as he came closer, moving with a peculiar ease on all fours, though it was only so he could press his cold, wet nose against me and start nudging me deeper into the alley.

Incredibly creeped out, I did as he urged, walking slowly through the multitudes of shifted Weres, who watched me with their hungry, glowing eyes. Chaz strode a little ahead of me, leading the way through the darkness. We didn't go far before he reached down and dug his claws under a manhole cover, lifting it with ease and setting it quietly to one side.

At first, I wasn't sure if he meant for me to follow until he crouched down to become eye level with me, pointing one of those curved talons at me and then to the opening of the alley. He then swept his hand around in a gesture that I took to mean the werewolves around us and himself and then pointed down into the sewer. I nodded, understanding. He and the others would find their way to the restaurant following the sewer lines. I would have to go in the front to allay any suspicion.

One thing you could say for Weres, they retain most of their human intelligence when shifted. I watched in fascination as, one by one, they crept on quiet paws past me and down the shaft leading into the dark tunnels below the city. Chaz went last, pausing to look back to me. I reached out a tentative hand to gently brush over his furred cheek, and he tilted his head, closing his eyes as he rubbed one of those pointed ears under my hand. I was amazed at how soft and thick the pelt was, though he turned away and was gone before I could analyze either of our actions any more closely.

I turned back toward the distant light beckoning at the mouth of the alley, shoving my hands deep into the pockets of my jacket and dragging the edges close around me so no one could see the guns, shoulder holsters, or stakes.

Consorting with Weres? I didn't take you for that sort, a by now familiar voice whispered in the back of my skull.

"Yeah, whatever. They're going to help tonight," I muttered, hoping any people on the street wouldn't think I was crazy and talking to myself. Except that this was New York, and chances were nobody would notice or care.

I looked up and down the street as I reached the end of the alley, turning toward *La Petite Boisson. We are going to fight vampires?* the voice asked.

Sighing and lifting one hand to run over my face, I glumly told it what I could. "Vampires, other Weres, and a sorcerer." I didn't like the twinge that last gave me, some touch of emotion or something like it from the belt that I couldn't readily identify. "They have my friend and a powerful magic item that I need to find and take away from the sorcerer."

Ah, the Dominari *Focus. That is troubling.*

It didn't speak again after that. I wondered how in the heck it was that every supernatural creature and even inanimate objects in this city seemed to know about this thing when I'd never heard of it.

Then again, vampires, Weres, and magi had been the stuff of cheesy movies and silly kids' novels up until a few years ago. If someone had told me even a week ago that I'd be working with a mage trying to save a vampire, while my werewolf boyfriend helped keep my ass out of the fire, I would have laughed myself silly. As it was, I was still having a hard time coming to grips with the fact that I was talking to a *belt*, for Christ's sake.

It seemed that Chaz's pack had scared off a good portion of the pedestrians, as the street was unusually empty for a block or so. Legally, packs were restricted to public or national parks or their own homes when shifted. They could shift at will, but most of the time didn't change fully, instead choosing the halfway point because they were forced to shift that much by magic or hormones or whatever it is during the full moon. Being locked into restricted areas while shifted was supposed to be for "their safety," but it was mostly because they scared the hell out of humans when they were something half-man, half-animal. And scared humans smelled like food. Which led to all kinds of problems, lawsuits, so on and so forth, that nobody, including the Weres, liked to deal with.

Not to mention that Animal Control had a field day when they picked up a Were in full animal form who then shifted to human in the back of the truck or the cages at their facilities. Usually it was teenagers who pulled that prank, though the last couple of snots who tried it got some hefty fines and even jail time for their trouble. Though you'd think the fact that there were timber wolves running around downtown Miami might have tipped someone off.

I didn't start seeing normal foot traffic again until I got within two blocks of the restaurant, and that was because of the line waiting to get in. Figuring they were expecting me, I bypassed the lot, heading straight up to the big guys with muscles straining their matching suits who were guarding the front door.

One of them headed toward me when he saw me coming, looking at a clipboard and nodding. "Shiarra Waynest?"

"That's me." I stopped about a yard away. He looked me over with disdain, not liking the look of my combat boots or trench coat, no doubt. Didn't fit with the diamonds and silk of the usual clientele. Tough titties.

"This way, please." Without bothering to hide his sneer, he gestured for me to follow him around the side of the building, away from the crowds. Not liking where this was going, I did so, my hands easing from the pockets of the trench to rest with a comforting kind of familiarity on the belt. For some reason, the brush of my fingertips along the leather grips of the silver stakes and the cool metal casings of extra rounds for the guns made me feel immeasurably better, more secure.

The guy pulled out a key and opened a locked, narrow passageway between the restaurant and the next building. It was well lit with small recessed lights trailing all the way to the end, and there was barbed wire protecting the top of the fenced wrought-iron gate. I noticed with unease that you needed a key to get *out,* as well as in, to the passage. The way led to another entrance on the side of the restaurant, which was covered by a short awning and up a few steps. He produced another key for it.

He unlocked the door and held it open for me, revealing a cheerfully lit stairwell leading above the main part of the restaurant. No way to go but up.

"Just follow the stairs. Someone will meet you at the top and show you the rest of the way. "

The guy sounded flat and bored. However, I could see the curiosity in his eyes as he looked at me. He didn't know what I was here for. Interesting.

I stood there for a moment, indecisive. Knowing it was a trap did not make it any easier to force myself to walk into the lion's den. It was the thought of what they would do to Sara if I turned tail now that goaded me into walking past the bouncer and taking the first step onto the stairwell, even as the door swung shut with an overloud "click" of a lock behind me.

Chapter 43

There was nothing overtly ominous about the stairs. None of the lightbulbs illuminating the way were out or even flickering. The stairs and banister were of a matching dark wood, the walls a nice, clean off-white. No artwork, no posters, no graffiti. Starkly clean.

When I got to the top (forty-two steps, I counted), there was another door. This one was also a plain, dark wood and had a brass handle with no lock. It opened easily under my touch.

My lips parted slightly in surprise and I glanced around the room with wide eyes. There were a number of Weres lounging on the carpets. They looked up immediately when I opened the door, raising their large, shaggy heads from their paws. There were far too many for me to possibly fight. I stood straighter, one hand sliding toward a gun as one of the Weres rose and approached me. I flinched but stood my ground, watching warily as it reached out one long, muscle-corded arm and pulled the door farther open. The door creaked alarmingly under its grasp and I couldn't help but notice that its claws left little indentations in the wood.

It made a sweeping gesture with the other paw—hand—whatever, baring its teeth at me in a silent snarl as it motioned for me to enter the room. Then it just stood there, waiting, slaver trickling down the side of its jaw as it stared at me with over-bright golden eyes.

The idea of running sounded really good right then, possibly even while shooting at it, but there was no way for me to outrun one of these things. Shooting at it would probably just piss it off, especially since I hadn't sprung for the silver-plated bullets back at the White Hat Weapons Emporium.

There were too many to fight, and since I wasn't interested in having it drag me wherever it meant for me to go, I reluctantly followed its direction and stepped into the room.

Five more Weres were watching, waiting, their tails and claws twitching as they crouched along the walls. Watching, but just that. I imagined they'd probably jump me quick enough if I tried anything funny. The first one turned, I guess assuming I'd follow it as it made its way across the room. Two more followed up the rear, and I had to try really, really hard not to look over my shoulder every few seconds as we made our way down a hall past several doors and to another room.

It looked like it had originally been a ballroom of some kind, large and echoing. The ceiling was high, domed, with an ornate chandelier dangling from the center and illuminating the softly glowing wood of lovingly waxed floors. Real candles on tall brass stands stood in alcoves around the room, adding to the cheerful warmth of the place. There were no windows, but I was pretty sure this room was over the main lounge and eating area downstairs.

A pentagram marred the floor directly under the chandelier. It was big, much bigger than the one in Arnold's apartment. That same ozone-ish smell hung heavy in the air, a shimmering haze rising up from the circle. Sara was in the center of it, lying on the floor with her eyes closed, unmoving.

A small, ugly sound rose from my throat, and I started to step forward but the lead Were put its arm out, barring my way. It pointed to something I hadn't seen at first, a small table at the other end of the room where a man and woman sat, another man standing a few paces behind them with arms folded. Another Were, bigger and far scarier looking than Chaz with a number of visible pink scars under its reddish-brown fur, was crouched next to the table, arms across its bent knees as it stared at me from across the room.

I did as I was directed and took a few steps toward them, skirting around the bubble rising from the floor. Sara didn't stir, and as I passed, I watched for a moment to make sure she was still breathing. Much to my relief, she was. Aside from a bruise I could see forming at her temple and her clothes being a little rumpled, she looked okay. I prayed that the one bruise was all they'd done to her.

I approached the table, jumping slightly as the

door thumped shut behind me. My heart skipped a beat when I saw that the standing man was Royce. He came around, face and eyes empty of emotion, pulling out a seat for me opposite the seated couple. The table held a decadent spread of food and drink. I came forward but remained standing before the table, mustering a glare for the two at the table.

The guy was smiling a secret little smile, mirth twinkling in his bright hazel eyes. He was dressed well in a charcoal gray suit, his dark hair neatly combed away from a narrow face. Slender, pale, and with an air of suppressed energy almost as frightening as what was exuding off the Were at his side, I started when I recognized him as the boy Sara had been sent to find by his crazy White Hat parents.

"David Borowsky," I whispered, noting his pleased nod. My gaze slid to the girl sitting next to him, her bright cherry lips curved in a sweet smile as she regarded me with a kind of insincere amusement. There was something dangerous glittering behind the flinty gray depths, her delicate china doll features showcased by her long chestnut hair, which was swept up into a cascade of artful curls. She was wearing a long evening gown the color of heart's blood that left her shoulders and neck bare, a single faceted ruby the size of my thumbnail hanging from a delicate gold chain at her throat. I was willing to bet the dress would swirl around her ankles when she stood up. My words for her were almost, but not quite as, surprised. Definitely confused.

"Tara. No, Anastasia Alderov. How?"

David gestured to the chair Royce had pulled out for me. "Please sit, Shiarra. Did I say your name correctly? It's rather unusual."

"Yeah, well, my parents were hippie gamers who liked fantasy novels." I stayed standing. "What do you want with me? With Sara?"

Anastasia laughed, a soft tinkling of bells. "Cuts right to the chase, doesn't she?" I was a bit surprised to note a rough Brooklyn accent lurking behind the mellifluous voice. It didn't match the china doll face, the delicate hands, or the pretty dress. She smiled at me, a dazzling curve of lips baring just a hint of pearlescent fang. "Oh, don't be so surprised. Born and raised in Brooklyn Heights, though I was living in Chicago up until recently." Malice dripped from the honey-dipped tones of her voice, and I knew without doubt that she had been the one to speak to me through Royce. She turned to look at David, and the two of them locked eyes in a sickeningly sweet way which said to me that, despite being evil and all that, they actually had feelings for each other.

This vampiress was not under the influence of the focus. Both of them used it. Both of them controlled the local vamps and Weres. And considering how many Weres greeted me on the way in, it looked like he was a lot better at it than she was. This kid was the sorcerer?

Fuck.

"Your parents have been looking for you, David," I said, realizing that he looked older and more sophisticated in the suit and with his hair slicked back than he had in the photo his parents had given me, taken of him in a ratty T-shirt with his hair dangling in his eyes.

Tight irritation lines appeared around his eyes, the hint of a pout curving his lips. "My parents don't own me. I'm old enough to do what I want. Go where I want." His gaze returned to Anastasia, softened. "See who I want."

Good God. The little emo freak was kidnapping and murdering and causing mayhem to spite his parents?

He turned back to me, and I backed away from the vicious force behind his gaze. "Anastasia doesn't like you. Royce wanted to turn you into one of his own, did you know that?"

I glanced at Royce. He remained as he had been, hands clasped behind his back, black eyes staring at nothing in particular somewhere off to the side of the table. No movement, no breathing, still as a stone and about as lifelike.

"Anastasia wanted to become a vampire but Royce wouldn't accept her. Thought she wasn't good enough for his tastes."

The vampiress narrowed her eyes, that glint of malice switching from me to Royce in a heartbeat. Suddenly, the reason she hated me so much became clear, if no more insane than any of the other reasons I had imagined they wanted me dead.

Incredulous, I spelled it out, seeing how they both glared at Royce and nodded while I spoke. "She was jealous of me. That he wanted me but not her. But how did . . . who made you a vampire then?"

"No one *you* would know. He was a patron of the arts. When I went to school out in Chicago, he saw me and took me under his wing. When I asked to come back here to negotiate a treaty with Royce, he let me go."

"So what does that have to do with you two being together? Or the focus?" Or me, I wondered. At least they were obliging me for the time being, answering my questions. Maybe if I kept them talking long enough, Chaz and the others would find a way to sneak in.

David smiled a pleased cat-that-got-the-canary smile, one I didn't like at all. "We went to high school together. Stayed in touch by e-mail when she went to Chicago. When she came back, we wanted to do something special, live the kind of life we dreamed about. So I made a new *Dominari* Focus."

My jaw went slack, eyes widening. This kid had the kind of power it took to make something like that? I mean, I was impressed with a talking belt, and it apparently took a whole coven of magi working together to make one. This was something entirely different.

He looked with something like pride to the gigantic Were panting at his side, then with a hardened, sadistic joy at Royce. "The vamp fought pretty hard not to kill you. You're lucky, you know. The last meeting you had really took the fight out of him. He would've made you his slave if he could've bound you instead of killed you. We would've just killed you quickly and kept using him to front this little empire of his, and live a nice, safe, happy eternity together. He would've made whatever was left of your life hell."

Oh, and that made me feel ever so much better. I shifted my weight, one hand stealing toward the stakes as he told me this. An air of tense readiness took over Royce and the Were, sensing I was up to something. That didn't stop me. "Well, aren't you the most kindhearted of souls. So what do you want with me now? Really?"

He slowly stood, the Were rising to tower at his side, Anastasia leaning back comfortably in her chair to watch. A calm, sly grin curved his thin lips as he reached one hand into the pocket of his dinner jacket, pulling out the ugly lump of the focus to set it on the table before him. He kept his fingertips on it.

"Why, I want to give you your reward for getting in our way, for making my baby jealous. For being so intuitive and resourceful. For helping my parents try to stop me, you redheaded little bitch." Despite what he was saying, his voice never wavered or grew angry. Just the same antagonizing calm, grating on my nerves.

Anastasia looked so pleased, I knew I was in deep shit. Alarmed, I tried to think of something to do, something, anything to stall them. "Look, I don't think—"

He cut me off as he offhandedly gestured in my direction with his free hand, chuckling softly. "I'm going to make you an Other so I can use you like the rest. What did you think I was going to do, make it easy and kill you quickly?"

I gasped and jerked back as Royce and the big werewolf both rushed at me at once, hands and claws reaching out to grab me.

Chapter 44

Without thought, I drew the guns in each hand, firing shots as I staggered back out of the immediate reach of Royce and the Were. Jesus Christ, the open mouth of that Were could've easily engulfed my entire head.

I twisted and turned, avoiding their grasping hands as I shot at them, doing what I could to ward them off while ignoring the commands Anastasia and David were shouting. Some part of me distantly heard the double doors across the room slamming open, the sound echoing across the great ceiling as a chorus of howls and yips and barks came spilling in to join the fray between me, Royce, and this monstrous Were I was starting to think must be Rohrik Donovan.

There wasn't much time for anything but reaction. I did everything I could to ignore the screams and inhuman sounds surrounding us. Royce made a grab to catch me around the waist and tackle me to the floor. When I dodged to the side, I twisted right into the swinging, hairy arm of the Were.

It was like being hit by a flying tree. A very large, very solid, very hairy tree. All the air rushed out of me as I flew across the room, coming to a painful landing against the table, with its lovely spread of flowers and expensive food and wines which were probably bottled before I was born.

On the bright side, I hit it on my side instead of my back, snapping a couple of ribs instead of my spine, and knocking the table over in the process. I could hear the dull crack of bones, but it was distant, like it came from somewhere else. At least, it felt that way until I tried to struggle up to my feet, gasping and fighting back tears as I hurriedly grabbed at the fallen table with one hand, trying to steady myself. The pain was incredible, blinding, but even now I knew Royce and Rohrik were both coming for me.

I managed to raise the one gun I'd been able to hold on to in time to catch Royce in the gut, making him gasp and fold over in pain. Despite myself, and despite the incredible pain of breathing against the jab of broken ribs into my lungs, I screamed in sheer terror and threw up one of my arms as the Were leapt on top of me, an unbearably heavy pressure on my legs and stomach. Its fetid breath washed over my face before it tilted its head and bit down on the arm I'd lifted to protect myself.

It didn't bite down very hard, only twisted its head slightly to one side like it was trying to catch and tear the fabric or skin. The weight of it crushed me, forcing the table under me to scrape with a high-pitched screech over the floor as the Were pushed me down, making it even harder to breathe than it was already.

All of a sudden, something else was on top of the Were, a grayish blur forcing it right over the edge of the table and off me. I heard a woman scream, and hoped to God whatever it was had landed on top of that bitch Anastasia.

Chaz stood over me, one clawed paw splintering the edge of the table as he leaned forward and howled a challenge to the Were that had attacked me. Rohrik came sailing over my head and crashed into him, the two of them gray and red blurs streaking over my head and tumbling in a roll across the floor, snarling and clawing and snapping at each other in movements so quick I could barely follow them.

I stood, panting, trying to get a handle on what was going on and clutching the gun to my chest like my life depended on it. There were furry bodies clashing against each other everywhere I looked, biting and snarling and clawing as they tumbled over and around each other and the bubble of energy, or whatever it was, in the center of the room.

Anastasia was nowhere in sight. David was a few yards away, dodging around the fallen table and running toward the circle, where it appeared Sara was stirring.

Though every muscle on my right side seemed to protest the movement, I slowly raised my arm and aimed the gun using the laser sight. I hadn't counted down the shots when I was fighting with

Royce and Rohrik, and I didn't know how many rounds were left. Just one more would have to be enough. Just one.

It seemed overly loud, even amid the pandemonium in the room. David staggered and fell gracelessly to the floor, the focus spilling from his fingers as he howled in pain and clutched at the knee I'd shot out. What do you know, it works just as well on sorcerers as it does on vamps.

Unfortunately, his dropping the thing didn't seem to have the immediate effect I was hoping for. Everyone else was still fighting. Even worse, he twisted around from his stomach to his back, hatred hot in his eyes, and flung his hand at me in an abrupt, angry gesture. A ball of snot green energy shot toward me. I yelped and dived to one side, scrambling around to hide behind the upended table even as the magic missile, or whatever it was, destroyed the top half of it.

To make my day complete, Anastasia was on the floor next to me, looking extremely rumpled and pissed off, particularly as she noticed I'd come to join her hiding behind the furniture. I was right, I thought dimly as she dived at me, fangs extended and nails curved into claws to gouge out my eyes. Her dress was ankle-length.

Her own momentum impaled her on the stake I had somehow pulled up to meet her charge, the gun falling to my side as both hands braced the slick metal against my stomach. The two of us howled in pain simultaneously; her for the stake shoved deep in her chest, ruining that pretty red dress, and me for the butt of the stake grinding against my broken ribs. I must have missed her heart. She was scrabbling at the stake and trying to yank it out, probably trying to avoid having it go any deeper and piercing her dead, shriveled excuse for a heart.

I let go of the stake and grabbed her shoulders, shoving her to the side and twisting so I could straddle her waist.

"Get off me, you bitch!" she screamed, one hand still curled around the stake while the other came at my face, red painted nails seeking to score my cheek.

I grabbed the hand with one of my own, catching her slender wrist and forcing it back to the floor. Then I snagged the wrist of the hand that was trying to yank out the stake, finding it much easier to subdue her than I had Royce. Either the belt was giving me more strength this time around, or she was a pushover.

She's young, an easy kill, it whispered. *Just twist the stake up and to the left and she'll be truly dead.*

"Not yet," I muttered, twisting to one side as she arched up in an attempt to bite me. Her fangs scraped harmlessly along my collarbone, unable to find purchase against the body armor. Unfortunately, I think she might have made holes in my nice new leather jacket. At least I was alive.

Using the leverage of my grip on her wrists, I stood and yanked her to her feet with me, twisting her wrists so that I had them locked at the small of her back with one hand. I was slightly annoyed to see that she was quite a bit taller than me, my head coming up only to her shoulder. I slid the other hand around to her stomach, grabbing the stake protruding from her. It was slick with blood, but I tried not to think about it, even as I had to choke back a gag reflex when I shouted at David.

"Yo, dumbass!" It was supremely gratifying that his pained gaze almost immediately locked on me, still glaring daggers in my direction but now with a touch of obvious concern for his ladylove. "Let Sara go, you fucking nutjob, or I swear to God I will finish what I started here."

To drive the point home, so to speak, I twisted the stake just a little to make Anastasia gasp in pain. Thank goodness the darn things had leather grips, or I wouldn't have been able to hold on against the slick flow of blood.

"Let her go or I'll kill Sara! I'll kill you all!" he shouted back, shrill, furious.

I glanced at Anastasia, who was staring up at the ceiling, mouth agape in pain and terror as she took deep, gasping breaths she probably didn't need. More an involuntary reflex than anything, I was sure. I racked my brains, trying to think of something to say that would convince him I meant business. "Do you really want to risk your girlfriend over a human?"

"No!" he screamed, lurching forward as if to stand and falling back with a pained cry as he clutched at his wounded knee. If he survived tonight's ordeal, he'd walk with a limp for the rest of his life.

Though there was a part of me that felt bad for

causing him that kind of pain, the rest of me knew he was the reason Veronica and Allison were dead, and Sara would be, too, if I gave him half a chance.

"Hurry up, let her go!" I shouted.

Anastasia tried to wrest her hands free, and I got her to stop that quick enough by tightening my grip on the stake and jiggling it just a little. Just enough to hurt.

I watched, suspicious, as he reached out a hand to the circle. Only then did I notice Sara was standing, pacing, on the other side of the shimmering curtain of energy. When David's fingertips brushed the surface, it was as if all that energy got sucked back into him through his hand. In seconds, it was gone, and Sara was racing in my direction. Smart Sara, stooping to pick up one of my fallen guns on her way, halfway between David and me.

Only when she picked it up, she took a shooter's stance and aimed it right at me.

Chapter 45

I pushed Anastasia sharply away from me and dived in the other direction to get behind what was left of the table as the first bullet whined over my head. It knocked Royce back to a kneel, snarling at me as he clutched his shoulder where the bullet had embedded itself. Guess she was still on my side after all. Glory Hallelujah.

I looked around frantically for the other gun, but somehow in the shuffle with Anastasia it had gone missing. Not only that, but both Royce and Anastasia were getting back to their feet. The stake made a disgusting slurping, popping sound as she slid it out of her stomach and flung it across the room. Judging by the look she was giving me, I'd better think of something else quick because she was going to flay me alive the second she got her hands on me.

Though every part of me screamed some kind of protest, from my chest down to my knees, I took to running, skittering around table legs to meet Sara. I tossed her some extra ammo while I ran, my breath coming in tight, wheezing gasps. My eyes widened when I saw the focus on the floor, just a few yards away, dangerously close to where Chaz and Rohrik were still fighting with each other. Both of them were covered with bites and claw marks, dripping blood on the floor, but I had no time to worry about it.

I ran past Sara and slid on my knees to scoop the thing up in my hand. Abruptly, the room seemed to *shift* like I was seeing two of everything.

No, not everything. The room itself was steady. It was the people in it that weren't. I could see the Weres, the vampires, and even David clutching at his injured knee and shouting something in a language I couldn't understand. Sara was shouting at me, too, but I couldn't hear her clearly over the snarls and yips of the Weres.

It was as if there were two of each of them, all moving and shuffling and fighting in motions too fast for me to completely make out. Like there was something solid and then a ghostly bluish-white "something" behind and a little above them. What were those things? Despite the danger, I took a second to try to focus on one of them, maybe figure out what it was and if it was something I could use.

Almost the second I did look at one, I had a complete awareness of the Were I was looking at. Mark Roberts of the Moonwalker tribe. Accountant and happily married father of two by day, werewolf by night. Not too high nor too low in the pack's pecking order. He was afraid, desperately, for himself and bleeding heavily from a bite in his throat. One of the not-pack had bitten him, tried to take out his throat. He could feel it, the pain, the blood, but he couldn't stop fighting. Something was making him fight, making him stay, even though he wanted to run, to be out of this vampire den that smelled like blood and death, to hide and lick his wounds.

I could feel his pain. His fear. His confusion.

I had no idea what I was doing. Didn't want to know. Just as abruptly as I'd come to focus on him, I lost whatever it was as something else, a sense of gathering power, nabbed my attention. The hair on the back of my neck rose, and I twisted to look in David's direction.

Another one of those balls of energy was coming at me fast—too fast. I had no time to dive out of the way and nothing to protect me. All I had time to do was clutch the focus close to my chest as the sickly greenish thing hit me square in the stomach. I screamed in agony as what felt like liquid fire splashed over my skin, spreading all over my body. Sara cried out, but I couldn't hear the words, couldn't think beyond the pain other than that I knew I couldn't let go of the damned piece of stone in my hands or I was dead, all of us were dead.

After a moment, the pain faded enough for me to stop screaming, and I lay there, panting and staring but not exactly seeing what was across the room from me. Except that something was wrong. Different. Quiet, except for my pained whimpers and a faint, angry chitter from Bob, who had somehow managed to cling to my jacket throughout all the fighting. I had just enough of my senses left to know it shouldn't be this quiet.

Every one of the Weres in the room had stopped fighting. They were shaking their heads a little, some clutching at their ears, looking around in confusion and fright.

"Give it back to me! Now!" David screamed, his hands in tight fists at his sides. Somehow, while I'd been distracted by burning into a crispy critter, he'd found his balance and managed to stand. "Give it to me before I kill you!"

"I think not," came Royce's smooth, angry voice from somewhere I couldn't quite see. My vision was too blurred, even without the weird haze of energy surrounding everyone in the room but Sara and me. I still tried to look, though just the simple act of turning my head made it feel like skin was being peeled off my neck and shoulder in the process. It took everything I had not to cry out in pain again.

Royce was holding Anastasia by the throat. He held her up and slightly to one side as easily as a child might hold a balloon, despite her nails clawing at his arm, making tatters of his shirt. She was snapping her fangs at him, her twisting body as sinuous and unnatural as a snake's. It looked for all the world like it took him no effort to casually heft her off the ground. Her feet were fourteen inches off the floor and even from here it looked like his fingers would leave permanent indentations in the skin of her neck.

David took a wobbling hop-step toward me, the fingers of one hand extended in my direction while the other arm was flung sideways for balance. His voice was urgent now, afraid. Not like before. "Give it to me, *now*, or we're all dead. They'll kill you, too, if they aren't controlled!"

Royce laughed, amused even as he was crushing the windpipe of the woman in his grasp. Her mouth was opening and closing like she was trying to scream. "No, my friend. She's not yours. Not one of your puppets."

A low, steady growling was building up. Not from Royce. From the Weres in the room. I could *feel* their attention swinging to David, knowing him for the cause of their fear, tasting his own on the air like a fine wine. He smelled like food, and in that moment, I knew, knew without a doubt, what his flesh and blood would taste like. I could almost taste the salty sweetness of blood on my tongue. I hoped to God that whichever Were I picked that stray thought from wouldn't become more solid in my consciousness. I didn't want to know who it was, his name or profession. Who he had killed.

"We'll kill you, but she'll be left alone."

"No!" David screamed, and I flinched as that green light started to form at his fingertips again.

Royce threw Anastasia like a rag doll, a casual gesture, and I winced in sympathy at the sound of the impact, the unmistakable crunch of breaking bone. I watched helplessly as the two lovers flew across the room, sliding in the Were blood spattered on the floor to stop in the midst of the werewolves. Immediately the beasts started to circle, closer, closer, and I closed my eyes as the mingling horrified screams of the vampire and sorcerer became frantic, animal, panicked. I managed to catch only a brief glimpse of their panicked faces as they clutched at each other when the Weres moved as one, converging on the two like a living carpet of fur, teeth, and claws.

The screams didn't last long. But by all that is holy, those sounds, the shrill wavering cries cutting off so abruptly, the sounds of cracking and ripping like wet cloth being torn apart, were going to haunt me in my nightmares. If I got out of this alive tonight.

I turned away, not wanting to see the roiling, furred bodies converging on whatever was left of Anastasia and David. The thick cracks and sounds of flesh tearing made me want to throw up, but I hadn't eaten anything in hours. Dry heaves made something grind low in my chest, and I had to fight the encroaching blackness in my vision as my mind tried to turn off the pain and horrors around me and just pass out.

That's when Royce came toward me. I also noticed Chaz, out of the corner of my eye, bleeding from numerous wounds but alive and stalking in my direction. And lo and behold, there was Arnold standing by the door, horrorstruck and unable to come closer due to the three dozen frenzied, feeding Weres between him and us.

Sara stepped between us and lifted the gun, shifting her stance so she could keep both the vampire and the Were in sight. They both froze. "You okay, Shia?"

I tried to answer. Bad move, trying to breathe.

After a brief fit of extremely painful coughing, I managed to choke out an answer. "I've been better."

She gave a faint laugh, forced, shifting her weight uncomfortably as Royce sidled another step closer. "You got any bright ideas on how to get out of here?"

Oh great. Sara asking me for ideas. Royce called out, his voice that same, melodic tone I remembered, just as friendly and smooth as it had been while he told David he was dogmeat. "I can escort you out. Just give me the focus, and I'll get the Weres out of here."

Chaz answered those words with an abrupt, angry growl, hackles rising and bloodstained teeth snapping at him in a truly frightening display. Royce didn't even flinch.

I wanted to say something witty. It hurt too much to talk, so I just settled on shaking my head. Bob made a small sound in my ear that seemed like a warning, though against what I had no idea. Both of the Others came closer still, Sara's voice shaking as she looked back over her shoulder at me for direction. "Shia . . ."

Enough was enough. This stupid focus was the cause of enough pain and misery to last several lifetimes. Thanks to this thing, two magi, a vampire, and a sorcerer were dead. Who knew how many Others or how many people had been killed due to David's handiwork, or what he'd had to do to get the power and knowledge to make it. If Royce got his hands on it, he'd use it to get the Weres out of here, all right. But then he'd use them, just like David had. If Chaz took it, he would take over the Moonwalker tribe, maybe others, and control his own pack on an entirely new level. I couldn't let Arnold have it, or he'd use it, too, manipulating everyone—maybe even Chaz this time—just like David had.

"Are you still with me?" I whispered, coughing slightly again and doing my best to keep my eyes open so I could keep an eye on Royce, Chaz, and Arnold. Sara was a good shot, but she wouldn't be able to stop them all in time.

The belt answered me, just as I'd hoped. Faint, but it was there. *Still here. You're bleeding internally—I can't do much more than slow it down. It's tough keeping you humans alive.*

I almost laughed, but the slight hitch of muscles in my chest and more of that grinding feeling, pressure and pain on one of my lungs, were deterrent enough. "Just a little longer," I promised it, twisting from my back onto my side, panting as I clutched the focus to my chest. It wasn't a lack of strength. It was the pain of my broken ribs and the sensation like my skin had charred, even though what I could see looked perfectly healthy, if a little pale. The pain of that spell David lobbed at me was all in my head, I guess. Didn't make it hurt any less.

Royce inched forward again, Chaz hesitantly following in his footsteps. "What are you doing?"

Sara backed up another step closer to me and lifted the gun, firing a warning shot into the ceiling. Glass tinkled and plaster rained down between her and the

Others. The two froze, the other Weres lifting their heads from their "meal" and turning toward us, ears pricked in alarm or curiosity. They were behind me, but I could "feel" them looking, the same way I knew Mark Roberts had been bleeding and afraid. Just like I could feel a mixed sense of hunger, elation, and fear from Royce. Funny to think that he was afraid. Funnier still that his fear was of me.

I coughed again and spat out a bit of blood, taking a few shallow breaths to compose myself before I looked up at the vampire and gave him his answer. "What needs to be done."

With that, I focused every last ounce of energy I could muster, doing what I could to pull more force with the help of the belt, lifting the focus as fast and high as I could then smashing it into the hardwood floor.

The last thing I knew before the world turned black around me was an intense backwash of energy from the bits of stone crumbling under my hand, throwing me back toward the gathered Weres to the sound of Sara's screams.

Chapter 46

I woke up. Which was both a pleasant and an unpleasant shock all on its own.

The low droning beeps, bluish-white curtain around the bed, and tubes strapped to my arms, nose, and chest told me more than the fuzzy, dream-like quality of my thoughts and vision that I was in a hospital. Every part of me ached abominably, but it was distant, like I was feeling everything through a curtain of cloth gauze.

I tried thinking back on what happened, how I got here. No such luck. The last thing I remembered was breaking the focus and passing out. Everything after that was just . . . empty. Blank.

Blinking my eyes to clear my vision, I turned my head to the side and found it in me somewhere to dredge up a smile at the sight of Sara seated at my bedside, her eyes closed as she leaned against the metal rail, head pillowed on her arm. She must have fallen asleep waiting for me to wake up. It was good to see she was alive and, aside from a bandage I could see winding around her other arm, unharmed.

"You're awake," came a surprised voice from behind the curtain. Chaz carefully brushed it aside, sidling around it to stand on the other side of the bed.

I nodded and tried to smile, my voice coming out no stronger than a faint whisper. "For what it's worth, yeah."

He smiled back at me, gently taking my right hand in both of his own. The left was tightly bandaged up and I could only see the tips of my fingers. Must've done more damage to it than I'd thought when I destroyed the focus. I lifted the bandaged hand to examine it, took a deep breath to sigh, then decided that was a bad idea and immediately expelled it.

"How long have I been out?"

"Your family was here. Visiting hours ended twenty minutes ago, but we snuck back in." Chaz said, not meeting my gaze. I stared hard at him until he finally capitulated, squirming like a kid caught playing hooky. The doctors probably told him he shouldn't tell me anything about the injuries to keep me from being worried. "We were all here yesterday, and the day before, too. You've been out for four days." So much for that.

I closed my eyes, fighting back the sudden sting of tears. We won. We came out alive, on top. Chaz was apparently okay. There wasn't even the hint of a scar to show where he'd been bitten or scratched during all that fighting. Chaz took the tears the wrong way, concern making his face fall as he reached up one hand to gently brush his fingers over my cheek. "Don't cry, please don't. Everything's okay now, the focus is gone and so is the holder."

I couldn't help it. Despite the pain it caused, the tightness in my chest, I started laughing. The soft, wheezy quality and the sharp pain made it hard to keep it up, but I did it anyway. Chaz looked shocked, even as I covered his fingers on my cheek with my bandaged hand. Tears spilling down, I laughed, and it felt good. Apparently it was enough to jar Sara, who lifted her head and blinked blearily at me before her eyes widened.

"We're alive. We won."

"You did. I owe you for that," came a new, unfamiliar voice, deep and rough with the hint of a smoker's husk behind the twang of a New Jersey accent. A man I didn't recognize was hanging back by the curtain. Chaz glanced over his shoulder, a wary look, but Sara didn't seem afraid.

He came forward to stand near the foot of the bed, keeping some distance between himself and Chaz while still keeping me from having to strain my neck to see him. He was tall, half a head taller than Chaz, with short black hair that had a touch of white threading through here and there, warm brown eyes showing little laugh lines at the corners, and skin burned dark by years in the sun. He wore jeans and a white T-shirt, along with a long-sleeved flannel shirt to cover his lean, muscled arms, and had a touch of stubble on his strong jaw. He looked like a forty-something construction foreman, and had the same air of casual strength, command, and lingering musk scent as Chaz did.

"The Moonwalker tribe owes you, girl. You saved them, me, from a nasty fate."

"You're Rohrik Donovan?" I asked after a moment, having to concentrate harder than expected to dredge the name up, absently wiping the tears off my cheeks. Man, whatever the doc had me pumped up on was making me slow.

He nodded and exchanged a look with Chaz, who didn't seem all that pleased that he was here. "I just came by to see how you were doing. Also, to let you know that you can call on any of the Moonwalkers when you're in need. We'll help you any way we can."

"Thanks," I said, though as much as I meant it, I was praying I would never be desperate enough to turn to a pack of werewolves for help again.

"I'm . . . uhh . . . I'm sorry about hitting you. Back there. The pack has taken up a collection to help defray any medical bills," he said, his gaze creeping off me to stare at the ceiling. My, was that a touch of red in his cheeks? He was embarrassed for hurting me. So much for being the Big Bad Wolf.

It hurt a little less when I laughed this time. Eventually he managed to look back at me, relief creeping into his features. It was good to see.

"I'll be in touch." He lowered his head and gave me a little salute, nodding to Sara and Chaz before leaving. Chaz watched him go, and I could feel his fingers tighten almost imperceptibly around mine. Mr. Sensitive today.

Sara spoke up next. "How do you feel?"

"Like warmed-over shit." I grinned at her to soften the words. Even that hurt. "I'll be okay, I think. As long as I don't have to fight any more Weres or vamps or insane sorcerers, my day is made."

Arnold cleared his throat from the door, carrying a bunch of coffee cups. Unfortunately, none for me. I guess he hadn't thought I'd be awake when he got back. "Hey, good to see you with your eyes open. Was that Rohrik Donovan who just walked out?"

I nodded, closing my eyes when the movement made my vision blur and head spin.

Arnold walked up to the bedside, carefully handing cups of coffee to Sara and Chaz before taking a sip of his own. I was pleased to note Bob's tiny triangular head poking out from under Arnold's shirt collar, whiskers twitching. Good to see the little furball survived.

Sara reached out to offer me some of her coffee, but I shook my head, figuring it would probably be better to stay away from caffeine while on whatever it was they were feeding me through the tube in my arm.

"I'm sorry I wasn't there to do anything in time. To keep you safe." Arnold sounded bitter, though part of me wondered whether it was for the focus or me. "I couldn't cast anything that might have helped with all those Weres in the way. It was all I could do just to keep Bob with you."

"Don't sweat it," I said, wondering if it was my

imagination or if my voice really was slurring the way I thought it was. It was getting harder to keep my eyes open.

Just then, a nurse strode in, though I was barely able to rouse myself enough to look over and see. "She's awake? All right, you three, let's give her some rest. You can all come back tomorrow."

I waved halfheartedly, smiling in amusement at their protests at being given the boot. I'd see them all when I woke up. Tomorrow.

Chapter 47

After a month and a half in the hospital, the doctors finally decided that I'd healed enough that I wasn't likely to start that nasty internal bleeding again and could go home. They were probably just getting sick and tired of my parents alternately threatening to kill me the minute I was well enough to withstand a beating and thanking God and everybody that I was alive. It was embarrassing as hell that my mom kept fluctuating between weeping with relief and berating the hell out of me for messing with Others, both loudly enough to disturb patients across the hall. I swear, I felt like an errant teenager again with all the new rules and restrictions they imposed on me, and I even had to promise my mom that when I was released from the hospital, I'd go to church with her for confession.

It helped my morale immeasurably that Chaz, Arnold, and Sara kept sneaking in after hours to see me every night.

Sara kept on top of things—paying my bills,

answering e-mails, watering plants—while I was in the hospital. I owed her big-time. Though I had saved her life back in that room, she saved mine by making sure my rent and car payment were sent in on time.

There was also a spike in phone calls and e-mails requesting my services after the news media reported on the ultimate showdown above *La Petite Boisson*. Arnold brought me the paper one night to show me my picture next to Royce's on the front page. I asked him, politely I thought, to burn it.

I had insurance, but it didn't exactly cover Were or magic attacks. There weren't any clauses in my crappy HMO that covered being beaten to shit by a werewolf.

So Rohrik Donovan and the rest of the Moonwalkers made good on their promise and helped pay off the sky-high medical bills. A couple of them also showed up to thank me in person, including a bookish, balding gentleman named Mark Roberts. It was odd seeing what he looked like as a man, but he seemed pleased to meet me and was kind enough to offer me a cut-rate deal on my bookkeeping and taxes.

Most of the rest of them sent me flowers. My hospital room looked and smelled like a goddamn florist shop. Even Janine stopped by at one point with a "Get Well Soon" card and a mumbled thanks and apology. I'm happy to report that she's warmed up to me quite a bit since I saved her sister's life.

Royce, thankfully, never showed up at the hospital. He did send a bouquet of white roses with a card bearing a picture of a sunrise or sunset on the front. I recognized his, or perhaps a secretary's, neat penmanship from the note he'd left me a lifetime or two ago when I first met him at his office.

Ms. Waynest:
My humblest apologies for these inconveniences you have endured.
Wishing you a speedy recovery.

—Alec

Inconveniences. Right.

When the doctors finally got around to answering all my questions, I almost wished they hadn't. Apparently I'd needed emergency surgery to fix my rib cage, pull bits of shattered bone out of one of my lungs, and some other nasty stuff that should have, but somehow miraculously didn't, kill me. Arnold told me it was a mix of the belt and his interference, via Bob, that had kept me alive. I'm thinking it was mostly the belt.

A mysterious benefactor anonymously paid the rest of my hospital bills. I haven't been able to figure out whether it was The Circle or Royce. Either way, it doesn't bear thinking about. If it was The Circle, it means they still want something from me. If it was Royce—that's the part that really doesn't bear thinking about.

A couple of days after I woke up, the police came to my hospital bed and took my statement about Veronica and Allison's deaths and the mess they found above Royce's restaurant. Turns out that sometime between Sunday and Monday, Mr. and Mrs. Borowsky had also been found murdered in their own home. No, I didn't know anything about that. Yes, the circumstances—bodies found in a circle burned into the floor and suffering a mix of vampire and Were bites—sounded like David and Anastasia's handiwork.

The police had taken statements from Royce, Arnold, Chaz, Sara, and a whole shitload of Weres at the time of the incident. Apparently, during the scuffle, a diner in the restaurant had called the cops when a stray bullet shattered his soup bowl and embedded itself in the table. Never mind the screaming or howling coming from above everyone's heads.

That's what saved my life, because an ambulance came with the cops to treat some guy who had a heart attack from the excitement of running for his life out of the fine establishment with the rest of the diners.

The police never found out which Were worked with Anastasia to kill Veronica Wright or Allison Darling. The bodies of David Borowsky and Anastasia Alderov? Never found. Presumed dead. Heh. So no charges were filed, probably because the cops couldn't figure out who the hell to arrest, and it was hard to keep a whole pack of werewolves, particularly during the full moon, enclosed in a jail cell. Plus, I imagine it must have been awkward taking the statements of a few dozen naked people who were bone tired from fighting for their lives, staying up all night, and going from furry to human in the course of a few hours.

So after a month and a half of going stir-crazy between physical therapy sessions and daytime soap operas, Chaz picked me up at the hospital and took me home. We swung by a grocery store so I could restock my fridge. My parents promised to drop my car off in a day or two. Everything was going back to normal.

Chaz helped me take everything upstairs, including the belt, holster, and body armor. Normally the hospital personnel just cut the clothes off you when they're trying to reach your vitals to save your life, but in this case they were too damned hard to cut. So I still had most of my ass-kicking outfit. Alas, the trench coat did not make it. They also sliced through, rather than take off, the gun holsters. The charm necklace never came off and was tucked safely beneath my T-shirt.

By the time everything was put away, it was almost eight and I was a bit sore and exhausted, but pleasantly so. I kicked Chaz out with the promise that he could come by the next night, and we'd watch some movies. For now, I just wanted to get some rest.

I puttered around a little, refamiliarizing myself with my home. All my plants were still alive. I had a ton of e-mail, mostly get well wishes, a few inquiries from journalists and the usual spam. The place was just as I'd left it; even the dirty clothes I'd forgotten to toss in the hamper were still lying on the bathroom tile. Damien's gift was still sitting in the back of my hall closet, untouched. Apparently nobody had busted in while I was gone. Everything was as it should be.

Except for the note I found on the bedside table. The neat block letters read:

DEAR HUNTER,

YOU'RE ONE OF US NOW. WHEN YOU'RE READY TO JOIN THE CREW, YOU KNOW WHERE TO FIND ME.

JACK

I crumpled the note and threw it in the trash before I slid into bed, gingerly touching the new scars on my stomach. They didn't hurt anymore but I'd never be able to wear a bikini again. Not really wanting to look at the scars and too tired to deal with the rest, I kicked off my sneakers, left my jeans and T-shirt on, and lay staring at the amber bars of light from the streetlamps reflecting through my blinds.

The White Hats could find someone else to play their games. I was done dealing with supernaturals. Except for Chaz, of course. And Arnold. And the Moonwalker tribe. Oh, hell, you know what I mean.

Chapter 48

Just as I was drifting off to sleep, there was a knock at my door. If it was Jack or some other White Hat, someone was really going to get hurt.

With a pained groan I got up, muttering darkly about the injustice of it all as I stumbled toward the door. Somebody knocked again before I was halfway there.

"For Chrissakes, I'm coming! Hold on." The knocking stopped.

Through the peephole I saw a man standing with his back to the door. I couldn't really make him out and was too tired to play games. I left the chain guard locked and pulled the door open a crack.

"What do you want?" I didn't quite mean for my voice to come out in such an unfriendly growl, but there it was.

Royce turned to face me, an amused smile curving his lips. He stood with one hand in the pocket of a well-cut black suit, which showed off his wide shoulders and flat, lean waist. The other hand held a bundle. I nearly backed up a nervous step but caught myself.

"I came to see if you were well. I didn't wake you, did I?" he said.

Bastard. "No. I'm okay. If that's all, thanks for stopping by." I started to shut the door, but he put his hand out, catching it before it could close. A herd of elephants couldn't have pushed it shut against that casual lean.

"Please. May we speak for a moment?"

I thought about it. Mostly I wanted to tell him to go to hell, but in a way I kind of owed him. Worse, he owed me for pulling his ass out of the fire and saving him from David and Anastasia's tender mercies. Also, he did say please. I wasn't *that* rude. After a purposely noticeable hesitation, I undid the chain and pulled the door open, stepping aside and folding my arms.

He slipped inside past me, black eyes glancing around, taking in the small kitchen, cheap dining set, and mismatched living room furniture. Him in his expensive suit, which probably cost more than all the furniture in the apartment put together, looked dreadfully out of place, but I wasn't about to apologize for my living standards. I shut the door and headed for the kitchen, carefully keeping my eyes off him.

"Possibly a stupid question, but can I get you anything?"

"Water would be fine," he said, his voice and manner deliberately bland. I wondered if it was for my sake or his.

I got him his water, and a soda for me, before easing myself down on the couch. He waited until I sat before choosing a place for himself, an overstuffed recliner, which tilted forward awkwardly when he sat down. I felt enormously frumpy in my I HAVE PLENTY OF TALENT AND VISION, I JUST DON'T GIVE A DAMN T-shirt and faded jeans but wasn't about to change on his account.

"So what did you want?" My voice was flat and unamused. I tucked my socked feet under me and leaned against the arm of the couch. I was tired, cranky, and in no mood to deal with vampires. Though I suppose one never is.

He tried, and failed, to hide a smirk behind the glass of water. After taking a sip he put down the glass, offering me the bundle of black cloth he carried. I hesitated again, just for a moment, before shrugging off my worry and taking it. My brows about lifted to my hairline when I unfolded the cloth and revealed my guns. They weren't with the stuff I took home from the hospital, so I'd assumed the police had found and confiscated them.

Now that I had my weapons back, I wasn't sure what I would do with them, but it did seem to warrant some kind of response. "Thanks," I said, carefully refolding the cloth and setting them aside.

"I wanted to apologize for my behavior," he said with what sounded like regret. His eyes still sparkled with suppressed mirth, but I wasn't about to point out the inconsistencies. A man like Royce apologizing for his behavior. Fancy that.

"I won't lie to you. David was speaking the truth.

I had thoughts of turning you, or at least binding you in the hopes that you would be able to maintain your will but still operate within my interests and perhaps take the focus from the two of them. It is probably for the best that it was destroyed."

"That's great," I said, shifting uncomfortably and looking away. This was not a subject I was comfortable speaking about. Particularly when I was alone and in pain from the beating of my life, with a vampire sitting five feet away. "So you came all the way to my neck of the woods to tell me this?"

He sighed and rubbed his fingertips against his forehead as if he were trying to rub away the first signs of a headache. A human gesture from an inhuman creature. No matter how good he looked, no matter how warm and sincere his smile, I couldn't put the thought out of my mind that it was the living, or maybe unliving, dead sitting across from me. When he looked at me, the amusement was fading, a small frown curving his lips.

"You do make things difficult. I'm trying to apologize. As you might imagine, I don't do this very often."

The first hint of sheepishness was creeping into my voice, but I bit back on it as best I could. I was pretty sure my cheeks were red, too. "Look, that's great. I'm glad you're getting in touch with your softer side. However, I'd like to remind you that you came damned close to tearing my throat out more than once and that doesn't exactly give me warm fuzzy-bunny feelings toward you right now, no matter how sorry you are."

He seemed to be a bit nonplussed, like he wasn't sure whether to be offended or amused. Eventually, he offered a neutral "As you say."

Warming up to my theme, I switched the soda to one hand so I could level an accusatory finger at him. "It's probably been a long time since you've been human, but I know you felt a very mortal kind of terror for me, not just when I got my hands on the focus but also back in your office. You want to control everyone and everything around you so you won't have to face the fact of your own potential mortality—it's why you wanted the focus for yourself."

He flinched as if I'd slapped him. In a way, I had. There was no way I could have known that without having had the focus to help me see into his thoughts. Maybe it was cruel of me to abuse the knowledge this way, but I needed to get my point across.

"As far as I'm concerned, there's a part of you that's still afraid that some nice, sunshiny day, I'll come find your daytime resting place and put an end to you. You know I'm not afraid of you anymore." The funniest part about that was how true it was. I hadn't been afraid of him, really afraid, since I realized that he was more scared of me than I was of him. "That's why you're here making nice now, to win me over so I won't turn you into a crispy critter. Am I wrong?"

He stared at me, his entire body gone into that odd, deathly stillness, only his eyes betraying some alien thoughts I couldn't comprehend. Eventually, he dropped his gaze and looked away from me. His voice, normally smooth and confident, came out in a whisper. "No. You're not wrong."

"Great," I said, though it seemed a hollow victory.

Summing up the reserves of whatever politeness was left to him, he straightened and looked pointedly into my eyes. Maybe he was trying to use his powers to spell me, or maybe he was just playing it straight. Either way, it was intense, charm or no charm to block his . . . uhh . . . charms.

"I would normally never turn someone without their consent. Believe what you will, but if I'd had a choice, I would not have done things the way I did. Like any other creature, survival is my priority. And—I mean this—I'm sorry for manipulating you the way I did."

I took a deep breath to steady myself, ignoring the dull ache it caused in my ribs. With as much graciousness as I could muster, I said, "I accept your apology."

He seemed relieved. Fancy that. "Good. There's one other thing I came for tonight," he said, dark eyes glittering with some emotion I couldn't place. Whatever it was, I didn't like it.

"What?" I finally prompted when he paused longer than seemed necessary.

In the blink of an eye, he was suddenly there, right in front of me, his lips pressed to mine and his fingertips lightly cradling the back of my head so I couldn't pull away. I was too shocked to think, move, breathe as he kissed me. I'd never seen anything move that fast. The only thing my mind managed to register around the cool, velveteen softness of his lips was the fact that there was not even the slightest hint of fangs behind them. That, and the desire I felt, brief and intense, that shocked me almost as badly as his touch.

Before the thought of struggling even entered my mind, he pulled back, the fingertips of one hand lightly trailing under my jaw, before he stood. I stared at him, open-mouthed, in pure shock. Just then, I didn't know whether to be angry, flattered, or afraid. So I simply gaped at him as a hint of that wicked, melt-in-your-mouth-sexy smile he'd won me over with back at The Underground curved his lips.

"Good night, Shiarra. I'm sure I'll be seeing you again soon."

With that, he turned, adjusting the lapels of his jacket as he walked over to and out my apartment door. I was still gaping when it shut quietly behind him.

Chapter 49

So that's the story of how I became a vampire hunter and came to see Others as just another, if scary, kind of people. I haven't actually hunted down any vampires since Anastasia but I keep finding little white cowboy hat pins in my apartment, my office, even one left on the passenger seat of my car one morning. I'm not sure how much longer Jack will let me ignore his little calling cards, but I'm willing to find out.

Arnold helped me put some spells on my doors and windows to keep the bad things out. Somehow, in the crazy aftermath of the fight, he and Sara had tumbled into each other's arms and are now dating steadily. Stranger things have happened, I suppose.

Like the fact that Chaz comes over any night we're both free. We've decided to give the whole relationship thing another shot. He promised not to come by during the full moon or shift in my apartment, and I promised not to freak out if he accidentally lost control and did it anyway. We go on double dates with Sara and Arnold sometimes. Talk about oddball relationships.

Royce has left me a couple of notes, sometimes in the mail, sometimes delivered as little cards with flowers. They're all invitations to see him again. I've done my best to ignore each and every one, though some perversity has led me to keep them in a little wooden box in my bottom dresser drawer, the same red cloth–lined box that cradles a pair of matched guns. Next to the box is a coil of leather with three identical silver stakes sheathed all in a row. I wear the belt when I'm alone at night so it has someone to talk to now and then. I won't tell if you won't.

Like I said in the beginning, I'm a private detective, not an assassin. Since I'm human, without outside help there's no competing with Others, so I'm doing my best to stay out of their world.

Unfortunately, they all seem to want in to mine.

Please read on for an exciting sneak peek of the next Shiarra Waynest novel, TAKEN BY THE OTHERS, coming in January 2011!

I don't usually have people pointing guns in my face. Or in my direction at all, really. I'm a private detective, so I know some people have certainly *thought* about shooting me after I reported their illicit activities to my clients or the cops, but looking down the barrel of a forty-five was a new experience for me.

"Jack, can we talk about this without the gun?"

Jack was precisely as I remembered him. Tall, slender, with close-cropped blond hair and the coldest blue eyes I'd ever seen. His flannel, long-sleeved shirt was rolled up to just above his elbows and left unbuttoned for easy access to his shoulder holster. He's clean-cut, looks like the poster boy for some white bread good ol' boy magazine, and crazy as a loon. He belongs to a group of extremists and vigilante hunters who call themselves the White Hats.

His thin lips quirked in a polite smile. No real emotion shone through the empty mask. I was praying he was just using some of his psycho scare tactics again. I deeply regretted leaving my own guns in my bedroom all the way across town. Fat lot of good they did me there. Maybe I should have our receptionist frisk the clients before letting them into my office from now on.

"Shiarra, I'm disappointed. I've left you a number of invitations to come work with us. Why didn't you get back to me? Did you succumb to Royce after the little fiasco this spring?"

That again. A few months ago I took a job I should've known well enough to leave the hell alone. When your business is failing and someone offers you a lot of money, sometimes you do stupid things. For example, accept a job trying to find some powerful magic artifact that a vampire was hiding from a bunch of magi. I suppose you could call accepting a proposition like that suicidal. These days, I just called it a bad business decision.

"No, I haven't gone to see Royce since the fight at his restaurant." One little white lie couldn't hurt. He'd come to see me, not the other way around. I'd stringently avoided Royce since the day I got home from the hospital, when he visited to apologize and thank me in his own way for pulling his ass out of the fire. "Listen, I don't deal in that shit anymore. Once was enough."

"You've taken on clients, done other jobs for supernaturals since your recovery. You have strong ties to two of the most powerful Were packs in the Five Boroughs. You're linked to the most influential vampire in the state. We need your expertise, and your connections."

The only reason the Moonwalker tribe had anything to do with me was because, like Royce, I saved their butts from a crazy power-hungry sorcerer. They owed me. They only reason the Sunstriker tribe had anything to do with me was because the leader of the pack was my boyfriend. Aside from that, the occasional (non-dangerous) case notwithstanding, I tried to keep my connections to anything furry or with fangs to a minimum.

I took a deep breath to steady myself while I thought about how to get Jack to get the hell out of my office, and take his gun with him. He'd tried this tactic before; I wondered why he'd never figured out that waving a weapon in someone's face was not a good way to get them to cooperate with you for any length of time. "You know I don't like vampires. I don't have much to do with Weres anymore, either. I don't take jobs that have anything to do with the supernatural, no matter what the papers say about me."

"You have the equipment and connections to be a hunter." He frowned. "We need you. I won't have you going to them, taking their side."

"Whoa now, who said anything about that?"

His eyes narrowed, something passing through them I couldn't read. "There's a new player in the game. It'll be down to him or Royce. Or us."

I stared blankly. "Who?"

"Word on the street is that Max Carlyle is coming to town." He stared back, expectant.

Silence. After a moment decidedly lacking any explanations, I urged him along. "And he is?"

"You really don't know?"

"Would I ask if I did?"

He grinned; the flash of white teeth against his pale skin was ominous. Predatory. Too much like the things he hunted—vampires.

"My, my. I hate to spoil the surprise." One hand reached up to rub his smooth-shaven jaw while he stared at me. After another long, drawn out moment of silence, he raised the gun, thumbed on the safety and tucked it away in its holster under his flannel. "Ms. Waynest, again, I must apologize for my methods. Unfortunately, your reputation leads me to worry about what needs to be done to ensure you're playing on the right side of the field."

Holding a knife to my throat in the dead of night after breaking into my bedroom didn't exactly give me warm fuzzies, and neither did holding a gun on me in broad daylight. I was hoping my expression was more neutral than pissed, but wasn't holding my breath.

"Look, for the last time—I don't want anything to do with Others. I don't talk to Royce, I don't give a shit what the White Hats are doing, and I'm not about to do the tango with things that could eat me for breakfast. I'm a private detective, and that's all. Someone go missing? Think your girlfriend is cheating on you? Great. I'll go look for them. But I will not," I stressed, leaning forward across the desk and pointing one admonishing finger in his direction, "be bullied into dealing with vampires and Weres again. Coming close to dying once was enough. You can't pay me enough to put my own life on the line. Not again."

"Oh, don't worry, Ms. Waynest. They'll be coming to you soon enough. And once they do, you'll come running to us for help."

I stood, a thread of fear trailing down my spine, even as I finally boiled over. I pointed at the door. "Get the hell out of my office! Stay away from me!"

He swung the door open and sauntered out of the room, his cool, arrogant laughter trailing behind him. My glare stayed trained on him until his shadowed frame was no longer visible behind the frosted glass of the front door.

Jen twisted around in her chair to peer into my office, staring at me with wide brown eyes over the rims of her glasses. "Jeez, Shia, what was that all about?"

I shook my head, coming around my desk to shut the door to my office. "Nothing. But if he comes back, or tries to make another appointment, I'm out of the office. No—out of the country."

She shrugged, muttered something, and turned back to her desk to work on the stack of papers in front of her. I glared at the frosted glass door with its gold leaf-inscribed "H&W INVESTIGATIONS," even though Jack was long gone.

As much as he pissed me off, he scared me more. Or maybe him saying the Others would come looking for me scared me more. Hell, I think I was entitled to be a little unsettled considering I'd had a gun waved in my face. Irritated and upset, I twisted around, calling over my shoulder as I shut the door,

"Hold my calls. If anyone asks, I've gone home for the day."

Some preventative measures needed to be taken about this Max Carlyle, I thought. I went to my desk and sat in the squeaky office chair, rolling it back so I could rifle through the back of the top drawer. After rummaging through a scattering of old Post-it notes, paper clips, pens and papers, I finally found the leather-bound notebook I kept business cards filed in.

I flipped through the pages until I found the neat, professional card for A. D. Royce Industries. It had all the data I needed to contact Alec Royce, the vampire I'd been doing my best to avoid the past several months. The one I'd ended up legally, contractually bound to, who'd been sending me invitations to a night on the town and, presumably, other things. All of which I'd carefully ignored up until now.

Daylight still shone through the window behind my desk, but I figured I could leave a message if he didn't pick up. I grabbed my cell, dug the card out of the little plastic holder, and dialed the handwritten number scrawled on the back.

Tucking the phone between my head and shoulder, I fixed my eyes on the framed photograph of Chaz and me on the corner of my desk. We were leaning back against the rail together at the end of the pier in Greenport and his arms were wrapped around me. I tried not to think about what Chaz would say about me calling the vamp, listened to the ringing, and finally, a click. "You've reached the desk of Alec Royce. I'm not in right now, but if you leave a message with your name and number, I'll get back to you."

That mild, friendly voice gave me the shivers, worse than anything that Jack had said or done. Did I really want to get back in touch with the vampire? Even though we were technically no longer enemies, maybe it wasn't such a good idea. Maybe he'd get the wrong idea about why I'd called him. After swallowing hard and hesitating a bit longer than I should have, I remembered I was supposed to be leaving a message and squeaked out a few words.

"Yeah, Mr. Royce, this—it's Shiarra Waynest. I'd like to ask you a couple of questions. I might need your help with something." I left him my cell number and was about to hang up, hesitated again, and added, "Thanks."

I set the receiver down, wondering if I'd done the right thing. Damn it all to hell and back, I was putting myself back in the fire by contacting him again. Regardless, I needed to know who Max Carlyle was, and what sort of danger he represented. Since Jack specifically brought up Royce when talking about Max, I had to hope Royce would have some idea about what was going on. After all, he was an elder, influential vamp. He had all sorts of connections that informed him well ahead of time when somebody gunned for him or planned to do something that would influence him or his properties. I knew at least that much about him from prior experience.

Depending on what Royce told me, I might have to lay low and hide somewhere out of town for a few days. Or a few months. Whatever would keep my ass out of the fire.